Thrall

Twilight of the Aspects

Don't Miss These Other Tales in the
WORLD OF WARCRAFT®

THE SHATTERING: PRELUDE TO CATACLYSM
by Christie Golden

STORMRAGE
by Richard A. Knaak

ARTHAS: RISE OF THE LICH KING
by Christie Golden

NIGHT OF THE DRAGON
by Richard A. Knaak

BEYOND THE DARK PORTAL
by Aaron Rosenberg & Christie Golden

TIDES OF DARKNESS
by Aaron Rosenberg

RISE OF THE HORDE
by Christie Golden

CYCLE OF HATRED
by Keith R. A. DeCandido

WAR OF THE ANCIENTS:
BOOK ONE—THE WELL OF ETERNITY
by Richard A. Knaak

WAR OF THE ANCIENTS:
BOOK TWO—THE DEMON SOUL
by Richard A. Knaak

WAR OF THE ANCIENTS:
BOOK THREE—THE SUNDERING
by Richard A. Knaak

DAY OF THE DRAGON
by Richard A. Knaak

LORD OF THE CLANS
by Christie Golden

THE LAST GUARDIAN
by Jeff Grubb

WORLD OF WARCRAFT®

THRALL

TWILIGHT OF THE ASPECTS

Christie Golden

GALLERY BOOKS

New York   London   Toronto   Sydney

Gallery Books
A Division of Simon & Schuster, Inc.
1230 Avenue of the Americas
New York, NY 10020

First Gallery Books hardcover edition July 2011

GALLERY BOOKS and colophon are trademarks of Simon & Schuster, Inc.

For information about special discounts for bulk purchases, please contact
Simon & Schuster Special Sales at 1-866-506-1949 or
business@simonandschuster.com.

The Simon & Schuster Speakers Bureau can bring authors to your live event. For more
information or to book an event, contact the Simon & Schuster Speakers Bureau at
1-866-248-3049 or visit our website at www.simonspeakers.com.

Interior art by James Ryman.

Manufactured in the United States of America

10   9   8   7   6   5   4   3   2   1

Library of Congress Cataloging-in-Publication Data is available.

ISBN 978-1-4165-5088-4
ISBN 978-1-4391-7143-1 (ebook)

Since this is a book about healing a wounded world,
I would like to dedicate it to some of the teachers and healers
who have given of themselves to help heal this one.

Jeffrey Elliott
Greg Gerritsen
Kim Harris
Peggy Jeens
Anne Ledyard
Mary Martin
Anastacia Nutt
Katharine Roske
Richard Suddath
David Tresemer
Lila Sophia Tresemer
Monty Wilburn

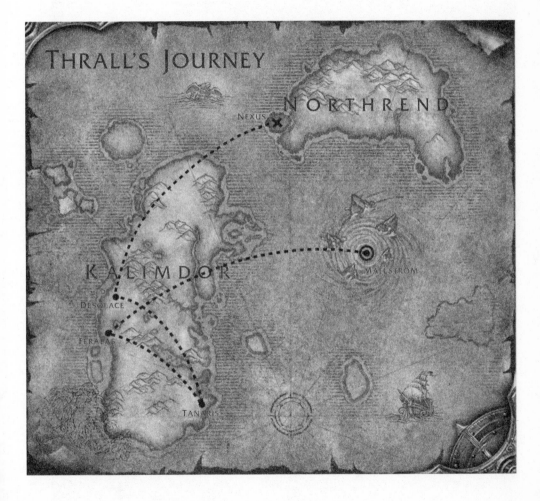

BLUE
DRAGONFLIGHT ASPECT

☠MALYGOS THE SPELL-WEAVER

☠SINDRAGOSA
Former Consort

SARAGOSA☠
Former Consort

KERISTRASZA☠
Unwilling Consort

CONSORTS

HALEH

MATRON PROTECTORATE

ARYGOS
Son; Mother Saragosa

KIRYGOSA
Daughter

BALACGOS☠
Son; Mother Unknown

CHILDREN

TYRYGOSA
Betrothed to Kalecgos

ANDORGOS

KALECGOS
In love with Anveena Teague

BLUE BROOD

☠ DECEASED

RED
DRAGONFLIGHT ASPECT

ALEXSTRASZA THE LIFE-BINDER

YSERA
SISTER

☠ **TYRANASTRASZ**
First Consort

CONSORTS

KORIALSTRASZ
Current Prime Consort

☠ **VAELASTRASZ**
Father Unknown

CHILDREN

CAELESTRASZ ☠
Son, Father Unknown

KANDROSTRASZ

KERISTRASZA ☠

CORASTRASZA
Sister to Raelorasz

RED BROOD

RAELORASZ
Brother to Corastrasza

☠ DECEASED

GREEN
DRAGONFLIGHT ASPECT

YSERA the AWAKENED

ALEXSTRASZA
SISTER

☠ **ERANIKUS**
CONSORT

MERITHRA
DAUGHTER

VETHSERA

VALITHRIA
GREEN BROOD

ITHARIUS

☠ DECEASED

BRONZE
DRAGONFLIGHT ASPECT

NOZDORMU THE **TIMELESS**

SORIDORMI
CONSORT

ANACHRONOS
SON / HEIR

ANDORMU
Brother; Co-Leader

KEEPERS OF TIME LEADERS

NOZARI
Sister; Co-Leader

EROZION

KEEPERS OF TIME

SA'AT

ZALADORMU

ZEPHYR

ZIDORMI

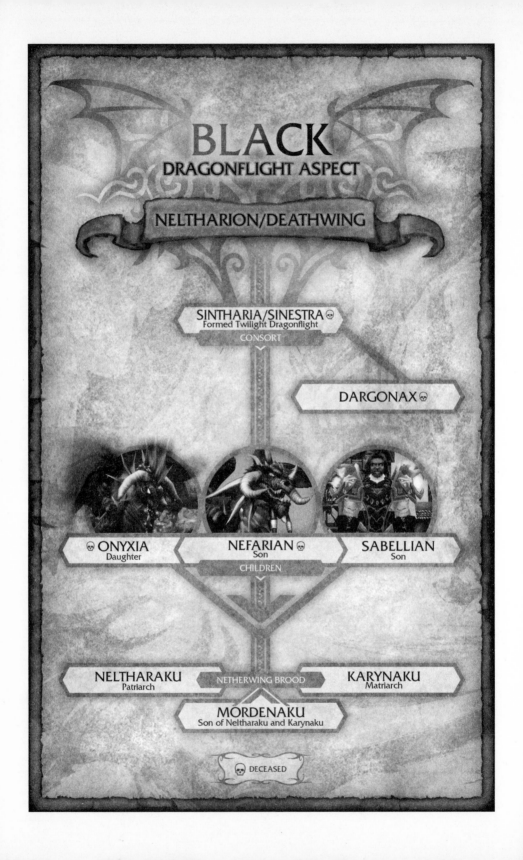

BLACK
DRAGONFLIGHT ASPECT

NELTHARION/DEATHWING

SINTHARIA/SINESTRA ☠
Formed Twilight Dragonflight

CONSORT

DARGONAX ☠

☠ **ONYXIA**
Daughter

NEFARIAN ☠
Son

SABELLIAN
Son

CHILDREN

NELTHARAKU
Patriarch

NETHERWING BROOD

KARYNAKU
Matriarch

MORDENAKU
Son of Neltharaku and Karynaku

☠ DECEASED

THRALL

TWILIGHT OF THE ASPECTS

ONE

Thrall, former warchief of the great and mighty Horde, now a shaman no greater than any of those with whom he currently stood, squeezed his eyes shut and struggled to stay on his feet. Beneath them, the earth bucked, a pathetically small piece of land jutting upward from an ocean roiling furiously around it, shaking and shivering in its pain.

Not long ago, an insane Dragon Aspect had torn his way into Azeroth, rending the world profoundly. The mad Deathwing was once again loose upon this world, and the violence of his return had left Azeroth with a gaping wound. To those whose minds were not beyond hope, Azeroth was not beyond healing, but it would never be what it once was.

In the heart of the world, a place called the Maelstrom, long-buried earth had been shoved violently to the surface. And it was here that those who were trying desperately to mend the broken lands had assembled.

They were shaman, each one powerful, members of the Earthen Ring who had left behind other serious duties and responsibilities to gather here. One alone could do little. Many, especially as highly trained and as wise as each one was, could do more.

There were dozens of them, standing alone, or in pairs or small groups on the slippery skerries, trying to stay on their feet on the bucking, shuddering earth. Their arms were lifted in gestures of both command and pleading. Though not linked physically, they were joined on a spiritual level, eyes shut, deep in the working of a healing spell.

The shaman were attempting to soothe the elements of the earth, as well as encouraging them to help heal themselves. True, it was the elements who were harmed, and the shaman who were not, but the elements had more power than the shaman. If the earth could be calmed long enough to remember this, it would be able to draw upon its own vast power. But the earth, the stones and the soil and the very bones of Azeroth, also wrestled with another wound: betrayal. For the black Dragon Aspect, Deathwing, once known as Neltharion, had been the Earth-Warder. He had been charged with protecting it and keeping its secrets. Now he cared nothing for the earth, casually and insanely ripping it to pieces, heedless of the havoc he wrought and the pain he caused it.

The earth mourned, and heaved violently.

"Stand straight and true!" cried a voice, somehow audible in Thrall's ears even over the rumbling of the earth as it quivered beneath them and the crashing of angry waves that sought to dislodge them from their precarious perches. The voice belonged to Nobundo, the first among his kind, the Broken, to become a shaman. This time it was his turn to lead the ritual, and so far he had done it masterfully.

"Open to your brothers and sisters! Sense them, feel them, see the Spirit of Life gleaming brightly inside them like a glorious flame!"

Standing with Thrall on one of the larger of the newly formed skerries was Aggra, a Mag'har and descendant of the Frostwolf clan Thrall had met in Nagrand and grown to love. Brown-skinned, her reddish-brown hair pulled back in a ponytail from an otherwise shaved head, she had strength in her hand as it grasped Thrall's own tightly. This was no gentle, subtle working they were doing now: this was triage.

They stood, daringly, close to the edge of sheer cliffs. Wind whipped up the ocean below them, sending the waves crashing to boom hollowly against jagged stone. All needed to calm before the healing could begin, but it was a risky choice.

Thrall felt his muscles lock, trying to hold him in place. It was much to juggle: staying upright on the wild earth, not toppling forward to the hungry ocean and sharp stones, and still trying to find the center of peace within that would enable him to connect on a deep and profound level with his fellow shaman. This was the space where, if the shaman was skilled and properly prepared, the Spirit of Life could enter—that energy that enabled the shaman to reach the elements, to interact with them, and to unite with others who were doing the same.

He could feel them reaching out to him, their essences an oasis of calm in the chaos, and he struggled to drop deep into his own inner core. With an effort, Thrall gained control of his breathing, refusing to surrender to the quick, shallow breaths that would only cause his body to taste worry and apprehension, instead forcing his lungs to inhale and exhale the damp salt air.

In through the nose . . . out through the mouth . . . extend from the soles of the feet into the earth, reach out with the heart. Hold tightly to Aggra, but do not cling. Close the eyes, open the inner spirit. Find the center and, in the center, find peace. Take the peace found there and link it to the others.

Thrall felt his hands sweating. His weight shifted and, for an instant, he slipped. Quickly he caught himself and tried to start breathing deeply again, to begin the centering ritual. But it was as if his body had a mind of its own and would not listen to Thrall's instructions. It wanted to fight, to do something, not stand and breathe and be calm. He—

A sudden light, so bright the orc could see it even with his lids tightly closed, flashed. A terrible *crack* shattered their ears as the lightning struck far, far too close. There was a deep rumble, and the earth quivered even more violently. Thrall opened his eyes in time to see a huge hunk of earth, scorched from the lightning strike only a few yards away, crumble beneath the feet of a goblin and a dwarf. They cried out in surprise, clinging to each other and the shaman on either side, swaying over the crashing waves and jagged rocks.

"Hang on!" shouted the tauren who had a death grip on the goblin's hand. He braced his hooves and pulled. The draenei clutching the dwarf did likewise. Gasping, the two shaman were dragged to safety.

"Pull back, pull back!" cried Nobundo. "To the shelters—quickly!" The gathered shaman needed no urging as a nearby skerry crumbled to pieces. Orc and tauren, troll and goblin, dwarf and draenei, all raced for their mounts, clambering atop the shivering beasts and urging them back to the shelters on one of the larger skerries as the skies cracked open and hurled stinging, fat raindrops upon the shaman's skins. Thrall hesitated long enough to make sure Aggra had climbed atop her winged mount, then he urged his own wyvern skyward.

The shelters were little more than makeshift huts, located as far inland as possible and protected by warding spells. Each individual and mated pair had their own. The huts were arranged in a circle around a larger, open ritual area. The warding spells protected the shaman from smaller manifestations of angry elements such as lightning, though the earth might open up beneath. But such was always a threat, no matter where the shaman were.

Thrall reached the shelter first, holding up the bearskin flap long enough for Aggra to charge inside, then dropping it and tying it closed. The rain pounded angrily on the skins as if demanding entrance, and the structures trembled slightly from the onslaught of the wind. But they would hold.

Thrall quickly began to remove his drenched robe, shivering slightly. Aggra did likewise in silence; the wet clothing would kill them more surely than a random strike of lightning, if not as swiftly. They dried their wet skins, one green, one brown, and then donned fresh, dry robes from a chest. Thrall set about lighting a small brazier.

He felt Aggra's eyes upon him, and the air in the tent was heavy with unsaid words. Finally she broke the silence.

"Go'el," she began. Her voice, deep and husky, was laden with concern.

"Say nothing," Thrall said, and busied himself heating water for hot beverages for them both.

He saw her scowl at him, then roll her eyes and almost visibly choke back her words. He disliked speaking to her so, but he was in no mood to discuss what had happened.

The spell had failed, and Thrall knew it was because of him.

They sat silently and awkwardly as the storm broke about them and the earth continued to rumble. At last, almost like a child that had cried itself to sleep, the earth seemed to subside. Thrall could feel that it was not at peace and far from healed, but it was still.

Until the next time.

Almost immediately Thrall heard voices outside their shelter. He and Aggra emerged into the gray day, the ground wet beneath their bare feet as they walked. Others were assembling in the main area, their faces reflecting grave concern, weariness, and determination.

Nobundo turned to Thrall and Aggra as they approached. He was a former draenei. His form was not proud and strong and tall, but bent, almost deformed, caused by exposure to fel energies. Many Broken were dark and corrupted, but Nobundo was not. Indeed, he had been blessed, his great heart opening to the shamanic powers, and it was he who had brought these powers to his people. Beside him were several draenei, their blue forms undamaged, sleek, clean. Yet, to Thrall and many others, Nobundo outshone them all because of who he was.

When the high shaman's gaze fell upon Thrall, the orc wanted to look away. This being—indeed, all the other shaman gathered here—was someone Thrall respected deeply, and had never wished to disappoint. And yet, he had.

Nobundo beckoned Thrall to him with an oversized hand. "Come, my friend," he said quietly, regarding the orc kindly.

Many were not so charitably minded, and Thrall felt angry gazes being cast his way as he approached Nobundo. Others came silently to join in this informal gathering.

"You know the spell we were attempting to work," Nobundo said, his voice still calm. "It was to soothe and comfort the earth. It is admittedly a difficult working, but one that all of us here know how to do. Can you tell us why you—?"

"Stop dancing around the subject," growled Rehgar. He was a massive orc, battle-scarred and hulking. One would not look at him and think "spiritual," but whoever made that assumption would be very wrong. Rehgar's life journey had thus far taken him from gladiator to slave owner to loyal friend and advisor to Thrall, and that journey was far from over. Now, though, a lesser orc than the former warchief of the Horde might have quailed before his anger. "Thrall . . . what the fel was going on with you? We could all feel it! You weren't focusing!"

Thrall felt his hands curl into fists and forced them to relax. "Only because you are my friend will I permit you to speak so to me, Rehgar," Thrall said quietly, but with an edge to his voice.

"Rehgar is right, Thrall," Muln Earthfury said in his deep, rumbling voice. "The working is hard, but not impossible—not even unfamiliar. You are a shaman, one who has been through all his people's true rites. Drek'Thar hailed you as the savior of his people because the elements spoke to you when they had been silent for many years. You are no inexperienced child, to be coddled and sympathized with. You are a member of this Ring—an honored and strong one, or else you would not be here. And yet you crumbled at a crucial moment. We could have silenced the quakes, but you shattered the working. You need to tell us what is distracting you so that we may aid you."

"Muln—" Aggra began, but Thrall lifted a hand.

"It is nothing," he said to Muln. "The work is demanding and wearying, and I have a great deal on my mind. Nothing more than that."

Rehgar uttered an oath. "You have a great deal on your mind," he spat. "Well, the rest of us do as well. Trivial things like *saving our world from ripping itself apart!*"

For a second, everything went red in Thrall's vision. Muln spoke before Thrall could. "Thrall was leader of the Horde, Rehgar, not you. You cannot know what burdens he bore and perhaps still does bear. And as one who until recently owned slaves, you cannot sit in moral judgment upon him!"

He turned to Thrall. "I am not attacking you, Thrall. I am merely seeking to see how we can aid you, that you can better aid us."

"I know what you are doing," Thrall said, his voice close to a snarl. "And I do not like it."

"Perhaps," Muln said, striving for diplomacy, "you are in need of some rest for a while. Our work is very demanding, and even the strongest must tire."

Thrall did not even grace the other shaman with a verbal reply; he merely nodded curtly and stalked off to his shelter.

He was angrier than he had been in some time. And the person he was most angry with was himself.

He knew he had been the weak link in the chain, had failed to put forth the ultimate concentration at the moment when it was most desperately needed. He could not yet drop deep into himself, touch the Spirit of Life within, which was what had been required of him. He didn't know if he would ever be capable of doing so. And because he could not do this thing, the effort had failed.

He was unhappy with himself, with the working, with the petty arguments—with everything. And he realized with a start that this unhappiness had been with him for a long time.

A few months ago, he had made a difficult decision: he had chosen to leave the rank of warchief of the Horde in order to come here, to the Maelstrom, to follow the path of shaman rather than leader. He had thought at first that it would be temporary. He had relinquished command to Garrosh Hellscream, son of the late Grom Hellscream, in order to travel to Nagrand to study with his grandmother, Greatmother Geyah. This was before the great Cataclysm that had shaken Azeroth; Thrall had sensed the uneasy elements and had hoped to be able to do something to calm them and prevent what had eventually transpired.

There, he had studied and learned with a beautiful but often irritating and frustrating shaman named Aggra. She had pushed him, forcing him to dig deep for answers, and the two had fallen in love.

He had returned to Azeroth and, once the Cataclysm had struck, decided to continue on to the Maelstrom to serve with his beloved.

It had sounded like the right thing to do—the hard choice, the best choice. To leave something familiar and loved, to work for the greater good. But now he was having doubts.

While Thrall had been traveling in Nagrand, Garrosh had killed Thrall's dear friend, the tauren chieftain Cairne Bloodhoof, in ritual combat. Thrall had later learned that Garrosh had been tricked by Magatha Grimtotem, a longtime rival of Cairne's, into fighting Cairne with a poisoned blade. Thrall could not shake the thought that had he not left Azeroth, Cairne would never have felt the need to rebuke Garrosh's leadership and would still be alive.

With Aggra, he had anticipated . . . he did not know what. A different sort of relationship from the one they had, at any rate. He had initially been put off by her bluntness and rough edges, then had grown to appreciate and love them. Now, though, it felt as if, instead of a steady companion to support and encourage him, he had found only another person to criticize him.

He wasn't even succeeding at helping the Earthen Ring calm the elements, if today's debacle was any indication. He had put aside the mantle of warchief and endured the murder of a beloved friend in order to come assist the Ring. And this, too, wasn't working.

Nothing was working; nothing was going the way it was supposed to; and Thrall—erstwhile warchief of the Horde, warrior, shaman— felt as if nothing he could possibly do could make any of it work.

It was not a sensation he was accustomed to. He had led the Horde, and led it well, for many years. He understood battleground tactics as well as diplomacy, knew when it was time for a leader to listen, when to speak, and when to act. This strange, belly-knotting feeling of uncertainty . . . this was new and alien, and he despised it.

He heard the sound of the bearskin being drawn back, but did not turn around.

"I would box Rehgar's ears for what he said to you," came Aggra's voice, husky and strong, "if I did not wish I had said it earlier."

Thrall growled softly. "You have a fine way of supporting," he said. "That helped *tremendously*. Now I shall go outside and be able to drop into my deepest self with no problem. Perhaps it is you who should have led the Horde all these years, instead of me. No doubt we would see a union of Horde and Alliance, with children of all races frolicking in Orgrimmar and Stormwind."

She chuckled, and her voice was warm, as was her hand when she placed it on his shoulder. He fought the urge to shrug it off angrily, but he did not soften, either. He stood in harsh silence, not moving. She squeezed his shoulder, then released it and moved around to face him.

"I have watched you since we met, Go'el," she said, her eyes searching his. "At first out of resentment, and then later out of love and concern. It is with love and concern that I watch you now. And my heart is troubled by what I see."

He did not reply, but he was listening. Her hand stroked his strong face gently, running along the furrows in his green forehead as she spoke.

"Despite all you have endured, these lines I now touch were not there when we met. These eyes—blue as the sky, blue as the sea—were not sad. This heart"—she placed her hand on his broad chest—"was not so heavy. Whatever is going on inside you, it is causing you harm. But because it is no external threat, you do not understand how to confront this enemy."

His eyes narrowed in slight confusion. "Go on," he said.

"You waste away . . . not your body—you are still strong and powerful—but your spirit. It is as if part of you is borne away with each gust of the wind, or washed away with the stinging rain. There is a hurt here that will destroy you if you let it. And I," she said, suddenly fierce, her light-brown eyes snapping, "will not allow that."

He grunted and turned away, but she pursued him. "This is a sickness of the soul, not the body. You have buried yourself so deep in the day-to-day running of the Horde that when you left, you left yourself behind with it."

"I do not think I care to hear anything more," Thrall said, his voice a warning.

She ignored him utterly. "Of course you do not," she said. "You do not like criticism. We must all listen to you, and if we disagree, we must do so respectfully. Yours must be the last word, Warchief."

There was no sarcasm in her voice, but the words stung. "What do you mean, I do not take criticism? I surround myself with differing voices. I invite challenges to my plans. I have even reached out to the enemy if it is in the best interest of my people!"

"I did not say those things were untruths," Aggra continued, unruffled. "But that still does not mean you take criticism well. How did you react to Cairne when he came to you in the shadow of Mannoroth's armor and told you he thought you were wrong?"

Thrall jerked. Cairne . . . His mind flashed back to the last time he had seen his dear friend alive. Cairne had come to him after Thrall had sent word to the old bull that Garrosh would lead the Horde while he was gone. He had stated, bluntly, with nothing to soften the words, that he thought Thrall was making a grave mistake.

I—need you with me on this, Cairne. I need your support, not your disapproval, Thrall had said.

You ask me for wisdom and common sense. I have but one answer for you. Do not give Garrosh this power. . . . That is my wisdom, Thrall, Cairne had replied.

Then we have nothing more to say to one another.

And Thrall had walked away.

He had never seen Cairne alive again.

"You were not there," Thrall said, his voice rough with the pain of remembering. "You do not understand. I had to—"

"Paugh!" Aggra said, waving away his excuses with her hand as if they were flies buzzing around her. "The conversation itself does not matter. You may indeed have been right, and at this moment I care not if you were or were not. But you did not listen. You closed him out, like drawing the skins tight against a rainstorm. You might never have convinced him, but can you tell me you listened?"

Thrall did not reply.

"You did not listen to an old friend. Perhaps Cairne might not have felt the need to challenge Garrosh, had he felt heard by you. You will never know. And now he is dead, and you cannot ever again give him the chance to be listened to."

Had she struck him, Thrall could not have been more shocked. He literally took a step backward, reeling from her words. It was something he had never voiced but something he had secretly wondered, late at night when sleep would not come. He knew in his heart that he had had to go to Nagrand and that he had made the best decision he could, given the situation. But . . . had he stayed and talked more with Cairne . . . what would have happened? Aggra was right . . . but he did not want her to be.

"I have always been able to listen when others do not agree. Look at the meetings I have with Jaina! She doesn't always agree with me, and she does not curb her tongue."

Aggra snorted. "A human female. What does she know about telling harsh things to an orc? Jaina Proudmoore is no threat, no challenge to you." She frowned, looking thoughtful. "Neither was your Taretha."

"Of course she was no challenge. She was my friend!" Thrall was starting to become angrier now that she had dragged Taretha Foxton into this strange fight she seemed determined to have with him. A human girl, Taretha had befriended him when she was a mere child; as an adult, she had found a way to help him escape his life as a gladiator, a slave of the human Lord Aedelas Blackmoore. She had paid for that deed with her life. "Few in this world have sacrificed as much for me, and she was a human!"

"Perhaps that is your problem, Go'el, and a problem others have with you. The most important females in your life have been human."

His eyes narrowed. "You will hold your tongue."

"Ah, and yet again you show me the truth of what I say: you will not hear disagreement. You would silence me rather than listen to me!"

There was truth in the statement, and it stung. With difficulty, Thrall took a deep breath and tried to rein in his anger.

"Then tell me: What do you mean?"

"I have only been in Azeroth a short while, and already I have heard the rumors. They outrage me to my core, and surely they should outrage you as well. Gossip pairs you and Jaina, or even you and Taretha, depending on the brew on tap, it seems." Her voice dripped anger and disgust—at him or at the rumors, Thrall wasn't sure and didn't care.

"You tread on dangerous ground, Aggra," he growled. "Jaina Proudmoore is a strong, brave, intelligent woman who has risked her life to help me. Taretha Foxton was the same—only she *lost* her life. I will not stand by and hear your bigoted slurs against them simply because they were not born orcs!"

He had advanced on her now, his face only inches from hers. She did not flinch, merely raised an eyebrow.

"You do not listen well, Go'el. I repeated rumors. I did not say I believed them. Nor did I say anything against either female other than they did not know how to criticize an orc. If anything, they have shown me that humans are capable of inspiring respect. But they are not orcs, Thrall, and you are not a human, and you do not know how to handle being challenged by a female of your own race. Or perhaps by *anyone*."

"I cannot believe I am hearing this!"

"I cannot, either, because until this moment, you have not listened!" Both their voices were rising, and Thrall knew that the little shelters offered no barriers to others' ability to hear their argument. Still Aggra pressed on.

"You have been able to hide behind the mantle of warchief. And that is why you are finding it so hard to free yourself of it now." She pressed her face even closer to his and hissed, "You bear the name of a slave, because you are a thrall to the Horde. A slave to what you think is duty. And you use that duty as a shield—a barrier between you and the dark places, between you and guilt, and fear, and second-guessing. And truly belonging to yourself—or to anyone else. You always plan ahead, and you do not take time to think about how far you have come, the amazing gift that your life has been. You strategize for tomorrow, but what about now? This moment . . . the little things . . . ?"

She softened, her eyes growing kind instead of angry, and with surprising gentleness reached for his hand. "What about this strong hand in yours?"

Irritated, Thrall yanked his hand away. He had had enough of this. First from the Earthen Ring, now from Aggra, who was supposed to stand by him and support him. He turned his back on her, heading for the entranceway.

Aggra's words followed him.

"You do not know who you are without the Horde, Go'el," she said. As always, she used the name his parents had given him—a name he himself had never used, given to him by a family he had never known. Suddenly, although she had used it a thousand times before, this time the name made him angry.

"I am not Go'el!" he growled. "How many times must I tell you to not call me that?"

She didn't flinch. "You see?" she said, and her voice was sad. "If you do not know who you are, how can you know what to do?"

He did not reply.

TWO

"This meeting," said Alexstrasza the Life-Binder, the great red Dragon Aspect, "will likely not be pleasant."

Korialstrasz chuckled. "My beloved has a gift for understatement."

Both the red dragons, the Great Aspect and Korialstrasz—her one remaining consort—had opted for more elven, less draconic forms as they spoke in the Ruby Sanctum. Each dragonflight had such a refuge, a place out of time and space that was a magical dimension unto itself. How each sanctum appeared was reflective of each flight. The Ruby Sanctum had once looked almost like the high elven lands did before the coming of the Scourge. The leaves of the trees were a warm crimson hue, the hills soft and rolling. The only way in or out of this special place was through a portal, guarded now more closely than ever after a recent attack by the black dragonflight and a single enemy calling itself a member of the twilight dragonflight. The sanctum had been badly damaged, but was beginning to recover.

They were alone, yet surrounded by their children. Hundreds of eggs were gathered here: the children of her body and her mate's as well as the children of others. Not all red dragons chose the Ruby Sanctum in which to lay their eggs. The whole world was home to them, indeed home to all the flights. But this was the heart, the sanctuary, a safe place and one uniquely theirs.

"Most of the blues are distraught that Malygos was slain, and I cannot say I blame them, even given the situation," Alexstrasza continued.

Malygos, the Dragon Aspect of Magic and the patriarch of the blue flight, had led a life fraught with tragedy. For millennia he had been mad, driven insane by Deathwing. Not so long ago, he had finally recovered from that dreadful condition, to the great joy of not just his own flight but all the flights save the hate-filled black dragonflight. The relief and happiness of his recovery lasted a poignantly short period of time. The other flights soon learned that, once he had regained his mind, he had put it to work analyzing the role of magic in Azeroth—and had reached a horrifying conclusion. Malygos had decided that arcane magic was running amok in the world—and that the mortal races were to be held accountable for its abuse.

And so he had started a war.

Malygos had diverted the magical powers that coursed beneath Azeroth to his own seat of power, the Nexus. The consequences had been violent, dangerous, and deadly. The world's crust had splintered, and the resulting unstable rifts had torn the very fabric of the magical dimension known as the Twisting Nether. Malygos's misguided attempts to "correct" the perceived misuse of arcane magic had to be halted . . . whatever the cost.

Dragon had fought against dragon in the bitter Nexus War, and it had been the Life-Binder herself who had reached the agonizing decision that Malygos—not long recovered from millennia of insanity—had to be destroyed.

Alexstrasza had taken her flight and allied with the magi of the Kirin Tor. With all that was at stake, the remaining flights had agreed to join the reds in their bitter task. The alliance of dragons became known as the Wyrmrest Accord. Together they had been able to defeat and slay Malygos, and the war had come to an end. Now the blue dragonflight was deep in grief, and without a leader.

And this meeting of the Wyrmrest Accord, which Alexstrasza was preparing to attend at Wyrmrest Temple, would be the first such since the fall of the blue Dragon Aspect. Since the end of that conflict, the Accord was even more precious to the flights—precious, and tenuous.

"I honestly do not believe they are ready as a flight to talk—or at least, to talk sense," Korialstrasz said.

She caressed his chin, smiling, her eyes warm with affection. "That is the tongue that has made you so *very* popular at recent gatherings, my love."

Korialstrasz shrugged a bit sheepishly, leaning affectionately into her hand. "I cannot deny it. I have never been the most popular of your consorts among our kind, and now that I am the only one, I fear I ruffle scales more often than not. But I must speak of things as I see them. It is my duty; it is how I can best serve."

"And it is one reason I love you so," Alexstrasza said. "But truly, it does not endear you to the other flights. This bias against the blues—it was Malygos who made the decision, not the entire flight. You cannot hold that against them. Surely they have suffered enough without the rest of the flights suspecting treachery from them at every turn simply because of the color of their scales."

He hesitated. "I—you know that I am fond of Kalecgos," he said. "And there are others who seem to be able to look at the situation with a clear head. But most of them cannot see past their loss—and their need to blame someone for it. And we are the flight they feel has most wronged them."

A frown marred the perfection of her brow for a moment, and her musical voice sharpened. "While I appreciate your bluntness, it is just as well that my whole flight does not think the way my consort does."

"You have the kindest heart in Azeroth. But sometimes a kind heart blinds one—"

"You think I do not see clearly? I? I led my flight against a fellow Aspect, in order to save beings whose lives are but a blink of an eye to us. You enjoy milling among the mortals, Korialstrasz, but do not think that means you are the only one who can see clearly."

He opened his mouth to retort, then closed it again. "I speak only out of concern."

At once, his mate softened. "I know," she said. "But perhaps your . . . concern about the blues will not be well received at this meeting."

"It never has been," he acknowledged with a small grin. "And thus we circle back to our starting point." He lifted both her slender hands and pressed kisses into each of the soft palms. "Go without me, then, my heart. You are the Aspect. Yours is the voice they will listen to. I will only be as a small pebble wedged between the scales—an irritant and little more."

She nodded her flame-colored head. "For this first gathering, tensions will be high. Later, when we begin speaking of plans, your insight will be welcome. Today, I think, is simply about reconnecting and healing."

Alexstrasza leaned forward. Their lips met, soft and sweet. One of the great pleasures of the elf-like forms they both felt so comfortable assuming was that skin was more sensitive to receiving a loving touch than scales. They drew back, smiling, the argument—if indeed it could even be called such—forgotten.

"I will return shortly with, I hope, good news." She stepped backward. Her smiling face shifted, a proud muzzle, gleaming crimson, jutting forward as the brilliant gold eyes enlarged. Almost faster than the eye could follow, her form changed from elven maiden to glorious, glittering red dragon.

Korialstrasz, too, changed. He enjoyed both forms, but his natural one was this—reptilian, massive, and powerful. A heartbeat later, two red dragons, now instantly recognizable for what—and who—they were, stood together in the Ruby Sanctum.

Alexstrasza tossed her horns, then nuzzled against her mate with a gentleness that other races might be surprised to see in a creature so massive. Then, with a grace belying her size, she leaped upward, and with a few beats of her mighty wings she was gone.

Korialstrasz's gaze followed her affectionately, then he turned to the eggs that were scattered about. He permitted himself to feel pride and love as he regarded his unhatched offspring. Humor made the corners of the great eyes crinkle for a moment as he said, remembering human customs of which he was so fond, "How about a bedtime story, hmm?"

Alexstrasza flew through the sanctum, concentrating on releasing her apprehension and instead letting her heart be filled with the restorative beauty of the place. Dragon eggs were nestled everywhere—in little hollows, beneath the red trees, in special nests near towering boulders. Keeping watch over the entrance to the sanctum, on both sides of the portal, were the wardens of the chamber: extremely powerful drakonid whose job was to protect the innocent whelps drowsing still in their shells. The future was here, and guarded lovingly, and her heart was glad. Because it was the future that was about to be built, beginning in this moment, with the meeting of four of the dragonflights.

The black flight, once so solid and stable and true, like the good earth it was to protect and be part of, had followed its mad patriarch, Deathwing, and permitted evil to enter its members' hearts. Black dragons no longer feigned interest in the other flights; not even the slyly smiling Nalice remained at the temple. Alexstrasza doubted that she would ever again behold a gathering of her kind and see red, blue, green, bronze, and black. The thought saddened her, but it was an old pain, one she was accustomed to bearing, and she did not let it dim her hopes for a positive outcome of the meeting.

Quickly she flew through the portal that kept the Ruby Sanctum safe and let her wings bear her upward to the top of Wyrmrest Temple, sacred to the dragonflights for millennia. Elegant, slim lines reached skyward, ice-coated arches and spires embracing but never enclosing the space. The temple climbed upward for several levels, each one smaller than the last. The Northrend sky arched above, a muted blue-gray with a few wispy white clouds. Below, the white snow was almost painful to behold, so pristine was it.

At the pinnacle of the temple was a circular floor inlaid with floral and geometric designs. Several yards above the floor hovered a beautiful, shimmering orb in shifting shades of blue and white. It served no real purpose save one very important one: it was a symbol of the unity of the Wyrmrest Accord itself.

Beneath the Orb of Unity, Alexstrasza saw dozens of reptilian forms milling about. Several of her own flight were already in attendance, as were some blues and not a few greens. The blacks, of course, would not be here—and if they were, blood would be shed—but Alexstrasza was dismayed, if not surprised, to see no bronze dragons were present, not even the cheerful but powerful Chromie.

Their Aspect, Nozdormu the Timeless One, had not been seen

for some time. The timeways had come under attack by a mysterious group calling itself the infinite dragonflight, whose motives were unclear but were focused on destroying the true timeway. Alexstrasza supposed that Nozdormu and the others of his flight had more than enough to deal with.

As she approached for a landing, sharp, angry voices reached her ears.

"An Aspect!" a voice was shouting. Alexstrasza knew that voice. It belonged to Arygos, a vigorous, outspoken member of the blue flight and child of Malygos and his favored consort, Saragosa. Arygos had openly sided with his father during the Nexus War, staunchly and unquestioningly supporting him. It would seem he was still his father's advocate even now.

"The red flight and a group of magi—non-dragons!—decided they should slay an Aspect. One of only five—four if we do not count Deathwing the Destroyer. How could you turn on your own? Who will be targeted next—gentle Ysera? Stoic Nozdormu? If there is anyone to be held accountable, it should be Alexstrasza. The so-called Life-*Binder* seems to have no compunctions about dealing death when it suits her."

Several heads had looked up as Arygos spoke, watching and saying nothing as the aforementioned Life-Binder approached. Alexstrasza landed gracefully near the younger dragon and said calmly, "My charge is to protect the sanctity of life. Malygos's decision and subsequent actions imperiled life. I grieve for your father, Arygos. The decision was a painful one. But what he was doing was harming far too many, and could have unraveled this world."

Arygos took a quick step backward, then narrowed his eyes and lifted his great blue head.

"Upon reflection, with the information we now have, I still cannot say my father's *motives* for the war were necessarily wrong.

The usage—or should I say improper and overusage—of magic was indeed of great concern. If you disagreed with his actions, and perhaps they were ill considered, surely there could have been other ways to have confronted Malygos!"

"You said it yourself—he was an Aspect," Alexstrasza continued. "And one who did not even still have the excuse of insanity to mitigate what he did. If you were so concerned with his safety, Arygos, then you should have helped us in finding those methods of restraining him."

"Life-Binder," came a voice, young and masculine and as calm as Arygos's was agitated. Another blue stepped forward, inclining his head respectfully but not subserviently. "Arygos did only what he believed was right at the time, as did many members of the blue flight. I am certain he is as eager as anyone else to move forward in rebuilding his own flight and accepting the responsibilities we all must," said Kalecgos.

Alexstrasza was pleased Kalecgos was here. This was the young blue her mate was so fond of, the one he said could speak sense. Which, she mused, he was already doing.

"I can speak for myself," growled Arygos, giving Kalecgos an irritated look.

Many of the blues felt that they were being persecuted and hounded by the other flights. In Alexstrasza's opinion, Arygos was even more elitist than most of his flight. She suspected this had to do with the young blue's personal history—one that had entailed reliance on other flights. Not for the first time, Alexstrasza lamented the loss of Arygos's clutch sister Kirygosa. Her mate had been killed, and she had gone missing before the war ended. The unhappy but realistic conclusion was that the young blue, pregnant with her first eggs, had fallen in battle. And because she had always dared to stand up to Arygos, and had sided with those few blues who had turned against Malygos, there was an extra layer of tragedy in that it was likely she had been slain by a member of her own flight.

"I do see that my late father's plan had negative consequences," Arygos continued, with obvious reluctance.

"We are still feeling those consequences," said Afrasastrasz, who had long been a particularly outspoken supporter of Alexstrasza. "The very *world* is. This is something that was directly caused by the decisions of the blue dragonflight's Aspect, whom you and others here supported. You need to do more than admit to being misguided, young Arygos. You need to make it *right*."

Arygos's eyes narrowed. "'Make it right'? Will *you* make it right, Afrasastrasz? Or you, Alexstrasza? You took my father from me. You left an entire flight without its *Aspect*. Will you bring him back?" His voice and entire body radiated anger and affront and a sincere, deep pain.

"Arygos!" snapped Kalec. "Malygos was not mad when he chose this course of action. He could have turned from it at any point and did not."

"I took no joy in the killing, Arygos," Alexstrasza said. "My heart still aches with the loss. We have *all* lost so much—all the flights, all the Aspects. Surely now is the time for healing, to turn toward one another instead of away."

"Yes," came a quiet voice that nonetheless carried, ending the argument immediately. "We should turn toward each other, and soon. The Hour of Twilight is coming, and we must be ready."

The voice was soft and lilting, and the green dragon who spoke stepped forward almost shyly. The other dragons drew back a few steps to allow her room to pass. She did not move with the strong, purposeful stride of most of her kind, but with almost dancing steps. Her eyes, which had been closed for aeons, were now wide open, rainbow hued, and she kept turning her head as if ready to behold something new each moment.

"What is this Hour of Twilight of which you speak, Ysera?" Alexstrasza asked of her sister. After millennia spent in the Emerald Dream, Ysera had awakened. Alexstrasza and many others were not sure how much of her had come back from that altered state; Ysera still seemed unanchored to this world, drifting and detached. Even her own flight, whose members, like their Aspect, dwelt nearly constantly in the Emerald Dream and were also guardians of nature, seemed unsure as to how to react to her. Ysera's integration into the waking world was uneven, to say the least.

"Is it something you saw in the Dream?" pressed Alexstrasza.

"I saw everything in the Dream," Ysera replied simply.

"That might be quite true, but it is unhelpful," said Arygos, seizing upon the distraction the Aspect of the green dragonflight had provided him. "You are no longer the Dreamer, Ysera, though you are surely an Aspect. Perhaps if you saw everything in the Dream, you saw also things that do not exist."

"Oh, that is very true," Ysera agreed readily.

Inwardly Alexstrasza winced. Not even she quite knew what to make of Ysera the Awakened. She was sane, yes—but was clearly having a difficult time putting together the pieces of the staggering multitude of things she had witnessed in any kind of coherent fashion. She would be of little help today.

"It would indeed be a good thing if we could work together—even before this Hour of Twilight." Alexstrasza regarded Kalec and Arygos. "The blues must determine how to select a new Aspect, and make restitution. You must show us that we can trust you again. Surely you see that."

"We must?" echoed Arygos. "Why 'must' we, Alexstrasza? Who are you to determine what the blue flight must and must not do?

To judge us so? You make no similar offer of restitution. Yet it is because of you that we need to find a new Aspect. What do you plan to do to show that you are to be trusted by us?"

Her eyes widened slightly at the insult, but Arygos plowed on. "How do we know you will not kill me? If I am chosen as Aspect, that is," he added hastily. "And your mate, Krasus, as he likes to go by—he is no friend to the blues. He has spoken out against us repeatedly. I cannot help but notice that he is not present at this meeting. Perhaps you didn't wish him to be here, either?"

"Korialstrasz saved your *life*, Arygos," Kalecgos reminded him. "When your father was so lost in his insanity that he abandoned you."

It was a very sore point for Arygos, and few were bold enough to remind him of it. The clutch of eggs that had contained both Arygos and Kirygosa had indeed been abandoned during Malygos's madness. It was Korialstrasz who had discovered that untended clutch, as well as many others, and taken it to Nozdormu to be cared for. Later, the clutches had been given to the red dragonflight. It was a glowing example of cooperation among three separate flights with a common cause: care of the unhatched, helpless whelps, be they red, blue, green, or bronze when they emerged from the shell.

"And even though he and I have certainly had our personal disagreements, that has not stood in the way of my learning to respect him. I have consistently found him to be reasonable and wise," Kalec continued as Arygos's eyes narrowed. "He has said nothing against our flight's behavior that I myself have not said."

"Really? And what does that then make you, Kalecgos?" Arygos retorted.

"Enough!" snapped Alexstrasza. She had not expected this meeting to go particularly smoothly, but she had hoped for better than this bickering. "Surely the flights have enough enemies out there that we should not waste precious time fighting among ourselves! Deathwing is back, more powerful than ever—and he has ripped Azeroth nearly to bits in the process. Now he has allies beyond his own flight: the Twilight's Hammer cult. Whatever the Hour of Twilight may be of which Ysera speaks, the twilight *dragons* are certainly an immediate threat. The Ruby Sanctum is still reeling from their previous assault. If we do not find out some way to put aside the petty differences and—"

"You *murdered my father*! How dare you call that petty?!"

Alexstrasza was slow to anger, but now she marched on the younger dragon and declared, "I say: enough! We must all move forward. The past is the past. We are in danger *now*. Did you not hear me? Do you not understand? *Deathwing has returned!*"

She was nearly nose to nose with Arygos now, her ears flat against her skull. "Our world has never been more fragile! Mighty beings are we dragons, indeed, but even *we* should be afraid of what will happen. We live in this world, Arygos. We must protect it, heal it, or even the dragons—including your blues!—will be destroyed. We must find—"

Other heads lifted on sinuous necks, turned skyward. And then Alexstrasza, too, heard and saw them.

Dragons.

For a brief moment, Alexstrasza dared hope that it was the bronze dragonflight. But an instant later she saw their coloration, and realized with horror what flight it truly was.

"The twilight dragons," she breathed.

They were coming for Wyrmrest Temple itself.

THREE

It was not in the manner Alexstrasza would have wished, but it did seem that the sudden presence of the twilight dragonflight galvanized the other flights into unified action. Without another breath wasted in argument among themselves, they lifted into the skies, charging to attack the enemy, to protect this sacred temple from danger.

It was an incongruously beautiful violence. Dozens of powerful forms in hues of ruby and emerald and sapphire wheeled and turned in midair. Their foe was all the shades of day turning into night—purple, violet, indigo—and grace and brutality combined into a bloody battle.

As they clashed, a voice seemed to echo in their very ears.

"How kind of so many of you to gather together in a single place, that I might destroy more of you weak creatures so readily."

Alexstrasza flew directly toward a cluster of three dragons, diving out of the way of their deadly breath, colored as purple as they were. Out of the corner of her eye, she saw one of the blues hover for a moment, casting a spell and then folding his wings and diving straight down. She swerved quickly and avoided the sudden storm of what looked to be icicles. One of the twilights managed to turn herself incorporeal, but the other two were too slow. Seizing the opportunity, Alexstrasza darted upward to clamp her massive jaws into the sinuous throat of one of them. Caught in his corporeal form with insufficient strength to transform, the twilight dragon let out a strangled scream and frantically beat the air with his indigo wings, trying to tear away from her. His black claws raked at her belly. Her scales blunted the damage from the attack, but white-hot pain still rippled across her stomach. She bit deeper, and the pain stopped. She opened her jaws and released the limp body, not sparing it a second glance as it tumbled downward.

"Who are you?" she cried, her own voice amplified and carrying on the cold, clear air. "Show yourself, name yourself, or be known for the coward and braggart that you are!"

"Neither braggart nor coward I," the voice came again. "I am known to my followers as the Twilight Father. They are my children, and I love them."

A chill rippled through the great Life-Binder, though she did not know why. If the name was true, and he was the patriarch of these beings—

"Then come forth and protect your children, Twilight Father, or sit back and behold as we slaughter them one by one!"

Two of them dove at her from opposite directions. So intent was she on locating the source of the voice she almost did not sense them in time. With barely a tail's breadth to spare, she folded her wings in and dropped like a stone, turning over as she did so. Directly above her the two twilight dragons shifted into their shadowy forms an instant before their collision, their two bodies passing harmlessly through one another.

Laughter, harsh and smug, enveloped her. "You are as a foolish little girl, for all that you are the great Life-Binder. It will be delightful to watch you crumble to pieces beneath what is to come."

A roar shattered her ears, and Alexstrasza's heart ached as one of her own fell in battle, great red wings still trying to bear him aloft although one of those wings had been ripped to ribbons. She dove toward her comrade's killers, bellowing and screaming fire. One of them immediately shifted from solid flesh and threw himself out of the path of flames. The other, either braver or more foolish, turned and hurled sharp daggers of dark magic at Alexstrasza before opting to shift. The arrogance cost him his life. She opened her jaws and breathed a sheet of flame along the full length of his body before the transformation was entirely complete. More powerful than the breath of an ordinary red dragon, the fire seemed to almost melt the bruise-colored scales, making them curl up as the flesh beneath them was burned to the bone. One side of his body scorched beyond recognition, the dragon fell, half in and half out of physical existence, but wholly in agony.

Out of the corner of her eye, Alexstrasza saw her normally gentle sister, Ysera, also fighting fiercely. Her jaws were opening, exhaling air that could be as sweet as summer flowers but had now turned sickly green and toxic. Two twilight dragons recoiled, gasping for breath, their wing beats faltering and their attention diverted long enough for Ysera, claws extended and great mouth gaping, to cast a quick spell. They howled in terror and began to fight each other, each one convinced that his fellow was the enemy. In a few seconds they would do Ysera's work for her.

Alexstrasza fended off another attack, diving and circling back over her foe to snap his neck with a mighty stroke of her powerful tail. As the lifeless body hurtled to the earth, she realized two things simultaneously.

First, there were two Aspects present, both in fine fighting form. There were far too few twilight dragons to realistically take them down, especially now that the elite drakonid who normally stood guard at the entrances to the sanctums had temporarily left their posts to join the fight. While they could not fly, any wounded twilight dragon who had the misfortune to land while merely injured was dispatched quickly. It was too easy.

And second, all the fighting was gathered in one spot.

Why?

A better tactic would have been to separate the various dragons, surround them, lure them away from any protective defenders, and utilize the architecture of the temple itself as a weapon. But the twilight dragons were clustered as thick as a colony of ants above the apex of the temple, right where they would make fine targets for Ysera and Alexstrasza.

Alexstrasza's gut twisted as a nameless, almost crippling fear shot through her. Something was horribly wrong.

"Break away from the enemy!" she cried, her voice clear and strong and belying her terror. "Lead them from the temple and attack them one by one!"

The defending dragons heard, and immediately scattered in all directions. The twilight dragons stayed clustered in a tight huddle, only a few of them breaking what now to Alexstrasza's eyes seemed almost like a formation to follow their prey.

And then she realized what it was. They had not come to attack. They had come to distract—

The explosion, both physical and metaphysical, was powerful enough to send Alexstrasza hurtling head over tail through the air, tumbling helplessly as a newly hatched whelp caught in a cyclone. She extended her wings and bellowed in sharp, surprised pain as they were almost ripped off, but managed to catch herself. Her entire body felt as if it had been pummeled by a living mountain, and for a long moment she could hear nothing.

But she could see. And as the pain ripped through her, she wished she could not.

Wyrmrest Temple still stood. Barely. Several of the glorious, graceful arches had been shattered, their remnants looking like melted ice. Red magical energy roiled upward from the base of the temple.

And at the base of the temple were—

"The sanctums!" someone cried. "Our children!"

Many of them broke and dove downward, and for a terrible instant that lasted an eternity Alexstrasza could not find her voice.

The Ruby Sanctum . . . the children . . . *Korialstrasz . . .* !

When she did finally find the ability to speak, she could not herself believe what she was saying.

"Hold fast!" she cried. "We cannot afford to lose anyone else! Drive off the enemy, my flight! Do not let them harm us further!"

More than her own red dragonflight rallied at her impassioned cry, funneling their rage and grief and terror at what they feared had just happened into their attacks. The twilight dragons seemed startled by the ferocity, and soon enough fled.

Alexstrasza did not give pursuit. She folded her wings and dove earthward, heart shaking her with its frightened pounding, deathly afraid at what she might find.

The Twilight Father stood on the top of one of the many mountains that jutted upward in the Dragonblight. He did not seem to feel the cold as the wind tugged at his hooded cloak, and kept the hood firmly in place with one hand. The other hand was closed tightly about a small silver chain, the links tiny and finely crafted.

From the shadowy darkness of the cowl, his eyes, set deep in a craggy, gray-bearded face, peered out. He had been watching the battle with pleasure, issuing his booming taunts to rattle the Life-Binder with an almost childlike glee.

But the explosion that had so devastated the dragonflights had also surprised and dismayed him.

Beside the large, stockily built man stood a beautiful young woman. Long, blue-black hair whipped in a wind that brought a pink hue to her otherwise pale cheeks. The thin chain that the Twilight Father held in his gloved hand culminated in a circle about her slender throat, almost like an elegant necklace. She, too, seemed impervious to the cold, although her tears had frozen on her face. Now, though, she smiled, and the tears cracked and fell to the cold stone beneath them.

Slowly, the hooded figure turned toward the girl. "How did you manage to get word to them? How did you do it? *Who helped you?*"

The girl's smile widened. "Your followers are too loyal to help me. I did not get word to them. But it seems that someone is smarter than you . . . *Twilight Father.*" She spoke the title, not with the respect that the cultists did, but with a defiant contempt. "Your plan has failed."

He took a step closer to her, then suddenly chuckled. "How stupid you are. There are always options. And a wise man always has more than one plan."

Casually, he tightened his grip on the chain. The girl gasped, her hands flying to her throat as the chain twisted, flared white, and began to burn her. He smiled at the smell of burning flesh, then, just as casually, released her from the spell.

She did not fall to her knees, not quite, but her gasping and shivering were sufficient to mollify him.

They had indeed suffered a setback. A tremendous one. But

what he had told his prisoner was true. A wise man always had more than one plan. And the Twilight Father was nothing if not wise.

He was far from defeated.

They were gone.

The sanctums—all of them. Gone, as if they had never been. Five miniature dimensions, sacred space to each flight—obliterated. And along with the sanctums were the unspeakably precious treasures they housed: their young. Thousands of lives had been snuffed out before they had even had a chance to breathe air or flex their wings.

Alexstrasza had accompanied the wardens; there was nothing left even to investigate. Somehow the twilight dragons had managed to cause each sanctum to implode, leaving nothing behind except traces of the energy used to destroy them. Discovering the how and even the why of this would be the work of another day, when heads were clearer and hearts were calmer. For now, the dragonflights were united indeed in their pain and loss.

There was no hope, and yet Alexstrasza had it. She reached out, with her heart, her Life-Binding magic, her depthless love, trying to find a trace of the one who had been first in her heart. Their bond was so great that even if he had been spirited away somehow, if he lived, she would sense him. She had always been able to before.

Korialstrasz?

Silence.

Beloved?

Nothing.

Gone with the sanctums, and the eggs, and the hope of the dragons' future, was Korialstrasz.

Alexstrasza crouched, stunned and reeling, on the snowy earth. Torastrasza, majordomo to the Ruling Council of the Accord, stood beside her, trying to offer comfort for something so horrific, so huge, that no solace could possibly be found, not for a long time. If ever.

Tariolstrasz approached Torastrasza. "A word with you?"

Torastrasza nuzzled Alexstrasza gently. "I will be back in a moment," she said.

Alexstrasza looked up at her with vacant eyes, briefly not comprehending Torastrasza's words. Then she nodded. "Oh, yes . . . of course."

My beloved, my heart, my life . . . why did I ask you to stay behind? Had you come with me, you might have survived. . . .

Angry voices were all around her, raised in rage and anguish, fear and fury. The only thing saving Alexstrasza from losing herself was merciful numbness, which was starting to wear off the longer this nightmare that could not possibly be real continued. She felt a gentle brush along her neck and turned to see Ysera looking at her with compassion in her rainbow-hued eyes. The green Dragon Aspect was silent, knowing there was nothing that could be said, and merely stretched out beside her sister, their sides touching.

"Life-Binder," said Torastrasza's voice after a time. Alexstrasza lifted her head with an effort and regarded the other dragon.

"Korialstrasz . . ." Torastrasza began, but she could not continue.

"I know," Alexstrasza said. Her heart broke a little more at the admission of it, as if saying the words were helping it to become more real. "He . . . was there. In the sanctum. My love is gone."

But oddly, Torastrasza was shaking her head. Sudden, irrational hope filled Alexstrasza. "He survived?"

"No, no, I—it seemed to be a suicide venture."

She stared at Torastrasza as if the majordomo were speaking

gibberish. "Your words make no sense!" she said, slamming her forepaw down.

"He was . . . he *did* this. What little is left bears his energetic mark. It is green and . . . and living."

"You are saying my sister's beloved consort destroyed the sanctums? Including the eggs and himself?" said Ysera, her voice still calm and detached.

"It—there is no other explanation."

Alexstrasza stared at Torastrasza. "This is not possible," she said, her voice harder than stone. "You *know* Korialstrasz. You *know* he is incapable of this."

"Not if he was working with the Twilight's Hammer!" Arygos's voice was filled with fury. "This whole time he was urging you to slay my father. Attack the Nexus. And all along he was plotting the extermination of our entire race!"

Anger exploded like a roiling fireball in Alexstrasza's blood. She leaped upward, her eyes on the blue dragon, and slowly advanced on him.

"While your father whimpered in his madness, Korialstrasz and I fought for Azeroth. We united with whatever allies we could find. We changed time itself; we risked death and worse for this world. Always he was beside me, his heart true and strong. He even loved you, Arygos, saving your life, and Kiry's, and that of so many others. Time and again, he has saved our world, our race. And now, you stand here expecting us to believe that he would ally with Deathwing? With a cult that wishes only the end of everything?"

"Arygos," urged Kalec, "there could be another explanation."

There could be . . . there was . . . there must be—Alexstrasza knew it. And yet—

"The battle tactics employed by the twilight dragons were designed to keep us fighting in the air high above the temple," Torastrasza continued, her voice as gentle as her words were ruthless. "It was a distraction, to keep us occupied . . . to lure out the Wyrmrest protectors so that—" Torastrasza broke off and looked down, unable to regard her adored Life-Binder as she spoke words that she had to know were ripping the Dragonqueen's heart to pieces.

"Alexstrasza," Kalec said gently, "tell us why Krasus chose not to come today. He surely . . . I am not certain, but you asked him to stay behind, did you not?" His voice was pleading.

She stared at Kalec, her heart breaking even further as she recalled the conversation—the last they would ever have.

Go without me, then, my heart. You are the Aspect. Yours is the voice they will listen to. I will only be as a small pebble wedged between the scales—an irritant and little more.

He was the one who had suggested he stay behind. "No," she breathed, both in answer to Kalec's question and in a desperate denial of what seemed now to be the truth—that Korialstrasz had indeed planned this.

Kalec looked at her in anguish. "I . . . even with the evidence— even with all it looks like—I cannot believe that Krasus would attempt genocide! This is *not* the Krasus I knew!"

"Perhaps madness does not confine itself to Aspects," sneered Arygos.

Something snapped inside Alexstrasza.

She threw back her head and screamed her pain, a keening sound that shattered the air and quivered along the frozen ground. She sprang upward, wings beating in time with her racing heart, eyes fastened on the beautiful Orb of Unity.

She flew straight for it.

Alexstrasza lowered her head at the last possible second, like a ram charging at its enemy. Her massive horns impacted the delicate orb. With an incongruously bright tinkling sound, the Orb of Unity shattered into thousands of shining pieces that fell like sparkling rain upon the dragons below.

She had to get away from here. Away from the dragons who were so quick to believe the worst of one who had always been the best of them. Not just the blues, or the greens, but her own flight, who should know better—

Should *she* know better? What if it was true?

No. No, she could not, would not, bear even the whisper of such in her heart, or she would betray one who had ever been most worthy of trust.

Torastrasza, Ysera, and Kalecgos flew beside her. They said something that she couldn't understand, and Alexstrasza whirled in mid-flight and began attacking them.

Startled, they veered away. She did not pursue. She had no wish to kill. She wanted them only to leave her alone, so she could escape from this place, this awful place that was now the site of unspeakable, almost unimaginable horror. She could never look upon the temple again without reliving this moment, and now—it was unbearable.

Everything was unbearable.

In her brokenness, Alexstrasza clung to one thing and one thing only: the hope that if she could fly far enough, fast enough, she could out-fly the memory.

Alexstrasza's attack was fueled by anger and fear, not a serious attempt to kill, and Ysera, Torastrasza, and Kalec dodged it easily. Ysera felt her own pain—many of the eggs destroyed in the explosion had belonged to her own flight, if not her own body—but she knew it was nothing compared to what her sister was experiencing.

Alexstrasza had lost mate, children, and hope, all in one terrible blow.

Ysera flew back to the temple sadly, her heart heavy, her mind—as ever, it now seemed—gnawing on pieces and bits of puzzles and enigmas.

The dragons were leaving in droves. Heartsick, furious, no one, it seemed, wished to linger here, amid what had once been so precious.

The Wyrmrest Accord had been shattered, as surely as the symbol of it had been, and the temple was meaningless now.

Ysera, though, did not flee. She flew slowly around the temple, peering at it almost in an impartial manner, then landed, shifted to night elf form, and walked around the structure on two feet. Corpses were everywhere: red and blue and green and twilight. The incongruous vitality and life energy of the magic Korialstrasz had used to destroy the sanctums were now seeping to the surface. Living plants broke the crust of the white snow.

Ysera shook her head sadly. Such vigorous life, to have dealt such death. She bent to caress a long green leaf, then continued her aimless ambling.

Her eyes were open, but she did not pay attention to what she saw with them. She had tried her best to communicate to the other dragons her incomplete vision. It was almost impossible to do so: the only way for anyone else to truly understand would be if they, too, had been asleep and dreaming for tens of thousands of years, and had only now awoken and were trying to make sense of it all. Ysera knew she wasn't mad, felt that the others knew this as well, but she had a certain empathy for insanity now.

The Hour of Twilight. She'd spoken of it at the meeting, tried to warn the others of it, but the warning had gotten lost; a little bright fragment of . . . something . . . had been briskly swept away like a broken bit of pottery beneath an industrious broom. It was—

She gnawed her lower lip, thinking.

It was the greatest challenge the dragonflights would face, but she did not know against whom they would be fighting. It might come soon . . . or aeons from now. Could it have something to do with the return of Deathwing? Surely it had to . . . did it not? This breaking of the world was one of the worst things that had ever happened to Azeroth.

How could she persuade others of the direness of the situation when she herself could not articulate it? She uttered a little noise of annoyance and frustration.

One thing she knew for certain. There were many pieces missing from this puzzle, but there was one core piece that was necessary before any of the others could fall into place. It was a very strange piece, an unlikely one at best, and she was uncertain as to how he would fit in. She only knew that he had to.

Ysera had seen him floating in and out of her dreaming. She had thought she understood his role in things, but now, peculiar as it seemed, something—some inner certainty that even she did not fully understand—was leading her to think she had not seen the full breadth of his contribution to Azeroth.

He was not a dragon. But he had the interests of the dragonflights in his heart—whether he knew it or not. He straddled worlds—but did not seek to rule or command or destroy them. He was unique.

She tilted her head, let the wind play with her long green hair. Perhaps that was why he fit in. Even the Aspects were not singular beings, although each had unique abilities. Not one but five there had been at the beginning, when the titans had come and shared their power for the good of Azeroth. Four there were now, but there would soon be five again, when the blues determined how to choose the one who would lead them.

But there was only one like this being.

There was only one Thrall.

FOUR

Thrall could not sleep. Aggra drowsed quietly beside him on their sleeping furs, but his mind would not be still. He lay on his back, staring up at the skins that covered the hut, and then finally rose, threw on some clothes and a cloak, and went outside.

He took a deep breath of the moist air and looked up at the night sky. The stars, at least, seemed to have some sort of peace about them, and the two moons—the White Lady and the Blue Child—were unaffected by Deathwing's violent rebirth into Azeroth. For the moment, the elements were as stable as they ever could be here in the Maelstrom—due in no part at all to Thrall's help, he knew, and he frowned to himself.

He began to walk, with no destination in mind. He simply wanted to move, in silence and solitude, and see if that calmed his thoughts enough so that he could finally sleep.

What had transpired during the spellcasting and afterward—both with the other members of the Ring and with Aggra in particular—had shaken him. He wondered if they were right. Was he truly helping here? He had given up everything to come—and yet it seemed that not only did he have no aid to offer, but he was disruptive. He had stayed behind today, "resting," while the others did workings all day. It was humiliating and painful. He growled low in his throat and picked up his pace.

He did not want to believe that Aggra was right—that he hid behind the mantle of leadership and was a "thrall" to duty. If that were so, then why could he not lose himself in the work here?

"What is wrong with me?" he muttered aloud, slamming one great green fist impotently into the palm of his other hand.

"That," came a lilting feminine voice, "I do not know the answer to. Maybe I will, at some point."

He turned, startled. A few feet away stood a tall but slender cloaked figure. The cloak, wrapped about her frame, revealed it to be a female, but her face was hidden in the shadow of the cloak's cowl. Thrall did not recognize the voice and frowned slightly, wondering who this stranger might be.

"Maybe I will too," he said. He inclined his head in greeting. "I am Thrall."

"I know. I've come for you." Her voice was musical, mesmerizing.

He blinked. "For me? Why? Who are you?"

"It's . . . hard to explain," she said, and cocked her head as if listening to something he couldn't hear.

"It's hard to explain your name?"

"Oh, that . . . no. It's the other that is challenging. You see . . . I have a small task for you, Thrall."

He found himself more amused than annoyed. "A task? Something for the Ring?"

"No, something for the villagers."

"The villagers?"

"In Feralas. It is little more than a small camp called"—she chuckled as if at a private joke—"Dreamer's Rest. There is suffering there. Suffering of the land, and an old-growth grove that has seen many years, and the druids who live near it. The elements there are out of control, as they are in many parts of this poor wounded world, and they are going to destroy the village if something isn't done. Only a shaman can talk to the elements and soothe them into harmony."

Thrall's amusement faded. He was beginning to suspect a joke. And he did not like it.

"Then let the shaman of the village do so," he said, somewhat sharply.

"There are no shaman there. It is too small, and there are only druids," the stranger said simply, as if that explained everything.

Thrall took a deep breath. What she was asking of him was trivial. It was the sort of thing novice shaman could handle. Why she had come to find him for such a task, he did not know and did not care.

"Surely there are others who can do that," he said, reining in his irritation and trying to maintain courtesy. If this was some sort of bizarre test by the Earthen Ring, he did not want to explode with erratic anger, no matter how much this dithering female was annoying him.

She shook her head vigorously, walking toward him. "No," she insisted, seemingly quite earnest. "*No* others. None like you."

This was getting ridiculous. "Who are you, to set me to such a task?"

Her face was still in shadow, but the glow of radiant eyes illuminated a smile of haunting sweetness. Was this a night elf? "Perhaps this will clarify."

Before he could retort, she had sprung into the air—high, higher than any true elf could go, the cloak falling from her as she spread her arms wide, offering her face to the sky. Her body began to shift faster than the eye could follow, and where before he thought a night elf had been, now there was a huge dragon gazing down upon him, wings beating steadily as she lowered herself to land.

"I am Ysera . . . the Awakened."

Thrall took a step backward, gasping. He knew the name Ysera. She had been the Dreamer, the guardian of the Emerald Dream. But now she dreamed no longer.

Much had changed with the recent Cataclysm, it would seem.

"Do this thing, Thrall," Ysera said. Her voice was still pleasant, though deeper and more resonant in her dragon form.

He almost answered, *Yes, of course*. But his recent failures haunted him. What she was asking seemed trivial indeed, but considering who she was, he guessed that it had to be very important. And he was not sure he could be trusted with something important right now.

"Mighty Ysera . . . may I meditate on this?"

She looked disappointed. "I had hoped you would say yes."

"It is . . . only a small camp, isn't it?"

Her disappointment seemed to deepen. "Yes. It is a small camp, and a small task."

Shame heated his cheeks. "Still, I would ask: Come again in the morning. I will have an answer for you."

She sighed, a great, melancholy bellow, and her breath smelled of fresh grass and mist. Then Ysera the Awakened nodded, leaped upward, and vanished with a few beats of her wings.

Thrall sat down heavily.

He had just been asked by a Dragon Aspect to do something, and had told her to come back tomorrow. What was he thinking? And yet—

He placed his head in his hands and pressed hard on his temples.

Things that should be easy were difficult, too difficult. His head was not clear, and it seemed neither was his heart. He felt . . . lost and indecisive.

Thrall had largely kept to himself since the argument with Aggra last night. But now, as he sat alone with only the moons and the stars for company, he knew he needed to seek her out. Aggra had wisdom and insight, although recently he found that he often disliked what she had to say. And he was clearly in no position to make a decision without support, or else he would have been able to say yea or nay at once to the mighty Aspect.

Slowly he rose and walked back to the hut.

"Did the moons give you guidance?" Aggra asked softly in the darkness. He should have known better than to think that his movements, however quiet, would not have awakened her.

"No," he said. "But . . . this shaman would like to ask something of you." He expected a sarcastic response, but instead heard the furs rustle as she sat up.

"I am listening," was all Aggra said.

He sat down next to her on their sleeping furs. Quietly he told her of the encounter, and she listened without interrupting, although her eyes widened at several points.

"This seems . . . almost insulting," Thrall said at last. "This is a minor task. To remove me from here, where my help is sorely needed, to save a tiny village in Feralas . . ." Thrall shook his head. "I don't know if this is a test, or a trap, or what. I don't understand any of it."

"You are sure it was Ysera?"

"It was a large green dragon," Thrall snapped, then added more quietly, "and . . . I *felt* that it was she."

"It doesn't matter if it is a test or a trap. It doesn't matter that this seems like a trivial task. If it is Ysera asking something of you, you should go, Thrall."

"But my help here—"

Aggra covered his hand with her own. "Is not needed. Not now. You cannot do what you need to do in order to be of aid to us here. You saw that yesterday—we all did. You are no good to anyone here at this point. Not to the Earthen Ring, not to the Horde, not to me, and surely not to yourself."

Thrall grimaced, but there was no scorn or anger in Aggra's voice. Indeed, it was gentler than he could remember it being in some time, as was her hand on his.

"Go'el, beloved," she continued, "go and do this thing. Go and obey the Aspect's request, and do not concern yourself as to whether it is a large thing or a small. Go, and bring back what you learn." She smiled a little, teasingly. "Did you learn nothing from your initiation?"

Thrall thought back to his initiation in Garadar, which seemed so long ago. He recalled the plain robes he had been asked to wear, how he was reminded that a shaman balanced pride with humbleness.

He was most assuredly *not* being humble in thinking of refusing the request of an Aspect.

Thrall took a deep breath, held it for a moment, then let it out slowly.

"I will go," he said.

The Twilight Father found himself a trifle disappointed at how quickly the reds, blues, and greens had fled. He'd expected that they'd put up more of a fight. Nonetheless, it made his task easier, and made him even more adored by the cultists, who obeyed his every command. Such was good, even if it lacked the sweetness that a more hard-fought victory would have provided.

He had watched, along with the girl, as the dragons had flown away, sometimes singly, sometimes in pairs or in groups. Now the only dragons that remained were quite lifeless, save for the ones directly under his command.

He had sent his lieutenants ahead to summon his followers, and now they gathered at the foot of the promontory and shivered in the cold. Their faces were so diverse, belonging to orc and troll, human and night elf—indeed, many of the races of Azeroth—and yet had a deep similarity in their expression of rapt adoration.

"And so our long journey has come, if not to its end, at least to a place where we pause, gather our forces, and grow strong. Wyrm-rest Temple was once a symbol of the unconquerable power of the unified dragonflights. It has been said it was made by the titans themselves, and the dragons regarded it as inviolable and sacred. Today, we saw them abandon it—including two of their Aspects. It is our home now, for as long as we choose to make it so. This ancient place of power, like all things, must fall!"

Cheers erupted from hundreds of throats. The Twilight Father raised his hands, accepting the wave of adoration that poured off of the crowd.

"It is fitting that part of this place is broken," he continued when the delighted uproar had started to die down. "The end of things is always with us, even at our moment of triumph. Now . . . let us take what has fallen to us, that it may serve our cause."

One of the great twilight dragons that had been hovering obediently came in for a landing. Like a subservient pet, she prostrated herself before him, pressing her pale purple belly to the cold stone so that he would have no difficulty in climbing atop her back. He stepped forward, and the chain binding the girl to him grew taut. He turned, mildly surprised.

The girl did not move at once, regarding the dragon with a mixture of loathing and pity.

"Now, now, my dear," he said, his voice making a mockery of kind words, "you mustn't hesitate. Although"—he smirked from beneath the cowl—"I daresay that this is not quite the homecoming you expected, eh?"

Kirygosa, daughter of Malygos, sister to Arygos, looked from the twilight dragon to the Twilight Father, her blue eyes narrowed in contempt, and kept her icy silence.

As they approached Wyrmrest Temple, Kirygosa noticed that something else was heading that way as well. Below her, an enormous sled, large enough to accommodate several dozen humans, moved across the landscape. The white snowfall elk that pulled it strained visibly at the task. Even as Kirygosa watched, one of them collapsed. The sled came to a halt. Four acolytes of the Twilight's Hammer moved forward, unbuckled the pathetic creature, and replaced it with another elk. The exhausted animal half walked, half stumbled as they tugged on its reins, leading it away from its fellows. When it again collapsed in the snow, lifting its head imploringly, one of the acolytes gestured. Several orcs dismounted from their large black wolves. The beasts waited, obedient, eyes fixed upon their masters until the command was given. Then the great beasts sprang as one, falling upon the hapless elk with shocking speed. Smooth white snow was churned up beneath the elk's struggles and suddenly blossomed with crimson, and the elk's pathetic cries were drowned out beneath savage growling.

Kirygosa looked away. No doubt such a fate was a trifle more merciful than simply leaving the elk to freeze to death, and the wolves did need food. They, at least, were innocent and natural creatures. Unlike their masters.

She returned her attention to the sled. A large canvas covered the top of it, revealing only a huge, lumpy form. It was the first time Kirygosa had seen it, and there was something about the shape—

"Curious, my dear?" said the Twilight Father, pitching his voice to be heard over the beating of their dragon mount's wings. "All will be unveiled in due time. This is the purpose of our being here. You will recall, I told you: the wise man always has another plan."

The tone of his voice chilled Kirygosa. The twilight dragon bore her steadily onward toward Wyrmrest Temple. She looked back over her shoulder at the sled fading into the distance below her. If its cargo was the sort of thing that the Twilight's Hammer considered its "other plan," she didn't want to know what it was.

The Twilight Father slid off the dragon's back onto the inlaid floor of Wyrmrest Temple, now covered here and there with the scarlet hue of dragon blood and the small, scattered, glittering shards that were all that remained of the Orb of Unity. Kirygosa followed in stony silence.

He handed Kirygosa's chain to an acolyte. They all knew how to control the dragoness: a single tug, in a certain way, with a certain firmness, would cause exquisite pain. The chain also prevented her from assuming her true form—a much more troublesome shape than that of a mere human female.

"Make sure she stays quiet, but do not hurt her for sport," he added to the troll, who looked disappointed. If Kirygosa was tormented too much, she might become desensitized to the pain, and that simply would not do. The troll led Kirygosa to a pillar and shoved her to the floor, then stood awaiting further commands from his Father.

The Twilight Father removed a small orb from beneath his cloak and placed it almost reverently on the bloodied floor. At once it began to pulse, glowing darkly, as if there were a seething black mist trapped inside it. Suddenly, as if the small orb were too tiny to contain something so powerful, it cracked open and the mist—no, no, not mist, *smoke*, thick and acrid and glinting here and there with orange-red embers—billowed upward. It formed a cloud, blacker than night and infinitely more unnatural, that swirled angrily until at last it took on shape and form. Baleful orange-yellow eyes, looking like liquid fire, peered out, impaling the Twilight Father with their gaze. A mammoth jaw, made of black metal, opened slightly in the hint of a mad, sly smile, and Kirygosa could not help but recoil.

Deathwing!

The Twilight Father knelt before the orb. "My master," he said humbly.

"You have succeeded?" said Deathwing without preamble. The deep voice seemed to shake the temple, shiver through the body, as if Deathwing were actually present.

"In . . . a manner of speaking," said the Twilight Father, fighting to control the slight stammer in his voice. "We have driven out the dragons from Wyrmrest Temple, including Alexstrasza and Ysera both. I have claimed it in the name of the Twilight's Hammer cult. It is your stronghold now, Great One."

The great, mad eyes narrowed. "That was not the plan," he hissed. "The *plan,* which you have failed to execute, was to destroy the dragons, not merely capture their temple!"

"This—this is true, my lord. The plan was . . . thwarted by something we could not possibly have foreseen." Quickly he explained. Deathwing listened with a silence that was worse than his angry shouting would have been. His features remained clear, though the smoke that formed them shifted, and once there was even heard a flapping of tattered, fire-limned wings.

When the Twilight Father had finished, there was a long, uncomfortable pause. Deathwing cocked his head, appearing to consider.

"This changes nothing. You have failed."

The Twilight Father began to sweat despite the cold. "It is a setback, Great One, nothing more. Not a failure. And there may be positive repercussions from it. It did drive the dragons away, and the Life-Binder—your greatest enemy—appears shattered by events."

"That is irrelevant," rumbled Deathwing. "You will find another way to achieve the goal I have set you, or else I will replace you with a general who does not fail me at a crucial juncture."

"I . . . understand, Great One." The Twilight Father's eyes flickered to Kirygosa; they narrowed in thought, then returned to regard Deathwing. "Leave it to me. Things are already in motion. I will begin right away."

"Do not think to cut me off, lesser creature," growled Deathwing.

Beneath his cowl, the Twilight Father felt himself paling. "I would never do such a thing, Great One. I am merely eager to be about serving you."

"You will serve me when I tell you to, and not a heartbeat before. Is that clear?"

The Twilight Father could only nod. But despite Deathwing's anger at having been interrupted, now he paused for a long moment before finally speaking.

"There may be . . . a new obstacle. I had *expected* that the dragonflights would not be able to stand against the combination of you, the Twilight's Hammer cult, and the one whom we seek to aid. I *expected* victory. You have told me that Ysera fled. It would have been better if she had not."

"My lord?" He couldn't help it: he swallowed hard.

"She lives, because of you," Deathwing snarled. "And because she lives, she has had the opportunity to speak with one who is destined to oppose me. His interference may tip the balance."

The Twilight Father's mind reeled at the news and its implications. What had the Awakened Dreamer done? Who, or what mighty power, had she summoned? Deathwing was deeply concerned—and that terrified the Twilight Father.

His throat dry, he managed, "What kind of being has she allied with?"

"A lesser creature," Deathwing said, biting off the words harshly.

The Twilight Father wasn't sure he had heard correctly. "What? But surely—"

"An orc!"

Both were silent now. Those mere two words told the Twilight Father all he needed to know. Once, long ago, Deathwing had been warned that an orc—seemingly the lowest of the low—would rise to challenge and possibly defeat him. No one, least of all the Twilight Father, had given it much heed.

He tried to shrug it off. "My lord, prophecies are notoriously cryptic. You are the mighty Deathwing. You have ripped this world asunder. We battle dragons—not just dragons, but the Aspects themselves! Mighty beings, not dust-eating orcs. Even a powerful one is no match for you."

"This one is different. He always has been. He has a remarkable variety of experiences to draw upon. He does not think like dragons do . . . and precisely because he does not, he might be able to save them."

The Twilight Father was dubious, but he did not let it show. "Tell me the identity of this short-lived enemy, my lord. Tell me that I may destroy him."

"You must do more than destroy. You must completely undo the one called Thrall—or this orc will be the undoing of everything. *Everything!*"

"It shall be done, I swear."

"Yes," agreed Deathwing. "It shall. You are running out of time"—he gave a macabre imitation of a draconic grin, lower jaw gaping open to display acres of jagged, metallic teeth—"*Father*. But do not despair. I may have aid for you. I am ancient, but I do not have limitless patience. Contact me again with better news."

The smoke that had formed Deathwing's image lost its solidity, becoming swirling black mist again. Slowly it settled to the floor, then coalesced into a black sphere. A moment later, even the darkness had disappeared. It was now, once again, a small, crystal-like orb. Frowning, the Twilight Father tucked it away and rose.

"You thought it would be so easy," came a clear female voice. "You and your huge, overly complicated plans. And now, as your master says, you are running out of time to undo this Thrall. The currents are shifting, Twilight Father, and your beard is gray. You are fooling yourself. You won't last long serving him. You will not win."

He turned to the enslaved dragoness and closed the distance between them. She gazed up at him defiantly while he regarded her for a long moment.

"Foolish little wyrm," he said at last. "You know but a small portion of my plans. Thrall is a flea that will soon be smashed more fittingly than you can imagine. Come," he said, and took her chain. "I have something to show you, and then we will see if I am fooling myself . . . or if *you* are the one being fooled."

He led her to the edge of the circular floor, and pointed. The mysterious sled had reached the foot of Wyrmrest Temple. Now that their services in hauling the vast vehicle were no longer needed, the snowfall elk had all been turned loose to feed the wolves. The hungry predators had done their job well: little was left now save bones. The acolytes were peering up, awaiting the signal from their adored Father. He lifted his hand, and with a flourish, the dark-robed cultists yanked off the fabric that had concealed what the wagon bore.

Kirygosa gasped, her hand flying to her mouth in horror.

Stretched out on the giant wagon was the corpse of a dragon. But just not any dragon: this body was enormous, far larger than even a Dragon Aspect. And it was misshapen, its dull scales the color of an ugly purple bruise on pale skin. And the most obscene, most horrific thing was that it did not have one head.

It had *five*. Even in the dim light with her human eyes, she could see that each head was a different color—red, black, gold, green, and blue.

Kirygosa knew exactly what it was.

"A chromatic dragon," she said in a choked voice.

Chromatic dragons were an abomination, a violation against everything natural. The monstrosities had been created by Deathwing's son, Nefarian. A mighty black dragon almost as evil as his father, Nefarian had tried to create a new dragonflight that would combine the powers of all five of the other flights—a dragonflight that could conceivably destroy all the others. The experiments were considered failures. Many whelps had died before hatching. Most of those that had survived long enough to hatch were unstable, volatile, and deformed in many ways. Only a few had reached adulthood, artificially aged by twisted magical processes.

The one before them now was definitely a mature dragon. Yet he did not stir.

"I thought they seldom survived to adulthood. Still . . . he too, is dead. Why should I fear a corpse?"

"Oh, Chromatus *is* quite dead," the Twilight Father said airily.

"Technically. For the moment. But he will live. He was Nefarian's final experiment. There had been many failures, as I am certain you know. But that is how one learns, is it not? By trying and failing?"

His beard parted in an avuncular smile as she continued to stare sickly at him.

"Chromatus exemplified the pinnacle of all Nefarian had learned through his various experiments," the Twilight Father continued. "Nefarian was, tragically, slain before he could give Chromatus the spark of life."

"A better deed was never done than the killing of Nefarian, that monster," muttered Kirygosa.

The Twilight Father gave her an amused look. "You might be surprised to know that just as the creation before you shall soon taste life, his creator does already. Yes—Nefarian has returned . . . in a manner of speaking. He is undead, but quite definitely active. For Chromatus . . . I have other plans."

Kirygosa could not tear her eyes away. "So this . . . *thing* . . . was the reason for everything you've done?" Her voice broke. "Bringing to life a monster who had no right to exist in the first place?"

"Come, now, Kirygosa!" chided the Twilight Father mockingly. "You should show more respect. You might prove to be very important in this task."

Her eyes widened. "No . . . no more experiments. . . ."

He leaned closer to her, handing over the chain to the troll acolyte who hastened up. "You see, my dear," he said gently, "the only one running out of time . . . is you."

FIVE

It was a long and arduous journey from the Maelstrom to Feralas. Thrall had emerged, as he had promised, to give Ysera his answer, only to find no sign of the green Dragon Aspect. He was at first bemused and irritated, then ashamed of his reaction: Ysera doubtless had many vital duties other than waiting on a simple shaman's answer. He was charged with this duty, had accepted it, and would see it through—though he could have wished Ysera had thought to leave one of her great green dragons behind to speed the journey. She had not, so he did the best he could with wyvern, ship, and wolf.

Ysera had told him that Dreamer's Rest was nestled against one of the great Twin Colossals. He rode along the overgrown road on his beloved, loyal frost wolf Snowsong, feeling the moist heat—so different from the temperate climes of Lordaeron where he had reached adulthood, and the dry heat of Orgrimmar—leach away at his energy.

He smelled and then saw the smoke from a long distance away, and urged his wolf on to greater speeds. The acrid stench was sharply at odds with the usual heavy, leafy scent of Feralas.

As he drew closer, Thrall felt his resentment and irritations at the task Ysera had given him melt away. These people, these druids, were in trouble. They needed help. And for whatever reasons the green Dragon Aspect had, she had wanted him to be the one to help them.

And so he would.

He rounded a turn, and the camp was suddenly there in front of him. Thrall came to an abrupt halt at what he beheld.

Carvings of owls . . . old ruins . . . a moonwell. . . .

"Night elves," he muttered aloud. Ysera had only mentioned "druids." She had apparently forgotten the small detail that this "Dreamer's Rest" was not composed of *tauren* druids, but possibly—probably—hostile night elves. Was this some sort of a trap? He had been imprisoned by the Alliance before, hauled off as "cargo" and saved only by the unlikeliest of rescuers. He would not permit himself to be so used again.

Thrall dismounted and with a hand signal instructed Snowsong to wait. Slowly, carefully, he moved forward to get a better look. As Ysera had told him, Dreamer's Rest was small indeed. It seemed to be deserted; perhaps the inhabitants were all off fighting the fire.

Ancestors knew, it was coming close enough. He could see several trees toward the far end of the camp, past a few dark-purple travel pavilions that had been erected. And again, as the Awakened had assured him, it was a small fringe of what looked to Thrall like a very old-growth grove indeed.

He could definitely sense the anger and anxiety in the elements here. It was almost buffeting, and his eyes watered at the smoke. If something wasn't done soon . . .

He felt something sharp and hard on the back of his neck and stood completely still.

"Speak slowly, orc, and tell us why you have come to trouble the

Druids of the Talon." The voice was female, hard, and brooked no argument.

Thrall cursed himself. He had been too distracted by the elements' pain, and he had been incautious. At least the elf was letting him speak.

"I was sent here to help you," he said. "I am a shaman. Search my bag if you like; you will find my totems."

A snort. "An orc, come to help night elves?"

"A shaman, come to help heal and calm an angry land," he said. "I work with the Earthen Ring. Both Horde and Alliance are trying to find a way to save this world. Druids have a similar organization in the Cenarion Circle. In my pack, I have a pouch that carries my totems. Search if you like. All I ask is that you let me help."

The hard pointed object was removed from pressing at his back, but Thrall was not foolish enough to strike. The elf would not be alone. He tensed as the Doomhammer, strapped to his back, was removed, but held himself in check. Hands rummaged through his pack and removed the pouch.

"Those are indeed totems," said a male voice. "And he wears prayer beads. Turn around, orc."

Thrall did, slowly. Two night elves regarded him. One was a Sentinel with green hair and violet skin. The other was male, clean-shaven, his green hair worn in a topknot. His skin was a rich, dark shade of purple and his eyes glowed a golden hue. Both were sweaty and soot-covered, obviously from trying to fight the blaze. Others now approached, looking cautious but curious.

The female was searching Thrall's face, and then recognition came to her.

"Thrall," she said, disbelieving. She looked at the Doomhammer lying on the earth, then back at him.

"Warchief of the Horde?" said another voice.

"No, not anymore, at least not according to rumor," the female said. "We have heard that he disappeared—left his rank as warchief. Where he went, the Sentinels have not been told. I am Erina Willowborn, a Sentinel, and this is Desharin Greensong, one of the Druids of the Talon. I was part of a diplomatic entourage to Orgrimmar once." Erina had been holding her glaive in a defensive posture; now she lowered it. "You are a very important personage, to come to our little camp. Who sent you?"

Thrall sighed inwardly. He had hoped to avoid mentioning the specifics of his task. "The rumors are true. I did leave, to help heal the damage caused to Azeroth by the Cataclysm. At the Maelstrom, working with other members of the Earthen Ring, I was found by Ysera the Awakened," he said. "She told me of the plight of Dreamer's Rest. That you had no shaman to help intercede with the troubled elements, and that you needed help."

"You expect me to believe that?" said Erina.

"I do," said Desharin. Erina looked at him, surprised. "Thrall was ever known as a moderate, even as warchief. And now that he serves the Earthen Ring, perhaps he was indeed sent here."

"By a dragon," said Erina sarcastically. "Excuse me . . . not just any dragon, but Ysera of the Emerald Dream. And carrying the Doomhammer."

"Who would wish to help druids more?" Desharin said. "And the Doomhammer is his, is it not? He may bear it wherever he wishes." The Sentinel had no response to that, and turned to another who had approached. He, too, had long green hair that hung unbound, but also sported a short beard. His face looked weathered and wise, and he regarded Thrall thoughtfully.

"This is your camp, Telaron," Erina said respectfully. "Tell us what you want us to do. He is an orc, and our enemy."

"He is also a shaman, and therefore friend to the elements," Telaron replied. "And the elements are so troubled that we cannot afford to deny them friends. We will put you to the test, Thrall of the Earthen Ring. Come."

Thrall followed as Telaron led him up the sloping hills closer to the blazing fire. The trees near the camp had mercifully not yet caught, and Thrall could see that they had been doused liberally with water. All the smaller scrub bushes had been cleared; only the old growth remained.

His heart ached to behold it.

Many of the great trees were already too badly burned to rescue. Others were just igniting, but the fires, angry and raw, were now spreading rapidly. Thrall recalled the blaze that had swept through Orgrimmar, and swiftly took out his fire totem from his pouch. He stepped forward, pressing his bare feet firmly into the good earth, lifting his hands skyward. He closed his eyes and reached out with his mind and heart.

Spirits of fire, what troubles you? Let me help. Let me take you away from where you harm things old and rare and irreplaceable, and bring you to where you can warm and comfort living, breathing beings.

There was a strange grimness to the essence of one elemental as it responded. It was similar to the dark anger of the spark that had threatened to destroy Orgrimmar some moons past, but there was something resolute in this one's nature.

I am doing what must be done. Fire purges. You know this. Fire burns away what is impure, so that it may be returned to the earth, and the cycle begun anew. It is my duty, shaman!

His eyes still closed, Thrall jerked as if struck. *Your duty? Surely you choose your duty, spirit of fire. And what has happened to these old trees, that you feel they need to be purged? Are they ill? Plagued? Cursed?*

None of these things, admitted the fire elemental, speaking in Thrall's heart.

Then why? Tell me. I would understand this, if I can.

The fire did not answer at once, burning suddenly hotter and brighter for a moment. Thrall had to turn his face away from the inferno.

They are . . . confused. Something is wrong with them. They do not know what they know. They must be destroyed!

Thrall himself was confused by that response. He was well aware that all things had a spirit. Even stones, which were not truly "living" beings; even fire, which was "speaking" in his head and heart. But he could make no sense of this.

What do they know? Thrall asked of the spirit of fire.

What is wrong!

"Wrong" as in unnatural, or "wrong" as in incorrect?

Incorrect.

Thrall thought frantically. *Could they learn what is correct?*

For a long moment he thought he had lost the attention of the spirit. It was agitated, erratic, distraught. If it would not listen—

They did know, once. They could learn again.

Then, spirit of fire, do not destroy. I urge you to pull back. If you must burn, burn as torches to illuminate the darkness, or as hearthfires, to cook meals and warm chilled bodies. Harm these trees no further, lest you forever destroy their ability to one day learn what is correct!

Thrall waited, muscles taut. He desperately hoped he was on the right track. The only way he would know would be if the fire obeyed him. For a long moment, nothing happened. The fire crackled and burned, and heat roiled off the consumed trees as they blackened.

Then: *Agreed. They must learn again what is true. Someone must teach them. If not, then burn they shall. Burn they must.*

And the fire slowly faded away to nothing. Thrall stumbled forward, his eyes flying open, suddenly exhausted by the working. Strong hands caught him as cheers went up.

"Well done, shaman," said Telaron, smiling approvingly. "Well done! You have our gratitude. Please—stay with us tonight. We would treat you as the honored guest that you are."

Weary from the journey and the intense working, as were the elves who would have normally been slumbering during daylight hours, Thrall accepted. That night, he found himself shaking his head in quiet amazement as he sat, accompanied by Snowsong, and ate and drank and laughed with night elf druids and Sentinels. He recalled the meeting not so long ago in which ten druids— five night elves, five tauren—had met to peacefully negotiate trade routes. They had been ambushed and slaughtered, the tauren arch- druid Hamuul Runetotem the only survivor. The action had in- flamed both the Alliance and the Horde. It was rumored that Gar- rosh Hellscream had sent the attackers, but such a thing was never proven, and despite Garrosh's hot temper, Thrall did not believe the rumors.

If that meeting had been successful, Thrall mused sadly, perhaps nights like this—singing songs and telling tales—would not be so uncommon between the two factions. Perhaps there would be more unity, and thus more healing of the world that both shared.

Thrall went to sleep while his night elf hosts were still singing songs to the stars, the sounds of the wilderness music to his ears, wrapped in sleeping furs with only his hand for his pillow.

He slept very soundly for what seemed like the first time in a long while.

Thrall was awakened at dawn by a gentle shaking.

"Thrall," came the musical voice of a kaldorei. "It is Desharin. Wake up. I have something to show you."

After so many years in battle, Thrall was not unused to waking swiftly and fully alert. He rose quietly and followed the elf, stepping carefully around and over drowsing night elf bodies. They moved past the moonwell and pavilions deeper into the old-growth fringe.

"Wait here, and be still," Desharin whispered. "Listen."

The trees, those that had been spared the worst of the blaze, moved and sighed, their branches creaking, their leaves murmuring. Thrall waited for a moment longer, then turned to his companion, shaking his head.

"I hear nothing."

Desharin smiled. "Thrall," he said quietly, "there is no wind."

And suddenly Thrall realized that the kaldorei was right. The trees were moving as if in a gentle wind—but the air was still.

"Look at them," Desharin said. "Carefully."

Thrall did, focusing intently. The knots and gnarls on the tree trunks . . . the spiky branches . . .

His eyes widened, and he suddenly understood what—who?—he was beholding. He had heard of them before, of course, but he had never seen one.

"These are ancients," he breathed. Desharin nodded. Thrall gazed in awe, wondering how it was that he had not seen this before. He shook his head slowly. "And here I thought I was coming only to save a forest. They seemed . . . just like trees."

"They were sleeping. You awakened them."

"I did? How?" Thrall didn't want to tear his eyes from the ancients. These were old, old beings, many of them keepers of wisdom from aeons past. They moved, and creaked, and appeared to be . . . talking?

Thrall strained to understand, and after a moment, he realized he could decipher the deep, softly spoken words.

"Dreaming, we were. Confused dreams that held us in our uncertainty. And so we did not awaken when the fire came. It was only when we heard the ancient ritual, of shaman to element, that we were awakened. By your actions, you saved us."

"The fire told me that it was trying to cleanse you. That it felt you were . . . impure," Thrall said, trying to recall exactly what it was the fire elemental had communicated to him. "It said you were confused. You did not know what you knew, and what you knew was incorrect. I asked if you could learn what was correct, and the spirit of fire thought you could. That was why it agreed to cease burning you."

Thrall realized, now that the fire was no longer a threat, that some of the ancients had small creatures nesting in their branches. They looked like tiny dragons with delicate, vibrantly colored wings like a butterfly's and feathery antennae adorning their bright-eyed heads. One of them flew out from the branches, fluttered about, and landed on Desharin's shoulder, nuzzling him fondly.

"They are called sprite darters," Desharin said, petting the small creature. "They are not dragons, but they are magical protectors and defenders of the Emerald Dream."

And suddenly Thrall understood. He looked at the ancients, at their little magical protector, at Desharin's green hair.

"You are a green dragon," he said quietly. It was a statement, not a question.

Desharin nodded. "My task was to watch you."

Thrall frowned, the old irritation returning. "Watch me? Was I being tested? Did I perform to Ysera's expectations?"

"Not quite like that," he said. "It was not an evaluation of your skills. I was to watch and see what was in your heart as you aided us, how you approached the task. You have a journey to make, Thrall, son of Durotan and Draka. We needed to see if you were ready to undertake it."

The ancients began to speak again in their strange, creaking language. "Long have we kept the memories of this world. Long have we tended knowledge that others have forgotten. But the spirit of fire was right. Something is amiss. The memories we bear are becoming hazy, confused . . . lost. Something has gone awry with time itself."

They must learn again what is true. Someone must teach them. If not, then burn they shall. Burn they must.

"That is what the spirit of fire was trying to say," Thrall said. "It knew that their memories were wrong, incorrect. But it thought they could learn the correct memories again. That means there's hope."

Desharin nodded, thinking aloud. "Something is wrong with the memories of the ancients. They are not as we are; their memories cannot be altered unless the things they remember *themselves* were altered. That means that time itself has been interfered with." He turned to Thrall, solemn and excited both. "This, then, is your journey. You must travel to the Caverns of Time. You must find out what has happened and help set the timeways right."

Thrall looked at him, stunned. "The timeways . . . so they *do* exist. I had suspected—"

"They exist. Nozdormu and the rest of the bronze dragonflight manage them. And he is the one you must go to with this information."

"I? Why would he talk to me? Wouldn't a fellow dragon be a better choice?" It was an almost overwhelming thought: to travel back in time, to alter or adjust history. He felt out of his depth. What had initially seemed like a trivial errand had now taken on dire significance.

"I will accompany you if you like," Desharin offered. "But the Aspect was adamant that you were important somehow. Do not take offense, but I am as puzzled as you are as to why she thought so." He gave a sudden grin that made him look much younger than he doubtless was. "At least your skin is green."

Thrall started to bridle, then found himself chuckling instead. "I would welcome any aid and illumination you care to give, and I am honored that Ysera regards me in such a light. I will do my utmost to help." He turned to the ancients. "Help all of you, if I can."

The ancients rustled, and Thrall heard the gentle sound of something dropping on the earth. It rolled down the slight incline and came to a stop at Thrall's feet.

"That is a gift for you," Desharin said.

Thrall stooped and picked it up. It was an acorn, looking to his eyes much like any other one. But he knew it was so much more, and felt a shiver as he closed his hand around it protectively for a moment before carefully putting it in his pouch.

"Take good care of it," Desharin said with sudden solemnity. "That acorn holds all the knowledge of its parent tree, and all the knowledge of that parent's parent tree . . . and on and on, back toward the beginning of all things. You are to plant it where it seems right for it to grow."

Thrall nodded, his throat closing up at the gift and the duty.

"I will do so," he assured the ancients.

"And now, friend orc," Desharin said, looking up at the lightening sky, "we head to the Caverns of Time."

Six

The trip would be swift on dragonback, Desharin said, and Thrall had to agree. Snowsong perforce was left behind. Telaron himself assured Thrall that she would be well taken care of. "Your friendship with the lady Jaina is well known," the night elf had said. "We will care for your wolf friend until arrangements can be made to return her safely. Snowsong is a noble beast, and deserves no less." Of course—druids would care greatly about an animal's welfare, and Jaina would be able to arrange a peaceful transfer. Snowsong could not be in better hands. Thrall gave Snowsong a final scratch behind the ears before turning to Desharin.

Desharin had assumed his true form and regarded Thrall as he approached.

"You honor me by bearing me," Thrall said to the green dragon.

"You are charged with a task by Ysera," Desharin replied. "The honor is mine. Do not fear. I will bear you swiftly and safely. You have my word. It would be more than my life is worth to disappoint my lady Aspect."

"She is terrible in her anger?"

"She can be, when she is roused to anger. She is an Aspect. The power she wields is tremendous. But her heart is gentle," Desharin said. "We serve her not out of fear but out of love. It would destroy me to give her any kind of sorrow." The words were filled with respect and admiration, and the deep loyalty that Ysera inspired in her flight touched Thrall.

Strange though this adventure was, he was glad he had agreed to accept it.

He climbed slowly atop the great being and then, with less of an effort displayed by any other creature Thrall had ridden, the dragon was airborne.

Thrall's breath went away at the feeling of magic and power that emanated from Desharin. His wings beat strongly, the breeze cool on Thrall's skin, and he rose upward seemingly effortlessly. When he could breathe again, Thrall almost wanted to laugh. Before, he realized, he had ridden beasts that could fly. Now he felt as if he were one such creature himself.

"Can you tell me more of yourself? Of the other dragons?" Thrall asked. "I know some, but to be honest, I do not know what is myth and what is fact."

Desharin chuckled, a deep, warm sound. "I will, friend Thrall, though as to most recent history, you must remember that I have been in the Emerald Dream and have only just awakened. But I will share what I know. One thing is for certain: Aspects only rarely intervene in the affairs of the short-lived races. The rest of my kind? Many are intrigued by what some arrogantly call the 'lesser races.' We sometimes enjoy taking your forms."

"Such as a kaldorei."

"Exactly," agreed Desharin, "although I may assume any one I wish. While we are individuals, of course, and each of us has a preferred shape, you'll find each flight gravitates toward a certain appearance more often than not. For instance, we green dragons tend to prefer kaldorei, because of our relationship with the great druid Malfurion Stormrage, who for so long shared the Dream with us."

Thrall nodded. It made sense.

"I have observed the reds are partial to the sin'dorei, and the blues often opt for human form. As for the bronzes, while their task necessitates a variety of shapes, they seem to enjoy appearing as . . . gnomes."

Thrall laughed. "Perhaps they enjoy being tiny and harmless-looking, given their natural form."

"Perhaps. Maybe you can ask."

"I . . . no, I don't think I will."

"You are wise."

"I have learned a few things," Thrall said. "Do any of you ever . . ." How to word it? He shrugged and said bluntly, "Take positions of power among the short-lived races?"

"Generally not, although Deathwing tried, and his daughter, Onyxia, actually succeeded," growled Desharin. "And Krasus is . . . was . . . a powerful member of the Kirin Tor."

"Was?"

"He met his end," was all Desharin said, and he fell silent. Clearly, it was a delicate matter.

Thrall changed the subject. "I have heard that there are other types of dragons than these five flights."

"Indeed, and these are the enemies of all of us, save the blacks whom they serve," Desharin said. "Deathwing's son, Nefarian, tried to create a new type of dragon called a chromatic dragon. He used magical experiments to combine qualities of all the other dragonflights. The resulting whelps were often deformed, and always short-lived, fortunately. None of them exists any longer. The twilight dragons had a similar sort of origin, except their creatrix, Sinestra, used ancient dragon artifacts and the powers of the nether dragons. They proved more stable and longer-lived . . . and also have an advantage in that they can turn incorporeal at will."

"A challenging enemy," Thrall said.

"Very," agreed Desharin, "especially when controlled by the black dragonflight."

Thrall watched as the greenery of Feralas gave way to the vast stretch of water that was now Thousand Needles. Thrall shook his head, gazing down at the dozens of small islands that used to be the pinnacles of the spiky rock formations that gave Thousand Needles its name. The world had changed so very much. He knew it had, of course; he had heard all the reports. But to see so much from the air . . . he wondered whether the others of the Ring had witnessed what he was seeing now, and if they had not, if perhaps they should.

Then Thrall and Desharin were flying swiftly over the desert of Tanaris, and Thrall could see the jagged teeth of sharp stones, part of a series of hills, jutting upward, and what looked like the tilted ruins of various strange structures. There was an angled tower, a broken domed structure, what appeared to be a typical orcish hut, and . . . the ragged sail of a ship? Overhead, Thrall could see two bronze dragons wheeling and turning.

"This area," said Desharin solemnly, "serves as the courtyard to the Caverns of Time. I will land and go in on foot. They will want to find out why we have come."

"I am sure they will," Thrall said.

Desharin alighted but remained in his dragon form. Thrall started to dismount, but Desharin said, "Stay where you are, friend Thrall. No sense in tiring your shorter legs unnecessarily." Desharin began to walk along the soft sand, heading for the arch of a domed building that appeared to manifest half inside, half outside of one of the jutting stones they had glimpsed earlier. Almost immediately, one of the wheeling dragons came to ground close to them.

"This is not your realm, green dragon," the bronze said in a low, angry voice. "Go, and go quickly. You have no business here."

"My bronze brother," said Desharin, with deep respect, "I am here on my lady Aspect's business."

The great eyes narrowed, and the bronze turned to glance at Thrall perched atop Desharin's back. He looked slightly surprised, then returned his attention to Desharin.

"You say you are here on behalf of Lady Ysera," he said, his voice slightly less intimidating. "I am Chronalis, and I am a gatekeeper of the Caverns of Time. Tell me why you have come, and perchance I may admit you."

"My name is Desharin, and I am here to aid this orc. He is Thrall, once warchief of the Horde, now member of the Earthen Ring. Ysera the Awakened believes he needs to find and speak with Nozdormu."

The bronze dragon laughed slightly. "Oh, I know of Thrall," he said, then addressed the orc directly. "And from what I do know of you, you are a not-inconsiderable personage for a short-lived being. But I do not think you can find Nozdormu, if his own dragonflight cannot do so."

Having been the warchief of the Horde, Thrall was not surprised to hear that he was known to the bronze dragonflight. What did startle him was the revelation that Nozdormu was missing.

"It may be that he can do what the rest of us cannot," said Desharin affably.

"She came to you? Ysera the Awakened?" Chronalis asked Thrall curiously.

Thrall nodded and explained his meeting with Ysera. He did not attempt to paint himself as better than he was, admitting fully that he had initially thought the task trivial, but that he now understood the importance of it, having realized that the grove was home to ancients. Too, he told Chronalis about the fire elemental's response to his plea to cease damaging the trees. Chronalis nodded, listening intently.

"I do not know how I will be able to find Nozdormu where others have failed," Thrall said bluntly. "But I give you my word, I will do the best that I can."

Chronalis considered. "We have let others into the Caverns ere now, to assist us in keeping the timeways true," he said, thinking. "Though the irony amuses me. If you wish to accompany him, Desharin, then you both may follow me."

"Irony?" Thrall asked, as the two huge dragons strode along a sandy walkway that seemed at first to lead into one of the listing buildings but quickly proved to enter the heart of the mountain.

"Indeed," Chronalis said, peering back at him over his folded wings. "You see, as I said before, sometimes we permit certain mortals to aid us in restoring the true timeway. The timeways have . . . come under attack recently, by a mysterious group called the infinite dragonflight. The bronze dragonflight, and particularly the Timeless One, Nozdormu, is charged with keeping the timeways as they are meant to be. If they are damaged or altered, the world you know could cease to exist. For reasons not yet known to us, the infinite dragonflight has infected various timeways, trying to alter them to their own ends. And your escape from Durnholde Keep, Thrall, is one of the events they sought to change."

Thrall stared at him. *"What?"*

"If you had never escaped from Durnholde, the world would not be as it is today. You would never have rebuilt the Horde or freed your people from the internment camps. And so you would not have been able to bring aid against the Burning Legion when the demons came. Azeroth could have been destroyed."

Desharin looked at Thrall with a new respect. "Well, no wonder the Aspect thought you important," he said.

Thrall was shaking his head. "Such knowledge might make me think more of myself, but instead . . . I feel humbled. Please . . . thank those who fought to preserve that timeway. To help me. And . . ." His voice trailed off. "If they see Taretha, tell them to be gentle to her."

"If they see Taretha, and all goes well, you will get to part with her as you once did," said Chronalis.

They went deeper into the mountain. Thrall felt as if he had imbibed a draft intending to send him on a vision quest, yet his mind was clear. To one side, a house looked as if it had materialized partway inside the stone of the cavern. Another house loomed at an awkward angle, the sky above it—sky? In a *mountain?*—purple and magenta and ribboned with strange energy. Columns jutted upward, supporting nothing; trees flourished in a place with no water or sunlight. They passed a graveyard on one side. Thrall wondered, but did not ask, who was buried there. On another side, he could see strange chunks of floating rocks, varied in shape. Here was a tower of orcish make; over there was a ship.

Too, there were beings that he realized were most likely bronze dragons. There were several children and adults of nearly all races, six-limbed golden-scaled dragonspawn patrolling against possible intruders, and of course, bronze dragons in their natural form flapping silently above them.

At one point Thrall looked over his shoulder and realized that after a few moments the dragons' pawprints had vanished.

"This is no ordinary sand," said Chronalis. "Your presence here does not leave a trace. Look there."

And Thrall's eyes widened.

It hovered in the air before him, a contraption worthy of a goblin or gnomish mind. It was an hourglass, but like none he had ever seen before. Three containers poured sand endlessly down.

And three containers poured sand endlessly *up*.

Wrapped about all six and their bases was a twining, twisting frame that embraced without touching. Slowly it turned, and the sands of time—for such Thrall now understood them to be—poured up and down.

"This is all so . . ." He groped for words, could not find them, and simply shook his head in amazement.

Desharin came to a stop, and Thrall took this as a cue to slip to the ground. Once he had done so, the green dragon assumed his elven form and placed a gentle hand on Thrall's shoulder.

"It is difficult for those who are not dragons to grasp," he said, adding with a grin, "It is difficult even for dragons other than bronzes to grasp. Do not worry. Your task is not to understand the vagaries of the timeways."

"No," Thrall said, letting a slight sarcasm creep into his voice. "I just have to find the Timeless One, who *does* understand the vagaries of the timeways, whom no one else can seem to locate."

Desharin clapped Thrall on the back. "Exactly," he said, laughing. Their eyes met and Thrall grinned. He decided he liked this green dragon. After Ysera's eccentric behavior and the clinical detachment of Chronalis, Desharin seemed very down-to-earth.

"I do not know how you wish to proceed," Chronalis said.

Thrall looked at Desharin. "I think perhaps some time to settle our minds before we begin would help," the green dragon said. "Clarity is often found in stillness, and Thrall is likely and rather understandably overwhelmed by all he has just beheld."

Chronalis dipped his golden head. "As you wish. You may roam wherever you like, but please—the timeways are nothing to enter carelessly. To do so may doom you. Under no circumstances should you enter them without speaking with one of us. I'm sure by now you can understand why."

Thrall nodded. "Indeed I do. Thank you for admitting me, Chronalis. I will do my utmost to aid you."

"Of that, I have no doubt," Chronalis said. He leaped upward and then suddenly seemed to blur. Then he was gone.

"What . . . ?" Thrall started to ask Desharin, then realized what must have happened. Master of time that he was, Chronalis had simply sped up time for himself and was now back at his post. Thrall shook his head, marveling.

They started walking away from the bronze dragons, who seemed to have pressing duties and tasks, even the children. It was easy to see that these were not real children; their faces and posture revealed the graveness of their roles. Trees grew here and there: evergreens, taking root in sand. It was but one of the oddities of this place, and Thrall shrugged and accepted it. The smell of pine was sharp and fresh. Immediately he was plunged back into his youth, growing up in Durnholde. When he had been permitted outside to train, this had often been the scent he had smelled. It was strange, how powerfully scent brought back memories, both good and bad: of a girl who had sacrificed everything to aid him, of a "master" who had beaten him almost to death in a drunken rage. . . . In Hillsbrad, Thrall had had his first glimpse of another orc, and deemed his brother a monster.

"You are agitated," Desharin said quietly. "And, if I am right, by more than these revelations."

Thrall was forced to nod. "I am reminded of the place of my youth," he said. "The memories are not necessarily pleasant ones."

Desharin nodded. "Come, friend Thrall. Let us find a place to be still and meditate before attempting to navigate these timeways. Unlike the bronze dragons, for us, the past is past, and should not be an undue burden. We will have challenges enough without bringing disquieting thoughts with us, I think."

They walked on for a little while in silence, until Desharin came to a halt. "This place seems quiet," he said, looking about. "We should not be disturbed here." He sat down beneath one of the towering trees and placed his hands on his knees. Thrall emulated him.

He was tense, not just because of what he had recently beheld and learned or the memories the scent of the trees were recalling, but because the last time he had attempted to drop into a meditative state with another, it had been an abysmal failure. The dragon noticed this.

"You are a shaman and have been for some time," he said. "This should be familiar to you. Why do you have such difficulty?"

"Well, you are a green dragon. You're more used to sleeping than being awake," Thrall shot back.

Desharin did not take offense, merely took a moment to brush back his long hair while Thrall continued to settle himself. The green dragon closed his eyes and took a deep breath.

Thrall found himself doing the same thing. Desharin was right. This was, of course, very familiar to Thrall. He watched the dragon for a moment, his thoughts not on dropping into a meditative state but on all that had transpired so very recently. Leaving the leadership of the Horde. Traveling to Nagrand and meeting Aggra. Cairne's death. The Cataclysm that had ripped open the world and turned it upside down. His irritation and inability to focus. Ysera's task and meeting the ancients . . . and this dragon, who sat before him, looking nothing like his true self and everything like a meditating night elf.

This place was unnerving, and compelling. Thrall did not want to close his eyes and explore his inner self. He wanted to explore the Caverns of Time.

But he would, and soon. He needed to embark on such an important task as prepared as possible. And so, reluctantly, he closed his eyes, and began to breathe slowly and calmly.

It happened so swiftly that by the time the sound of wind whistling across the flat of a blade alerted him to danger and he opened his eyes, Desharin's head had already been severed from his shoulders.

Thrall dove to the side, somersaulting and landing on his feet. He did not spare the corpse of his new friend a glance. Desharin was dead, and Thrall would soon join him if he was not careful. He reached for the Doomhammer, grasping it and wheeling it around with the ease and speed of long familiarity. His eyes were firmly fastened on the suddenly appearing threat as he swung: large, but not as large as an orc, wearing heavy black plate mail. Spikes jutted out here and there from elbows and shoulders and knees, and gauntleted hands clasped a huge, glowing two-handed broadsword. But what should have been a blow across the stranger's midsection, crushing his armor like a cheap tin mug, instead met empty air.

His foe lurched away, missing the Doomhammer's heavy head by less than a finger's breadth. Surprised, Thrall lost a precious second in attempting to halt the powerful swing and bring the hammer around for a second strike. His attacker had already recovered and now bore down on him with the massive broadsword, which gleamed with enchantment. The strike was much swifter than Thrall would have given him credit for, encumbered by armor as he was. The orc knew a flicker of apprehension. Who *was* this unknown enemy? Fierce, fast, strong—

Acting on instinct, he let the swing of the Doomhammer carry him out of the path of the charging adversary. Releasing one hand, he lifted it and summoned a strong, concentrated gust of wind. The human—for Thrall was starting to guess it was one, based on the size and style of armor—stumbled and nearly fell in the soft sand. Another request to the spirits of air, and several handfuls of sand suddenly rose to scour the front of the helm. It offered some protection, but not enough: the sand, precisely directed by Thrall, penetrated the eye slits and would temporarily blind. A shout came from behind the helm, the voice of a human male snarling in agony and anger, lifting his sword not to attack but to shield his face.

The broadsword's glowing aura pulsed, red and as angry as its master, and then it was descending toward Thrall.

Thrall realized that he was facing, not just an enemy surprisingly agile and strong on his own, but one who held a weapon that might be as powerful as the Doomhammer.

Desharin had been taken unawares—but he should not have been. What had this man done to so cloak his presence, to hide himself from a green dragon and the former warchief of the Horde? Where were the other bronze dragons? Thrall thought about calling to them, but they would likely be too far away: he and Desharin had—foolishly, in retrospect—sought an out-of-the-way location for their meditation.

Spirits of earth, will you aid me?

A sinkhole opened beneath the black-armored man's feet. He stumbled and fell to one knee, all his grace and power turned into desperate clumsiness as he fought to free his leg. Thrall snarled, lifting the Doomhammer and bringing it smashing down—

—to clang and halt against the blade of the two-handed sword. One gauntleted hand grasped the blade. Magic crackled along the weapon, and the human shoved hard enough to send Thrall hurtling backward as if thrown by a giant's hand.

The human was on his feet now, standing over Thrall and lifting the glowing weapon. He plunged it down toward the earth.

Thrall rolled to the side, but not fast enough. The sword missed spearing his torso but still carved a groove along his side. Thrall leaped to his feet.

At that moment, a huge shadow fell over them. Before he even realized what had happened, Thrall had been caught up in a giant claw. The dragon was far from gentle.

"We will deal with the intruder!" the dragon cried. "Your task is to find Nozdormu!" And indeed, Thrall saw that the dragon was heading straight for the whirling, churning outline of a portal to one of the timeways—which one, he did not know.

Before Thrall could say anything—could even draw breath in his compressed lungs to speak—the bronze dragon dropped close to the earth and all but threw the hapless orc into the portal.

Before he disappeared inside it, though, Thrall could hear his foe shouting behind him in a voice that sounded strangely familiar.

"You will not escape me so easily, Thrall! You cannot hide in there for long, and when you emerge, I will find you! I will find you and I will slay you! *Do you hear me?!*"

SEVEN

Beneath his running feet, the sand that had so treacherously slowed Thrall down abruptly became solid earth and grass. Above him, instead of the bizarre skyscape of the Caverns of Time, he saw pine trees, black sky, and twinkling stars. Thrall slowed and came to a halt, attempting to get his bearings.

The familiar smell of pine and earth, the scents made all the sharper for being borne on the misty and slightly chilly air, confirmed Thrall's location. A stream splashed a few feet away, and Thrall caught sight of the white-tufted tail of a fox. Thrall had never been to this specific place, but he knew the area. He had grown up here.

He was in the foothills of Hillsbrad, in the Eastern Kingdoms.

So, he mused, *I know where I am. But the more important question is . . . when?*

He had done something few had ever done, something he hadn't been sure was possible until a short time ago.

When was he?

He leaned heavily against a tree, letting the Doomhammer slip to the earth as the realization sank in. He had been too distracted by Desharin's sudden death and the violence of the attack to truly notice and appreciate the magnitude of what he was doing.

The slice in his side demanded attention. Thrall placed a hand over the wound, asking for healing. His hand glowed softly, tingling with warmth, and the wound closed beneath it. He removed his robe, rinsed it clean of blood in the stream, bundled it up in his pack, and had just finished shrugging into a fresh robe when voices came to him.

The voices of orcs.

Quickly he wrapped the too-recognizable Doomhammer in the old robe and stuffed it as best he could into his pack, hoping to catch a glimpse of the orcs while also desperately thinking of a plausible story. His eyes widened slightly, and he was suddenly very glad that the Doomhammer was in his pack, safely out of sight. He recognized the banner one of them bore. A black mountain silhouetted against a red background. It was the banner of the Blackrock clan. That meant one of two things, depending on when in his world's history he was. Most of the members of the Blackrock clan were not individuals for whom Thrall had respect. He thought of Blackhand, cruel and domineering, and his sons, Rend and Maim, who had gone on to dwell inside Blackrock Mountain.

But there was one Blackrock who, in Thrall's opinion, redeemed the clan. That orc's name was Orgrim Doomhammer. Thrall's heart lifted as the thought occurred to him that he had perhaps gone back to a point in time when his mentor and friend still lived. The orc who had picked a fight with him while disguised as a simple traveler. Who had gulled him into attacking with good, honest orcish anger . . . and who had been pleased to have been bested by Thrall. Who had taught him orcish battle tactics and who, with his last breath, had named Thrall warchief of the Horde and bequeathed to the younger orc his famous armor . . . and the Doom-hammer.

Orgrim. Thrall was suddenly seized with a longing to see the mighty orc—his friend—once more. And such a thing was possible, here . . . now.

The approaching orc drew an axe. "Who are you?" he demanded.

"Th-Thra'kash," Thrall said quickly. He could not announce himself as a shaman, not here, not in this era. How could he? "A warlock."

The guard looked him up and down. "With an interesting taste in robes. Where are your skulls and embroidered cloth?"

Thrall drew himself up to his full height and took a menacing step toward the guard. "The purpose of operating in the shadows is to not be noticed," he said. "Trust me. It is only the insecure who must announce how dangerous they are with black clothes and bones. The rest of us *know* what we can do, and do not need to boast of it."

The guard took a step backward, then looked around carefully. "You were . . . sent to assist with the mission we are to carry out later?"

There was an edge to his voice that Thrall did not like, but he needed to divert suspicion quickly. So he nodded and replied, "Yes, of course. Why else would I be here?"

"Odd, to send a warlock," said the guard, his eyes narrowing for a moment. Thrall endured the scrutiny, and then at last the guard shrugged. "Oh, well. My job is not to ask questions, just to carry out my orders. My name is Grukar. I have some things to attend to before it is time. Come with me up to the fire near the tent. It's a cold night."

Thrall nodded. "My thanks, Grukar."

Thrall followed Grukar as the other orc took him up farther into the foothills area. There was a small tent erected in hues of red and black. The entrance flap had been pulled down, and two orcs stood guard on either side of it. They looked curiously at Thrall, but as he was clearly with Grukar, they soon lost interest in him.

"Wait here for me," Grukar said quietly. "I will not be long." Thrall nodded and went to the bonfire a few feet away. Several other guards huddled there, holding out their hands to the flame. Thrall imitated them, trying to draw as little attention to himself as possible. And then he heard voices.

Or rather, a single voice. Thrall could not catch all the words, but someone was speaking of Gul'dan. Thrall's eyes narrowed as he listened. Gul'dan had betrayed the orcs. He had allied with demons in order to increase his own personal power and formed the Shadow Council to undermine the clans. Worst of all, he had persuaded the highest-ranking orcs of Draenor to drink demonic blood. It was this stain that had hounded them for so long. Even those who had not partaken found themselves developing an unquenchable thirst for slaughter, their skin turning green with the taint, until Thrall's friend Grom Hellscream had finally, fully freed the orcs by slaying the demon Mannoroth, whose blood had been the cause of so much torment.

But that heroic act was many years in the future, Thrall knew. In this timeway, Gul'dan's treachery was still new. And someone had come to persuade Orgrim Doomhammer to overthrow Gul'dan.

At last, the grim tale wound down. For a moment there was silence.

And then Thrall heard a voice he had never thought to hear again. It was younger, slightly higher than what Thrall remembered, but he knew it at once, and a lump crept into his throat.

"I believe you, old friend."

Orgrim Doomhammer.

"And let me reassure you, I will not stand for Gul'dan's plans for our people. We will stand against the darkness with you."

Thrall suddenly wondered: Had he even been born when this conversation took place? Who had had the courage to come to Doomhammer with such—

And then he knew, and the knowing suddenly took his breath away.

"One of my personal guards will escort you to a safe place. There is a stream nearby and much game in the woods this time of year, so you shall not go hungry. I will do what I can on your behalf, and when the time is right, you and I shall stand side by side as we slay the great betrayer Gul'dan together."

But that wasn't what had happened. What had happened was—

The tent flap was drawn back. Three orcs emerged. One was Doomhammer—younger, fit, strong, and proud. In his face Thrall could see the older orc he would one day become. But although he had thought just a moment ago he would hunger to look upon Orgrim's face once again, he found his eyes riveted on the other two orcs.

They were a mated pair, donning fur clothing that was much too heavy for this climate as they emerged from the tent. With them was a large white wolf—a frost wolf, Thrall knew. They stood tall and proud, the male powerful and battle-toned, the female every inch the warrior that her mate was.

And in her arms, she bore an infant.

Thrall knew the child.

It was he . . . and the orcs who stood before him now were his parents.

He simply stared at them, joy and shock and horror racing through him.

"Come, Durotan, Draka," said Grukar. "Thra'kash and I will escort you to your safe camp."

The baby fussed. The female—

... Mother ...

—looked down at the child, her strong, proud orcish features softening with love. She then looked back at Thrall. Their eyes met.

"Your eyes are strange, Thra'kash," she said. "I have only seen blue eyes in this little one before."

Thrall reached for words, but Grukar suddenly looked at him oddly. "Let us make haste," he said. "Surely a discussion of eye color can wait until you are safely at your new location."

Thrall had never felt so lost before in his life. He followed mutely as Grukar led his parents down to the same spot where he had entered this timeway. His mind reeled with the implications.

He could save his parents.

He could save himself from being captured and raised as a gladiator by the cruel yet pathetic Aedelas Blackmoore. He could help them attack Gul'dan, perhaps free them from the demonic taint decades before Hellscream would do so. He could save Taretha.

He could save them *all*.

He had spoken with Orgrim Doomhammer about the murder of his family. Words came back to him from that conversation— long ago to him now, but still in the future in this timeway.

Did my father find you? Thrall had asked.

He did, Orgrim had replied. *And it is my greatest shame and sorrow that I did not keep them closer. I thought it for the good of both my warriors and Durotan as well. They came, bringing you, young Thrall, and told me of Gul'dan's treachery. I believed them. . . .*

He knew he was staring at the pair, but he could no more stop doing so than he could stop breathing. He was famished for this sight—a sight he should have been granted growing up, a sight that would be forever taken from him by the actions that were about to occur shortly if he did not prevent them.

They finally noticed. Durotan seemed curious but not hostile, and Draka was openly amused. "You appear interested in us, stranger," she said. "You have never seen Frostwolves before? Or perhaps this blue-eyed babe intrigues you?"

Thrall still could not find words. Durotan saved him the trouble. He had looked about and judged the site to be good. It was secluded and verdant. He turned to Draka, smiling. "I knew my old friend could be trusted. It will not be long before—"

And then Durotan broke off in mid-sentence, suddenly going very still. Before Thrall realized what was happening, the chieftain of the Frostwolves screamed his battle cry and reached for his axe.

It happened so fast.

There were three of them, each charging in a different direction—one to Durotan, one to Draka, and one to the wolf who sprang forward to protect his companions. Thrall cried out hoarsely and reached for the Doomhammer, determined to help his family.

A strong hand seized his arm and jerked hard. "What are you doing?" snarled the guard. And then Thrall realized two things at once as more fragments of his conversation with Doomhammer returned.

Though I do not know for certain, I am convinced that the guard I entrusted to lead Durotan to safety summoned assassins to kill them instead.

The guard was in on the attack. And he had assumed Thrall was too.

The second thing Thrall realized was worse.

He could not stop what was about to occur—not if he wished to preserve the true timeway.

His parents had to die. He himself had to be found by Blackmoore, had to be trained in battle, if he was to free his people from the internment camps. If he was to keep the world as he knew it from destruction.

He froze in mid-step, agonized. Every fiber of his being told him to fight, to destroy the assassins, to save his mother and father. But it could not be.

Draka had placed the infant Thrall on the ground and was now fighting fiercely to defend both her child and herself. She shot Thrall a brief glance filled with fury, contempt, and hatred. He knew he would bear its sting to his grave. She returned her attention to her struggle, uttering curses upon the orc attacking her and upon Thrall for his betrayal. A short distance away, Durotan, blood pumping from a brutal cut in his leg, attempted to choke his soon-to-be killer. There was a sharp howl, cut off abruptly as the wolf fell. Draka continued to struggle.

And the infant Thrall, lying helpless on the earth while his parents fought, wailed in terror.

Sickened, Thrall watched, unable to alter history, as his dying father fought with renewed strength and managed to snap the neck of his enemy.

At that moment, the assassin who had killed the wolf whirled on Grukar. The traitor was so surprised by the turn of events that he didn't even think to draw his own weapon.

"No!" he cried, his voice high with surprise and fear. "No, I'm one of you; they are the target—"

A massive two-handed sword sliced through Grukar's neck. The severed head went flying, blood spurting in a pattering spray over Thrall's robes. Now the assassin turned on Thrall.

It was a grave mistake.

This, at least, Thrall could do: defend himself. His day would come, certainly. But not today. Thrall uttered a battle cry and charged, channeling his grief and horror and outrage into an attack that startled his would-be killer. Still, the assassin was a professional, and he rallied. The fight was close and intense. Thrall swung, ducked, leaped aside, kicked. The assassin hacked, growled, dodged.

His attention focused on his own survival, Thrall's heart nonetheless ached as he heard Durotan's cry of pain at the sight of Draka's mangled corpse. The sound did not weaken Thrall. Instead, he felt a surge of renewed energy and focus. He increased his attack, pushing his now-alarmed opponent back, back, until the other orc stumbled and fell.

Thrall was on him at once. He pinned the assassin to the ground with one foot and lifted the Doomhammer high. He was about to bring the mighty weapon down to smash the orc's skull, when he froze.

He could not alter the timeway. What if this vile creature needed to live, for some purpose he couldn't imagine?

Thrall growled and spat in the orc's face, then leaped off him. He stepped on the huge sword the other had wielded. "Go," he said, "and never, ever let me see your face again: Do you understand?"

The assassin was not about to question his good fortune, and he took off at a dead run. As soon as he was certain the wretch had truly gone, Thrall turned back to his parents.

Draka was dead. Her body had nearly been hacked to pieces, her face locked in a snarl of defiance. Thrall turned to his father just in time to see the third assassin cruelly lop off both of Durotan's arms—denying him even the ability to hold his son before he died. Thrall had seen many atrocities, but this horror froze him in place, unable to move.

"Take . . . the child," Durotan rasped.

The assassin knelt down beside him and said, "We will leave the child for the forest creatures. Perhaps you can watch as they tear him to bits."

Later, Thrall would not be able to recall how he had gotten from one end of the small clearing to the other. The next thing he knew, he was shouting so loudly his throat hurt, the Doomhammer moving so fast it was but a blur. This killer, too, he let go, though everything in him burned to tear the bastard to tiny pieces of bloody pulp. Clarity came back to him as, on his hands and knees, he gulped in air in great racking sobs.

"My child," Durotan whispered.

He was still alive!

Thrall crawled over to the infant and picked him up. He gazed into his own blue eyes and touched his own small face. Then, as he knelt beside his father, Thrall rolled him over onto his back. Durotan grunted once in pain. Thrall placed the infant, wrapped in a swaddling cloth that bore the emblem of the Frostwolves, on Durotan's chest.

"You have no arms to hold him," Thrall said, his voice thick, tears filling his own blue eyes as the child that he had been wept. "And so I place him on your heart."

Durotan, his face drawn in torment that Thrall could barely imagine, nodded. "Who are you? You betray us . . . you . . . let me and my mate die . . . yet you attack our killers. . . ."

Thrall shook his head. "You would not believe me, Durotan, son of Garad. But I beg you . . . by the ancestors, I beg you to believe this: *your son will live.*"

Hope flickered in the dimming eyes.

Thrall spoke quickly, before it was too late. "He will live, and grow strong. He will remember what it means to be an orc, and become both a warrior and a shaman."

The breath was coming rapidly, too rapidly, but Durotan fought to cling to life, listening raptly.

"Our people will recover from the darkness Gul'dan inflicted on them. We will heal. We will become a nation, proud and powerful. And your son will know of you, and his brave mother, and name a great land after you."

"How . . . can you know . . . ?"

Thrall forced the tears back and placed a hand on his father's chest, beside the infant version of himself. The heartbeat was fading.

"Trust that I do," Thrall said, his voice intent and shaking with emotion. "Your sacrifice was not in vain. Your son will live to change his world. This, I promise."

The words had simply poured forth, and Thrall realized as he uttered them that they were true. He *had* lived, and he *had* changed his world—by freeing his people, by fighting demons, by giving the orcs a homeland.

"I promise," he repeated.

Durotan's face relaxed ever so slightly, and the faintest of smiles touched his lips.

Thrall gathered the baby and held him to his heart for a long, long time.

The infant slept, finally. Thrall held and rocked him through the night, his mind and heart filled nearly to bursting.

It was one thing to hear that his parents had died trying to protect him. It was another to witness such devotion. As a suckling babe, he had been dearly, deeply loved, without having to do anything. This infant had no accomplishments. Had saved no lives, fought no battles, defeated no demons. He was loved simply for being himself, tears and fussing, laughter and smiles.

More than anything in his life, Thrall wished he could have saved his parents. But the timeways were merciless. What had happened must happen, or else it had to be put right by the agents of the bronze dragonflight.

Put "right." Letting good people die, innocent people; that was putting things "right." It was cruel. It was devastating. But he understood.

He glanced up, winced, and looked away from the sight of his butchered family—and blinked. Something was reflected in the water—something gold and shining and scaled—

Thrall tried to see where the reflection was coming from. There was nothing—only trees and earth and sky. There was no mammoth dragon as expected. He rose, holding the infant, and looked into the water again.

One great eye looked back at him.

"Nozdormu?" The river was far too small to house the dragon—it had to be a reflection—and yet . . .

Thrall's concentration was broken by a sudden squalling sound. It would seem the infant Thrall was awake—and hungry. Thrall turned his attention to the child, trying to murmur something soothing, then looked back to the water.

The reflection was gone. But Thrall was certain he had seen it. He looked around. Nothing.

A human voice broke the stillness of the forest. "By the Light, what a noise!"

The voice was full of respectful courtesy and apology, although the noise issued by the infant Thrall was none of the speaker's making. "Might as well turn back, Lieutenant. Anything that loud is certain to have frightened any game worth pursuing."

"Haven't you learned anything I've tried to teach you, Tammis? It's as much about getting away from that damned fortress as bringing back supper. Let whatever it is caterwaul all it likes."

Thrall knew that voice. Had heard it offering praise. More often had heard it hurling curses, lowered in angry contempt. This man had helped shape his destiny. This man was the reason he still bore the name of Thrall—a name to show everyone precisely what the orc no longer was.

The voice belonged to Aedelas Blackmoore.

Any moment now, Blackmoore and his companion—who had to be Tammis Foxton, Blackmoore's servant and father to Taretha Foxton—would come to this clearing. Blackmoore would find the baby Thrall now held in his arms and take him for his own. He would raise Thrall to fight, to kill, to learn strategy. And then one day Thrall would kill him.

Gently, Thrall placed his infant self down on the ground. His hand lingered a moment on the tiny black head, caressed the not-yet-worn fabric of the swaddling cloth.

"Such a tender yet bizarre moment."

Thrall whirled, seizing the Doomhammer and placing himself between the infant and the owner of the voice.

The mysterious assassin who had attacked him in the Caverns of Time now stood a few paces away. Thrall had thought the bronze dragons would have dealt with this man, but it would seem that, despite his words of frustration as Thrall had escaped earlier, he had eluded the bronzes and found a way into this timeway after all. And a way to Thrall.

Again Thrall could not shake the strange sense of familiarity. The armor—the voice—

"I know you," he said.

"Then name me." It was a pleasant, booming voice, tinged with humor.

Thrall growled. "I cannot name you—not yet—but there is something about you . . ."

"I should thank you, really," the assassin continued to drawl.

"My master set me a task. To slay the mighty Thrall. You've already slipped through my fingers once. And you might again. But
you've forgotten one . . . *little* . . . thing. . . ."

With each of the last three words, the assassin took a step forward, and Thrall suddenly realized what he meant. He tightened
his grip on the Doomhammer and drew himself up to his full
height. The human was large for his race, but nowhere near as
large as an orc.

"You shall not harm this infant!" he snarled.

"Oh, I think I shall," said the black-armor-clad figure. "You see . . .
I know who is just a few moments away from being here. And it's
someone you won't want to harm—because then this timeway
would be just as violated as if you'd let your parents live. You know
Aedelas Blackmoore will be here, and that he's going to pick up
this little green baby and raise him to be a gladiator. And you most
certainly don't want to be around for that particular reunion."

Curse the bastard, he was right. Thrall couldn't let himself be
seen. And he couldn't fight Blackmoore and risk injuring or even
killing him.

Not yet.

"So you need to go. But you also need to protect your younger
self. Because if my job is to kill you . . . it's ever so much easier to
chop a baby in two than it is a full-grown orc. Although I've done
that quite a lot, if I do say so myself. What to do, what to do . . . ?"

"It's not going away," complained Blackmoore. He was closer
now, though he was still a few steps away from the clearing.

"It could be an injured creature, sir, incapable of crawling away,"
Tammis suggested.

"Then let's find it and put it out of our misery."

The stranger laughed, and suddenly Thrall realized his course
of action.

Silently, though his whole soul ached to shout his battle cry, he lunged at the assassin. Not with his hammer but with his powerful body. The human was clearly not expecting such an attack and did not even manage to raise his weapon before Thrall slammed into him, the force propelling them both into the briskly flowing stream.

"What's that splash?" Lieutenant Aedelas Blackmoore took a long drag from the bottle.

"Probably one of the large turtles that live in the area, sir," Tammis said. Already tipsy and about to head into drunk, Blackmoore nodded. His horse, Nightsong, came to an abrupt halt. Blackmoore stared at the bodies of no fewer than three adult orcs and that of a huge white wolf.

Movement drew his eye, and Blackmoore suddenly realized the source of the horrible noise. It was the ugliest thing he had ever seen—an orc baby, wrapped in what no doubt passed for a swaddling cloth among the creatures.

He dismounted and went to it.

EIGHT

S everal days had passed since the debacle at Wyrmrest Temple. Kalec had thought—foolishly, perhaps, but sincerely—that with the tragic but necessary death of Malygos, some kind of healing, some kind of peace and unity, could occur among the dragonflights. He had come to that meeting with hope in his heart, only to see more than his own personal dream shattered.

The loss of so many eggs, from all the flights, all at once—exterminated by one of their own, no less—was a devastating blow from which Kalec wondered if any of them would truly recover. Korialstrasz, a friend of his for some time now, someone Kalec had completely and utterly trusted . . . Kalec shook his head, lowering it slightly on his great neck in sorrow.

Ysera was awakened, but still unfocused and unclear, and had, according to what he could learn from her flight, gone wandering. Nozdormu had been missing for some time. Alexstrasza, shattered by Krasus's betrayal, had vanished as well. Malygos was slain, and Deathwing was loose in the world, plotting the destruction of all of them.

Even the oldest among them admitted that not since Deathwing's initial betrayal had there been such a time of despair and chaos.

Each flight had withdrawn unto itself. Kalec had friends among most of them, but even contact with them had been laden with tension. While the green, red, and bronze flights did not know where their Aspects might be, they at least had living ones. The blues did not, and their focus in these last few days had been in rectifying that.

The blues had converged on the Nexus, the site that had always been their home. There, in their cold caves, there had been a great deal of talk, and analyzing, and theorizing, and discussion of magical protocol. But very little had actually been done.

Kalecgos thought his flight was much more interested in the theory of how they might go about creating or choosing a new Aspect than in the pressing need for one. He supposed he shouldn't be surprised. The blues loved intellectual challenges. It was only their contempt for the "lesser races" that prevented them from—as the late Krasus had done—adopting different forms to mingle with other users of magic such as the Kirin Tor magi. Arcane magic— cold and intellectual—was their birthright, thanks to the titans' decision to make Malygos the Aspect of Magic in this world. The younger races, really, had no business meddling in it, according to those who thought this way. And too many of them did for Kalec's comfort.

There seemed to be as many different proposals for how creating or selecting a new Aspect would occur as there were blue dragons themselves. Or, Kalec amended, nostrils flaring in annoyance, as many different proposals as there were *scales* on each dragon.

An early fear had been quickly calmed when one of the younger blues had asked worriedly, "What if there can be no new Aspect? The titans made Malygos into the Aspect of Magic. What if only the titans can make another, and the other flights have forever doomed us to living without an Aspect?"

The older dragons had shaken their heads, completely unconcerned. "We all know that the titans were very powerful, and very wise," one of them had said. "We must assume that they anticipated this might one day happen. Our scholars are certain that, with enough research, they will be able to discover what we should do."

Kalecgos believed this; he believed in the wisdom of the titans, who had charged all the Aspects so very long ago. Other blues, though, believed more in the superiority and capability of the blue flight itself. They could not possibly fail to come up with something. They certainly did not lack for theories.

According to legend, when the Aspects were first created, the moons had been in a rare conjunction. A repeat of this same alignment, not seen for centuries, was due to occur in just a few days. One popular theory, which played to the sense of the dramatic, espoused that this celestial event was of import to their task. Some felt it was "crucial to the proper working of the magic necessary to facilitate the alteration of a normal blue into an Aspect"; others simply deemed it good timing.

Others wanted a majority of blues present at the ceremony. "We will have an Aspect, one way or another," one of the more pragmatic magical scholars had said. "If there is no physical transformation bestowed by the conjunction of the two moons, at the very least we can decide, as a flight, who we think would be our best leader."

"Too, it is not as if the great Malygos died without leaving those of his brood behind," Arygos had said. "I myself am a child of Malygos and his prime consort. It could well be that the ability to become an Aspect is in the blood. We must consider this to be of great importance."

"There is nothing that points to that," Kalecgos had said. "Not all the Aspects were kin originally." He disliked Arygos's attitude and knew that the son of Malygos felt threatened by one he saw as an "upstart." If there was division among the dragonflights, there was also division within the blue dragonflight. Malygos's ghost yet lingered. There were those, like Arygos, who would prefer to follow in that Aspect's footsteps and withdraw as much from the world as possible, and those who thought as Kalec did: that being in this world, connecting with the other races and flights, only served to strengthen and enrich the blue dragonflight.

It had been a subtle division before the attack of the twilight dragons. But now it was a glaring, open schism, one Kalec did not like but was not naive enough to ignore.

He disliked this whole new concept of a "vote," of the title of Aspect simply being that: an empty title, without any of the real powers behind it. This was something that had been part of this world since before the memories of nearly anyone or anything, except perhaps the ancients. To turn it into a sort of contest, to reward the blue dragon who was most liked or could sway most of the flight—

He shook his head angrily and moved away from the discussion. Arygos noticed and called out, "Kalecgos! Where are you going?"

"To get some fresh air," Kalec called over his shoulder. "It is too close in here for me."

The human, with his heavy armor, sank like a stone, although he struggled valiantly. He released the enormous sword, instead grabbing hold of Thrall's robe with one gauntleted hand. They sank together. Thrall tried to bring a weapon down on the man's arm, but his movements were slowed by the water. Instead, he seized the human's hand and, utilizing his superior strength, bent back the fingers.

Bubbles escaped from the human's helm as he lost his grip on Thrall's robe and reached out with his other hand, but Thrall kicked hard and swam out of reach.

That was when he realized that this stream was much deeper than it had appeared. Much deeper than it could possibly be. He caught a glimmer out of the corner of his eye and turned his head.

It was the glittering gold of a great bronze dragon's scales—the same image he had seen in the water earlier. Thrall suddenly realized that the hot, burning sensation of his lungs craving air had ceased. This was somehow timeways magic, and he knew it and accepted it. He kept his eyes on the alluring scales and struck out toward them.

The water about him shimmered, and he felt a strange, tingling warmth all along his body. The scales disappeared. He shot to the surface—

—of the sea. As he glanced around, trying to orient himself, he recognized several ships. Or, at least, what was left of them.

These were the vessels he, Grom Hellscream, and the other orcs had stolen from the humans in order to follow the advice of a strange prophet—a prophet who had urged them to depart the Eastern Kingdoms to come to Kalimdor.

Thrall was slogging ashore with the rest of them now, glancing at the floating debris. He seized a crate and hauled it ashore. As he set it on the ground, someone called out to him.

"Warchief!" How long, Thrall mused, had it been since he had answered to that title? Nonetheless he turned—only to see an orc striding up to . . .

"Me," Thrall said. "It's me. . . ." Just as he had seen himself as an infant what seemed like a short while ago, he now realized that he was looking at another version of himself. He listened to the conversation, trying not to get caught staring at the Thrall of this timeway. This was much stranger than when he had simply seen his other versions during his vision quest. This time he was physically standing only a few feet away.

"Our ship sustained heavy damage when we passed through the raging Maelstrom," the orc reported.

Again a strange twinge. The Maelstrom . . . the place he had left. The place where Deathwing had ripped through: the place the Earthen Ring was trying so desperately to heal. He shook his head in wonder at how much change a few years had wrought.

"It's unsalvageable," the orc grunt continued.

Thrall-of-this-timeway nodded. "I knew it. Can we confirm our location? Is this Kalimdor?"

"We traveled due west as you instructed. This should be it."

"Very well."

Still watching surreptitiously, Thrall thought back to this moment eight years past, recalled what had been uppermost on his mind.

"Has there been any sign of Grom Hellscream or the other ships?" Thrall-of-this-timeway asked.

"No, Warchief. Not since we got separated."

"Hmm. Prepare to move out. If our comrades did make it here, we should be able to find them along the coast."

Thrall turned back to look at the long, sandy stretch.

And saw a glimmer of gold. It was brief, and vanished; it could have been nothing more than the haze of sunlight on sand. But Thrall knew better.

The others were busy scouring the damaged vessels and bringing supplies ashore. Soon camp would be built. Thrall would leave that to his old self.

He headed west, following the glimmering scales.

This time he found a small hole in the earth the size of an animal burrow. And encircling it . . . the now-familiar glimmer of a timeways portal.

Was Nozdormu truly trapped? Thrall wondered as he stepped forward. Or was he merely leading Thrall on some sort of chase? The hole grew to accommodate him. He fell, but even before he had a chance to be alarmed, he emerged on the other side of the portal, climbing out of it to see a huge black bird sitting in the grass before him. It cocked its head and fixed him with gleaming red eyes.

The bird's beak opened. "Greetings, son of Durotan. I knew you'd find your way."

Medivh! The great mage had come to Thrall in a dream, telling him to follow. Thrall had obliged, and Medivh had rewarded his persistence. Except hadn't he been human during this conversation?

Thrall tried to remember what he had said. "It was you I saw in the vision. Who are you? How do you know me?"

The raven cocked its ebony head. "I know many things, young warchief, about you and your people. For instance, I know that right now, you are looking for Nozdormu."

Thrall's jaw dropped.

"You are out of time . . . in many ways. Know that I have seen the future and beheld the burning shadow that came to consume your world. And in glimpsing that future, I have seen others. I will tell you what I may, but you must do the rest."

Thrall suddenly laughed, wondering why he was at all surprised. This was, after all, Medivh. Whatever he was, jumping around in time was probably not beyond him.

"Listening to you served me well once," he said. "I cannot think but that it will serve me well again."

"Are you familiar with weaving, Thrall?"

Surprised at the question, Thrall answered, "I . . . have seen loom work done, but it is most definitely not a skill I possess."

"You do not need to have the skill to understand it," the raven-that-was-no-raven said. "The warp and the weft. Seeing the pattern. Guiding the shuttle. Understanding that something that did not exist before is being created, and that the loom is a miniature world. And being aware that to unravel part of the piece, all you need to do is pull on a single loose thread."

Thrall shook his head slowly. "Mage, you confound me. I have witnessed today the murder of my parents. Have fought against a mysterious assassin sent likely by the infinite dragonflight. And I am trying to find the Timeless One, who seems to be leading me on a fruitless hunt. And the best advice you can give is to think about weaving?"

The bird gave what looked like a shrug, ducking its head and lifting its shoulders.

"Listen to me, or do not. I know what you are chasing. Be careful you are chasing the right thing. This place is full of illusions. There is only one way you can find what you truly seek—only one way you can find yourself. Farewell, Go'el, son of Durotan and Draka."

The bird's wings flapped, and in a few seconds it had flown completely out of sight.

Thrall was at a loss. Words escaped his lips, and he was surprised at their content. "None of this makes sense, but the spirits tell me . . . that I should trust him."

Those were the exact same words he had said at the end of his actual first meeting with Medivh. And he realized with a start that the words were as true this time as they had been then. The spirits *were* telling him that he should trust the mage. He closed his eyes and opened to them, to the elements of earth, air, fire, water, and the last element, life, which was always in his heart.

He still did not truly understand what the mage had been getting at. The words still seemed nonsense. But Thrall was calmer and knew that somehow, when the moment was right, he would understand.

Guide me, he asked of the elemental spirits. *I wish to help, I truly do, but I cannot seem to find this great being I was sent to find. I see images of him, hints, but each time I only fall further into my own life's situation and am no nearer to reaching him.*

He opened his eyes.

Nozdormu was before him. Or rather, a translucent image of him was. The great dragon had opened his mouth and was saying something, but Thrall heard nothing.

"What is it you wish, Timeless One?" he cried. "I am trying to find you!"

Nozdormu extended a foreleg, palm turned up, and beckoned to Thrall. The orc raced forward—

And there it was, coming faster each time: the twinkle of sunlight on Nozdormu's bronze scales. This was not yet the place in time that Thrall was supposed to be, it would seem.

He recalled something that Cairne had once said to him long, long ago. *Destiny . . . it will find you in time. . . .*

Then where is the right time? Thrall wanted to shout. He was sick, soul sick, of chasing this mysterious illusion, who seemingly appeared only to tease and trick and plunge Thrall into yet another timeway.

Each time he followed the image of the Timeless One, it led him to a different point in his life. Some were pleasant to relive; others, far from it. But each one was a significant moment, a profound place in time. And in every one of these moments Thrall saw Nozdormu. Thrall was alert for the reappearance of the mysterious assassin, but there seemed to be no sign of the persistent human.

Thrall hoped that the bastard had drowned, sunk with the weight of that oddly familiar armor in a stream that was much more than a stream. But hope that another encounter would not happen did not make him any less alert.

Thrall realized that he had gone for far too long without food or sleep when he stepped through another portal into a twilit forest. It was familiar . . . too familiar.

"Hillsbrad again," he muttered to himself, rubbing his face. Well, at least he knew his way around. The forest had changed since he had last been here—how long ago? His rumbling belly and weary body told him it had been almost a day. The trees were older-seeming, which made him think that years had passed since— since he had seen his parents fall. And the season was different. It was full-on summer. That meant plentiful game and berries and fruit to be harvested, so at least he would not starve while awaiting whatever past moment he was to experience to show itself.

He quickly rigged a snare to catch rabbits and then went for-aging for a time, enjoying the quiet, long twilight. One noose was successful. Thrall expertly built a small fire to roast the small animal—though many orcs enjoyed raw meat, he preferred his cooked—and then stretched out by the fire for some desperately needed sleep.

He awoke some time later, instantly alert. He did not move; something cold and metallic was pressing against his throat.

"Stupid, filthy orcs," came a voice. It was female, and rough somehow, as if it had not been used in some time. "If it weren't for the money you're about to bring me, I'd kill you where you lie."

Money? She must be talking about some kind of bounty. Was there one on his head now, in Alliance lands, and had she identi-fied him so readily in the darkness? No, she would have said so, not made a general, all-encompassing statement against orcs.

"I will not harm you," Thrall said, keeping his voice as calm as possible. It was a blunderbuss barrel she had pressed to his neck. He calculated the odds that he could move swiftly enough to seize it and direct it away from him before she fired, and suspected he couldn't.

"Oh, I know you won't, because I'll blow your brains out. Now: Get up, move slowly. You're worth more to me alive than dead, but don't think I wouldn't settle for a lesser bounty if you give me any trouble."

He obeyed, moving slowly as she had ordered, keeping his hands where she could see them.

"Over by that tree, to your left, then turn around and face me," she ordered.

Thrall complied, turning slowly—

And gasped.

The woman in front of him was thin, almost gaunt. Her short, close-cropped hair was pale. She appeared to be in her early thirties and wore practical pants, boots, and shirt. The moonlight made her face look haggard, casting shadows beneath her cheekbones and under her eyes, but Thrall did not think sunlight would be any kinder. She might have been beautiful once. In fact, Thrall knew she had been.

"Taretha," he breathed.

NINE

Taretha's eyes narrowed as she aimed the blunderbuss straight at his broad chest. "I won't miss," she said. "How do you know my name?"

For a wild moment Thrall was totally confused. And then he understood. He must have stumbled into one of the wrong timeways—one of the ones that the bronze dragonflight was trying to repair. Because, painful as it was, he knew that Taretha Foxton, his only friend in childhood, had never lived beyond her midtwenties.

"This is going to sound very strange, but please, I urge you to believe me," he said, trying to sound as calm—and as sane—as possible.

An eyebrow lifted. "You speak well . . . for a stinking greenskin."

It hurt to hear Taretha, who had always thought of him as a brother, use such ugly words to Thrall, but he did not react.

"It is because I was educated—by humans," he said. "I was raised by Lord Aedelas Blackmoore to be a gladiator. He made sure I learned how to read and write, the better to understand war strategy. Your mother, Clannia, saved my life, Taretha. She nursed me when I was an infant. My name . . . is Thrall."

The gun wavered, but only for an instant. Thrall could tell by the way she handled it that Taretha was no stranger to firearms.

"That's a lie," she said. "That orc died after a few days."

Thrall's mind reeled. So he *had* existed in this timeway . . . but had died in infancy. It was all so hard to take in. He tried again.

"Have you heard about dragons, Taretha?"

She snorted. "Don't insult me. Of course I have. What do they have to do with an orc I'm rapidly losing patience with?"

She was so harsh, so bitter. Still, Thrall pressed on. "Then perhaps you know that there is one group of dragons called the bronze dragonflight. Their leader is Nozdormu. They make sure that time unfolds the way it is supposed to. In another timeway, as I told you, I survived and became a gladiator, just as Blackmoore wanted. You sneaked me notes, hidden in books. You became my friend."

"Friend to an orc?" Disbelief made her voice climb higher. "Not likely."

"No," he agreed. "Most *unlikely*. And most wonderful. You remembered the baby your mother nursed, and you were fond of him—of me. And you hated what they did to me. I have only just met you, yet I say I already know something about you. I believe that you do not like violence done to beings who cannot defend themselves."

The gun wavered a second time, and her eyes flickered away for just an instant before she turned her gaze upon him again. Hope filled Thrall's heart. Whatever had befallen her to make the gentle young woman he had known so tough and hard, he could tell that she was still Taretha underneath it all. And if she was still Tari, maybe he could reach her. Could help her, somehow, some way, in this timeway, in a way he had been unable to in his own.

"You helped me escape," he continued. "I freed my people from the internment camps. I defeated Blackmoore and razed Durnholde. And later, humans and orcs and others united to defeat an attack on our world from a demonic force called the Burning Legion. All of this was because of you, Tari. My timeway owes so much to you."

"It's a nice story, and much cleverer than any I would have expected from an orc," Taretha said. "But it's a lie. The world is certainly not that way here. And that's the only world I know."

"What if I could prove it to you?" he said.

"That's impossible!"

"But—if I could?"

Taretha was still wary, but he could tell she was growing curious. "How?" she asked.

"You did meet the infant orc," Thrall said. "You remember what color his eyes were?"

"Blue," she said at once. "No one had ever seen an orc with blue eyes before or since."

Thrall pointed to his face. "My eyes are blue, Taretha. And I, too, have never known of any other orc with blue eyes."

She snorted. "Like I'd come close enough to look into your eyes at night," she said. "Nice try." She jerked her head to the left. "Start walking, greenskin."

"Wait! There is one more thing . . . to prove to you I'm telling the truth."

"I've had enough of this," she said.

"In the bag," he persisted. "Look in the bag. There's a small pouch in it. In that pouch . . . I think you'll find something you'll recognize."

He prayed he was right. The small pouch contained only a few items. His totems. The acorn, of course—the gift of the ancients. A makeshift altar, with representations of each of the elements. And . . . something precious. Something that had been lost to him but had been found again . . . something that he would keep with him until the day he died.

"If this is a trick, I'll blow a hole in you so big . . . ," she muttered, but, scowling and obviously despite her better judgment, she knelt carefully and began to rummage through the bag. "What am I looking for?"

"If I'm right . . . you'll know it when you see it."

She muttered again, shifting the musket to her right hand and dumping out the satchel with her left. She combed through the items, obviously seeing nothing that meant anything.

"All I see is a rock, a feather, a—"

Taretha fell silent. She stared at the small piece of jewelry glinting in the moonlight. She seemed to have completely forgotten all about Thrall as one hand, trembling, picked up the silver necklace. A crescent moon swung from the chain. She looked, open-mouthed, at Thrall, and instead of the anger and underlying fear and hatred that had distorted her pretty features earlier, there was shock . . . and wonderment.

"My necklace," she said, her voice soft and small.

"You gave it to me," Thrall said. "When you helped me escape. There was a fallen tree you told me to hide it in. Near a boulder shaped like a dragon."

Slowly, not even looking at him anymore, she put the gun down. With her other hand, Taretha reached into her worn linen shirt and pulled out a necklace identical to the one she held.

"There was a dent I made in it when I was young," she said. "Right . . . here . . ."

Both necklaces had the exact same dent: a slight misshaping of the bottom horn of the crescent.

She looked up at him, and for the first time he could see the Taretha he remembered gazing back at him. Slowly he went to her, kneeling down on the ground beside her.

Her hand closed upon the second necklace, then she held it out to him. She released it, and it crumpled gently into his huge green palm. She looked at Thrall, no fear in her face, and smiled slightly.

"Your eyes," she said quietly, "*are* blue."

Thrall was pleased, but not surprised, that Taretha believed him, despite how ludicrous he knew his story sounded. He had given her proof she could not dispute. The Taretha he had known would have looked without bias on such proof. And this woman before him was still Taretha, though much different from the gentle, sincere young woman he remembered.

They talked for a long time. Thrall told her of his world, although he did not tell Taretha what eventually became of her. He would not lie if she asked, but she did not. He told her of his history, and the task that Ysera had set him on.

And she told him, poking at the fire, bits and pieces of information about this new, twisted timeway that had sprung up.

"Oh, Blackmoore is definitely in this timeway," she said bitterly when the conversation turned to that wretched man. "Except I think I like the one in yours better."

Thrall grunted. "A crafty, selfish drunkard trying to create an army of orcs to use against his own people?"

"In this timeway he is a crafty, selfish, sober general who doesn't *need* an army of orcs to use against his own people," she said. "From what you have told me"—she turned her short-cropped head to eye his powerful build—"you are a mighty warrior. And I believe it. It sounds like Blackmoore relied upon you and his secret scheme too heavily. When you died, he had to do the work himself."

"Normally, that is an admirable trait," Thrall said.

"Normally. But he is hardly . . . normal." She turned away as she said it.

There was something in her expression that made Thrall instantly alert. A personal anger, and . . . shame?

"He . . . you were his mistress in this timeway too," he said. "I am sorry."

She laughed harshly. "Mistress? A mistress gets to attend parties, Thrall. She gets jewelry, and dresses, and goes hunting with her master. Her family is well taken care of. I was nothing so *respected* as a mistress." She took a deep breath and continued. "I was just a diversion. He tired of me quickly. I can at least be grateful for that."

"Your parents . . . what happened to them?"

"They were punished." She smiled, but it did not reach her eyes. "For 'letting' you die, not very long after we lost my brother, Faralyn. Father lost his position and was demoted to the basest task of cleaning the stables. Mother died when I was eight. Blackmoore wouldn't even let her see the doctor that winter. Father died a few years later. I took what meager savings they had and left without a backward glance. By then Blackmoore couldn't have cared less. He was too busy ruling."

"Ruling?" Thrall gaped at her.

"No one recognizes his claim to the throne of Lordaeron, of course. But no one dares topple him from it."

Thrall sank back, trying to make sense of this. "Go on," he said, his voice hollow.

"He was so popular. He started only with his own men, training them, driving them to perfection."

Thrall thought of the endless gladiator matches he had been forced to endure. This did, in a twisted and bizarre way, sound like Blackmoore.

"Then he hired mercenary soldiers and trained them the same way. And after the Battle of Blackrock Spire, well, there was no stopping him."

"What happened there?"

"He slew Orgrim Doomhammer in single combat," Taretha said offhandedly, and took another handful of berries from those Thrall had gathered earlier.

Thrall could not believe his ears. Blackmoore? That sniveling, drunken coward? Challenging Orgrim Doomhammer, warchief of the Horde, to single combat? And *winning*?

"The defeat completely disheartened the greensk—I'm sorry. The orcs," Taretha quickly corrected herself. "They've become slaves, Thrall. Their spirits are broken. They're not even kept in camps like you told me about. Any found wild are purchased by the kingdom and either broken to servitude or, if they prove too defiant, killed."

"That's why you wanted me alive," Thrall said quietly.

She nodded. "If I turned in a wild orc, I could live on what they paid me for more than a year. It's . . . that is how my world is, Thrall. It's how it's always been. But . . ." Taretha frowned. ". . . I've always felt . . . well, it never felt *right*. Not just morally, but . . ." Her voice trailed off.

Thrall understood what she was trying to say. "It never felt right because it isn't," Thrall said firmly. "This timeline is wrong. Blackmoore is dead; the orcs have their own land; and I have made friends among humans." He smiled. "Starting with you."

She smiled a little in return and shook her head. "It's strange, but . . . that seems right to me, now." She hesitated. "I notice that you never mentioned what happened to me in that other timeway."

He winced. "I had hoped you would not ask. But I should have known you would."

"I, um . . . I take it I don't end up like this Jaina Proudmoore woman you spoke so highly of," she said, attempting lightness and failing.

He eyed her thoughtfully, then said, very seriously, "Do you truly wish to know?"

Taretha frowned, poking again at the fire, then shoved the branch in and sat back. "Yes. I do want to know."

Of course she would. Taretha did not shrink from the uncomfortable. He hoped that what he had to tell her would not turn her against him, but it would be wrong to tell her anything other than the absolute and complete truth.

He sat for a moment, gathering his thoughts, and she did not interrupt. The only sounds were the crackle of the fire and the soft murmurs of night creatures.

"You died," Thrall said at last. "Blackmoore found out that you were helping me. He had you followed when you went to meet with me, and when you returned . . . he had you killed."

She made no sound, but a muscle in her face twitched. Then, her voice strangely calm, she said, "Go on. How did I die?"

"I don't know, exactly," Thrall said. "But . . ." He closed his eyes for a moment. First witnessing the butchering of his parents, and now this. "He cut off your head, and put it in a bag. And when I came to Durnholde and asked him to release the orc prisoners . . . he threw it down to me."

Taretha put her face in her hands.

"He thought it would break me. And in a way, it did—but not the way he wanted." Thrall's voice deepened as he remembered the moment. "It made me furious. For what he had done—for the sort of man he had proven himself to be—I would show him no more mercy. In the end, your death meant his. I have relived that moment many times. Always I wondered if there was something I could have done to save you. I am sorry that I could not, Taretha. So very sorry."

She kept her face covered, and when she at last spoke, her voice was thick and muffled.

"Tell me one thing," she said. "Did I make a difference?"

He couldn't believe she was asking that. Did she not understand everything he had said?

"Taretha," he said, "it was because of your kindness that I was able to understand that some humans could be trusted—and that's why I was willing even to consider allying with Jaina Proudmoore. It was because of you that I believed I was more than . . . than a green-skinned monster. That I and therefore my people—all orcs— were worthy of something more than being treated like animals."

He placed a hand on her shoulder. She lifted her head and turned toward him, tears streaming down her face.

"Taretha, my dear friend," he said, his voice shaking. "My sister of the spirit. You didn't make *a* difference. You made *the* difference."

To his astonishment, she gave him a shaky smile.

"You don't understand," she said brokenly. "I've never made any kind of a difference. I've never *mattered*. I've never done a single thing that affected anything or anyone."

"Your parents—"

She made a dismissive sound. "The parents from your world sound more caring than mine. I was a female, and little use to them. We were all too busy trying to survive. The schooling you talked about—I never got it. I can't *read*, Thrall. I can't *write*."

Thrall couldn't imagine Taretha being illiterate. Books were what had bound them to each other in the first place. Without her notes, he might never have escaped. He had thought her fate in the true timeway a brutal one, felt that it was unjust to one who was so kind and greathearted. But in a way, the life she had been leading here was almost worse.

Aggra had accompanied him on his shamanic vision quest, and had, in a fashion, "met" Taretha.

She should not have died, Thrall had said on that spiritual journey.

How do you know this was not her destiny? That perhaps she had done all she had been born to do? Aggra had replied. *Only she knows.*

And Thrall realized with a lurch in his heart that Taretha—in both timeways—did know.

"To hear this from you—to know that my being alive mattered to anyone, let alone to nations, to . . . to the history of the world—you don't know what it means to me. I don't care if I died. I don't care *how* I died. At least I mattered!"

"You did, and you do," Thrall said, his voice urgent. "You may not have made a difference . . . yet. But that doesn't mean you can't."

"If I turned in a wild orc, I could live on what they paid me for more than a year. It's . . . that is how my world is, Thrall. It's how it's always been. But . . ." Taretha frowned. ". . . I've always felt . . . well, it never felt *right*. Not just morally, but . . ." Her voice trailed off.

Thrall blinked. "So you have said." It was an important insight, but he did not understand why she had chosen to repeat it now.

She frowned. "Said what?"

The air felt . . . different. Thrall got to his feet, and picked up Taretha's gun. It was to Taretha's everlasting credit that she did not panic, but instead was instantly on her feet and at his side, looking out into the surrounding woods for the threat. "Did you hear something?"

"You did, and you do." Thrall was sitting beside her. "You may not have made a difference . . . yet. But that doesn't mean you can't—"

He stopped in mid-sentence. And then he understood.

"This timeway is wrong," he said. "We both know that. And there's something *so* wrong with it, so amiss, that it's not even flowing correctly anymore. Things are . . . repeating. Things may even be unraveling."

Taretha paled as he spoke. "You mean—you think—this world's just going to *end?*"

"I don't know what's going to happen," Thrall said honestly. "But we need to figure out how to stop it, and how to get me out of this timeway. Or else everything—your world and mine, and who knows how many others—will be destroyed."

She was frightened. She looked down at the fire, gnawing her lower lip, thinking.

"I need your help," Thrall said softly.

She looked up at him, and smiled. "You have it. I want to make a difference . . . again."

TEN

The world was silent.

There was not a cry of anger, or pain, or delight. Not the soft sound of a breath. Not the single beat of a pair of wings, or a heart. Not the nearly imperceptible sound of a blink, or a plant taking root.

No, not quite silent. The oceans moved, their waves curling upon the shore, then drawing back, although nothing now existed in their depths. The wind blew, rattling the eaves of dwellings that housed nothing, rippling grass that was turning yellow.

Ysera moved, the only living thing in this place, the unease stirring, becoming worry, becoming fear, becoming horror.

The Hour of Twilight had come.

Her paws fell on earth that had ceased to support life. Would *not* support life, ever again. No longer would a breath from her bring verdancy. She walked on each continent, desperately hoping that someplace, somewhere, had been spared.

Dead, all dead. No dragons, no humans or elves or orcs, no fish, no birds, no trees, no grass, no insects. With each bitter footfall, Ysera trod upon a mass grave.

How was she alive?

She shrank from the question, fearing the answer, and moved on.

Booty Bay, Orgrimmar, Thunder Bluff, Darkshire, Desolace—corpses were everywhere, rotting, uneaten by the carrion feeders as they, too, lay rotting where they had fallen. Ysera felt madness brush her at the enormity of it all and pushed it away ruthlessly.

Our temple . . .

She did not want to see, but had to see—

And there she was, standing at the base of the temple, her great, once-slumbering eyes now open wide.

There were wing beats here. And breath, and cries of hate-filled victory. The air thrummed with them, the twilight dragons, the last things left alive and utterly triumphant on a corpse of a world. At the foot of Wyrmrest Temple lay the bodies of the mighty Aspects: Alexstrasza, burned to death, her ribs charred and thrusting upward. A blue Aspect whose face she could not see, frozen solid in a spasm of agony. Nozdormu the Timeless One, locked firmly in time now, still as stone. And her own body, overgrown with what had once been green and living, but now even the vines that had wrapped around her throat to choke her were themselves dead. Each Aspect appeared to have been slain by his or her own unique powers.

But that was not what made her grow cold with terror.

Ysera the Awakened stared at a single, massive body. It was illuminated by the dim, somber light of the twilight skies of Northrend, a limp and too-still thing.

It was impaled upon the very spire of Wyrmrest Temple as the swollen red and orange sun set sullenly behind it.

Ysera sank down to the earth, trembling, wanting to tear her eyes away and unable to.

"Deathwing," she whispered.

She jolted herself back to reality, her mind clearing even as her body still trembled from the vision. She shook her head, whispering, *"No, no, no . . ."*

It was a vision, but one she somehow knew was not yet set in stone. One that might yet be changed . . . but only if one orc changed it.

Thrall, I know not what role you have to play, but I beg of you . . . please, please, do not fail.

Do not let this world become so very, very silent.

The question was . . . how did they make the timeway right?

"Tell me everything that happened, starting from when I died," Thrall said.

"That's . . . a lot, but all right," Taretha replied. "Like I said, Blackmoore threw himself into his goal. He trained and honed his men, and then mercenaries. After the Battle of Blackrock Spire, he didn't dismantle his own personal military. As soon as the orcs surrendered, he made a secret deal with them—a deal that left the rest of the Alliance horrified. Join with Blackmoore's private army, turn on King Terenas and the others, slaughter them—and they got to live. Guess what they did?"

Thrall nodded. "Of course they would. All they were doing was still fighting the enemy. And so Terenas fell."

Taretha nodded. "So did Uther the Lightbringer and Anduin Lothar."

In Thrall's timeway, Lothar died fighting Doomhammer at the Battle of Blackrock Spire. "What of Prince Varian?"

"Both Varian and Arthas, Terenas's son, were too young to fight. They fled to safety and both survived."

Arthas. The fallen paladin . . . the Lich King.

"Have there been any strange illnesses in the land? Poisoned grain, plagues?"

Taretha shook her fair head. "No, nothing like that."

The impact struck Thrall like a blow. This was a world in which Blackmoore lived; that much was true and to be despised. But Taretha lived, too . . . and so did untold numbers of innocents who would become neither Scourge nor Forsaken.

"Do you know the name Kel'Thuzad?" he asked. Kel'Thuzad, a former member of the ruling council of Dalaran, had sought power in Thrall's timeline. That lust for power had taken him down dark paths. Paths that had had him experimenting with the lines between life and death. After such a flirtation, it was grimly fitting that Arthas had raised Kel'Thuzad's body as a lich.

"Oh, yes," Taretha said, grimacing. "Blackmoore's chief advisor."

So Kel'Thuzad had succumbed to the lure of power in this timeway too. Except here it was mortal, political power, not an ancient evil, that had seduced him.

"Antonidas and Dalaran have severed all ties with him," Taretha continued. "They like to appear impartial, but rumor has it that their allegiance is more with Stormwind than Lordaeron, even though they are physically so close to us." She shrugged. "I don't know how accurate that is. I just hear things now and then when I venture into Southshore."

Dalaran was still here, too, then, with Antonidas still at the head of the magi. The city had not fallen; it had not been relocated to Northrend.

"Where are Arthas and Varian?"

"Varian rules Stormwind. Arthas is with him. They are as close as brothers. Varian was best man at his wedding."

"To Jaina Proudmoore," Thrall said quietly.

Taretha nodded. "They have a child, a little boy. Prince Uther."

There was no plague, no Lich King. Not yet, anyway. Arthas was a married man, and a father. Lordaeron had not been transformed into the Undercity, populated by the undead, but instead was ruled by Blackmoore sitting in a good man's throne.

"To think of him having so tight a grasp on this world," he muttered.

"Which makes it all that more peculiar that he has suddenly disappeared," Taretha said.

"Disappeared?"

"Yes. His advisors have tried to cover it up, of course. They said he's gone on some mission or other, to roust out more orcs, or kill some dragons, or sign a peace treaty, depending on what you want to believe. But he's vanished."

"Perhaps someone killed him," Thrall said. He smiled slightly. "One can hope."

"If so, then there would be great fanfare," Taretha pointed out. "That throne would be filled by someone—either Arthas as the rightful heir, or by Blackmoore's killer. No, something odd is going on. But it won't last long. I am certain that Arthas and Varian are already planning an attack. They must have spies."

She was right. Though denied her education, Taretha was still a highly intelligent woman. There would, of course, be spies, and Arthas and Varian would likely move as quickly as they were physically able to take advantage of this mysterious "absence."

Thrall paused a moment, thinking hard. He knew he had to restore the timeway or else all would unravel. Perhaps it was a good thing that Blackmoore was gone; perhaps this would open up some way for the timeway to restore itself somehow.

And yet—that would mean such great tragedy.

The plague would have to sweep through the land. Thousands would be either corpses or worse.

Arthas would need to become the Lich King. A thought made him break out in sweat: What if, in this world, Blackmoore was to become the Lich King? He had Kel'Thuzad whispering in his ear.

Antonidas would have to die, and Dalaran must fall, as must Quel'Thalas.

And Taretha—

He rested his forehead in his hand for a moment. The task seemed impossible. If only he could find one of the bronze dragons, talk to him or her, explain what was going on. Even a green or red dragon would be of aid. They knew of the charge of the bronzes; they would believe this story of fouled timeways, at least in theory.

"Do . . . do you think we can make a difference?" Taretha asked quietly.

He laughed hollowly. "I think we need to find a dragon," he said. "One who would actually listen to an orc without killing me first and—"

His eyes opened wide.

"—and I know where we can find one."

Krasus sat in his private study, seldom more happily ensconced than here. It was a warm-feeling room, smaller than he could have commandeered given his position in the Kirin Tor, but comfortable. Currently, every flat surface, from desk to small table to top of a bookcase, was covered with an open book of some sort. Only when he was at the side of his mate, Alexstrasza, did joy fill his heart more than when he was here. He disliked the necessity of being away from her, but no one understood "duty" better than the Life-

Binder. She understood that his work here among the Kirin Tor would aid the flight, and, more importantly in his beloved's eyes, aid Azeroth. The humans, high elves, and gnomes with whom he worked might have assumed that dragons, living as long as they did, would grow bored with one another and welcome chances to spend time apart.

They would be wrong.

An orb hovered nearby, its shades of green and brown and blue revealing it to be an accurate and immediately current representation of Azeroth. Scattered hither and thither were tools, trinkets, and other priceless items. At present, he was busily scratching on vellum notes from a very ancient tome that, should it be handled more than was necessary, would crumble into dust. Magic held it together for now, but Krasus was practical, and knew that making a copy of the key elements in the book would be a wise backup against the ravages of time and broken spells. It was a task that an apprentice could accomplish, but Krasus preferred to do it himself. It appealed to his scholarly, magical soul to sit quietly and revisit ancient lore.

There was a knock on his door. "Enter," he called, not looking up.

"Lord Krasus?" It was Devi, one of the young high elf apprentices.

"Yes, what is it, Devi?" Krasus inquired.

"There is a young lady here to see you. With her slave. She insisted I bring you this. But . . . may I speak freely?"

"You always do," he said, smiling a little. "And I always value it. Please."

"There seems something . . . off about her. Nothing hostile, but . . ." She shook her raven head, frowning a little, gnawing on the problem. "She told me to give you this."

Krasus was instantly alert. Devi had good instincts about people. The apprentice approached and dropped something small and brown and completely ordinary-looking into his outstretched palm. A simple acorn.

Krasus inhaled swiftly.

Knowledge—so much knowledge! Aeons of knowing, of witnessing, contained in this tiny, deceptively unimportant thing. It tingled against his palm, and he closed his hand about it for a moment, not wanting to release it.

Devi watched him intently. Of course, she was still an apprentice. She wouldn't be able yet to recognize what Krasus had—that this was the acorn of an ancient. It was like a whisper that only trained, sharp, and listening ears could hear.

"Thank you for your observations, Devi. Show her in," Krasus said, revealing nothing.

"You should be aware that she insists on bringing her orc," Devi said.

"Why do you think she wishes to do so?"

Devi tilted her head, analyzing. "Honestly, sir, I cannot think why. He seems completely cowed, and the woman says it is very important. I do not think they are planning to harm you in any way, but I cannot even hazard any other guess. It is puzzling." A frown marred the beauty of her dark-skinned face. Devi did not like puzzles.

"Then show the orc in too. I think I might just be a match for a girl and a broken-spirited orc." Their eyes met and she grinned. Others might deem the sharp-tongued elf impertinent, but Krasus liked that she did not seem intimidated by him.

"Right away, sir," she said.

The acorn of an ancient. Krasus unfolded his long fingers and regarded it again. A rare thing, a beautiful and powerful thing. Who was this girl, to have come by it?

The door opened again, and Devi brought in his guest, bowing and closing the door as she left. Krasus rose and looked at the young, fair-haired girl searchingly.

She was slender, and would have been pretty had she not borne the unmistakable signs of having lived a very hard life. The dress she wore—a simple frock and cloak—was clean, but had obviously been mended more than once. She was well groomed, but her hands had calluses and broken nails. She stood straight but was clearly very nervous. She dropped a deep curtsy.

"Lord Krasus," she said, "my name is Taretha Foxton. I thank you for seeing us."

The name meant nothing, but what an interesting choice of words. . . .

"'Us'?" Krasus said mildly, walking over to them, hands clasped behind his back. In truth, the orc was more impressive than the human. Larger than most, he was powerfully muscled, yet wore a simple brown robe. His hands, too, looked callused—but from grasping weapons, not from working in fields. There was a difference in how one gripped a weapon versus a tool, and Krasus had seen enough human warriors to recognize the signs of one when he saw him. Too, the orc was not as stooped as most of his kind were, and he met Krasus's gaze evenly.

With blue eyes.

"Remarkable," Krasus murmured. "And who might you be?"

"My name," the orc said, "is Thrall."

"An apt name for a slave, but frankly, I deem you none such," Krasus said. He held out his hand, which still contained the acorn. "Very clever, to use this to gain admittance to me. You knew I would be able to sense the knowledge contained within. How did you come by such a precious thing?"

He was not surprised when Taretha looked to Thrall for a reply.

"I have . . . a tale to tell you, mage," Thrall said. "Or perhaps I should call you . . . my lord dragon?"

Krasus kept his face calm, but shock shuddered through him. Very few knew of his true identity as Korialstrasz, consort to Alexstrasza. And until this second he had been certain that he knew every one of those individuals.

"This day," Krasus said with forced mildness, "is getting more and more interesting. Come sit, and I will have something to eat brought in. I suspect this tale you speak of will be long in the telling."

He was right. Taretha and Thrall sat—the latter rather gingerly, in one of the larger chairs—and began to speak. There was a pause for food—simple tea and cakes, which the poor girl fell upon like a starved wolf—but other than that, the story unfolded with little interruption for the better part of the afternoon. Krasus interrupted occasionally to ask questions, or to clarify something, but for the most part he simply listened.

It was mad. It was absurd. Ludicrous.

It also made perfect sense.

Mad tales, Korialstrasz had learned, having heard his share of them in his many millennia of life, had holes in them. They had notes that did not ring true. But while this strange orc, Thrall, spoke of things that seemed impossible, Korialstrasz knew they were not. As Krasus did, Thrall knew the nature of Ysera the Dreamer and of her flight. Thrall said that the acorn Krasus still held was a gift. Krasus could tell: there was a peace about it that would not be present had it been randomly picked up or taken by force. The orc knew how the timeways worked. He even knew names of bronze dragons who were friends to Korialstrasz and his queen.

No orc slave would know of such things.

When Thrall had finished, Krasus took a sip of tea, examined the precious acorn in his hand, then reached over and dropped it into Thrall's palm.

"This is not for me," he said quietly. "Not really. Is it?" It was a statement, not a true question.

Thrall looked at him for a moment, shook his head, and returned the acorn to his pouch. "I was to plant it where it seemed right," he said. "I do not think Dalaran is the place."

Korialstrasz nodded. He had sensed the same thing from the acorn.

"I dislike Aedelas Blackmoore heartily," the dragon mage continued. "Nearly everyone does, unless they are in his pay, and I would wager that even they love the money, not the man. I would not mourn his loss if he were sliced from stem to stern, as you described doing. But simply doing that is not going to correct things, Thrall. While I understand the need to restore the true timeway, I will tell you that you will find few who think your world superior to their own. Plagues, a Lich King, Dalaran destroyed and remade, orcs having their own homeland—you have an uphill battle, my friend."

"But it is the right thing to do," said Thrall. "If it is not corrected, then my timeway—the real one—will be destroyed! And this one is already doomed!"

"I know that. You know that. A few of my fellow Kirin Tor members know that. The bronze dragonflight certainly knows that. But you are talking about mass upheaval of an entire world." He gestured to the hovering sphere that was Azeroth.

Thrall rose and walked over to the globe, watching as wispy, miniature white clouds passed over the surface. He regarded it intently, but made no effort to touch it.

"This . . . is real, isn't it?" he said. Curious, Taretha rose and joined him, her eyes widening as she regarded the slowly turning globe.

"In a manner of speaking," Krasus said. "You couldn't wipe out the world by smashing it with your fist, if that's what you're asking."

"No . . . but that would solve the problem, would it not?" Thrall said wryly.

"It might at that," Krasus agreed, his lips twitching in slight amusement.

"But . . . are we on it? Or representatives of us?" Thrall asked.

"Yes, right here," Krasus said. "Our . . . spirit essence, for want of a better term, can be detected."

"And you could find Arthas, or Varian?"

"Not specifically. I know where we are because . . . well . . . I know where we are," Krasus said. "I can detect that Arthas is in the world, but—" His dark eyes widened. "I see what you're getting at."

"Do the dead leave . . . signature traces?"

"They do," Krasus said. "You want me to look for Blackmoore."

The orc nodded. Krasus raised an eyebrow, then lifted a hand. He spread his fingers gently and held them about six inches over the white clouds as the representation of Azeroth turned. He frowned. He stepped around the globe slowly, holding his hand over it, moving it about. Finally, he lowered it and turned to Thrall.

"Your hunch was right," Krasus said. "Aedelas Blackmoore is nowhere to be found on this world."

"What does that mean?" asked Taretha in a small voice.

"Well, it could mean any one of several things," Krasus said. "He could have found a way to hide his signature. Or his spirit could have been stolen. It does happen from time to time. He could physically not be on this world. We both know there are gateways to others that could exist."

Krasus glanced at Thrall as he spoke, and frowned. The orc looked very unsettled and was making a visible effort to calm himself. "Thrall, what is it?"

Thrall didn't answer him. He turned instead toward Taretha, putting a huge hand gently on her shoulder. "Tari . . . you said that Blackmoore defeated Orgrim Doomhammer in single combat."

She nodded. "Yes, that's right."

"Did he . . . take the Doomhammer? Or Orgrim's armor?"

"The hammer was shattered in combat, or so everyone says," Taretha said. "And the armor was too big for him."

Thrall relaxed slightly. He seemed relieved. "Of course it would be. He couldn't possibly wear it."

Taretha nodded. "That's why he only took a few symbolic plates of it. He had them be part of a new set of armor designed especially for him."

The orc's hand fell from Taretha's shoulder, and he stared at her.

"Thrall?" she asked, worried. "What is it? What's wrong?"

The orc slowly turned his head to regard the spinning miniature Azeroth. For a long moment he didn't speak.

Finally, he said in a heavy voice, "I know what happened to Blackmoore."

Taretha and Krasus exchanged glances and waited for Thrall to continue.

"He's not here because he's not in this timeway anymore. He escaped. He's free of it. He doesn't have to obey its laws any longer. And he's got a purpose. One thing that's driving him."

He turned to face them. "And that one purpose is to kill me."

Eleven

"It makes sense," Krasus mused. "You are able to traverse the timeways. Though you must be very careful. It is easy to be trapped by illusions."

"I can indeed traverse the timeways," Thrall agreed. "But I'm not out of *my* timeway completely. I know because I've visited it at various points. Blackmoore *is* out of his own timeway completely. And that's because he's had help. It's got to be the infinite dragonflight behind this; that's the only explanation that makes any sense. That's why the ancients were so troubled. Why their knowledge is flawed now."

Krasus rubbed his temples. Thrall watched him keenly, only now fully aware of how much he wanted this red dragon mage to give him a solution.

"What would happen if he killed you, Thrall?" Taretha asked, directing the question to both of them.

"My best guess? Disaster," said Krasus bluntly. "I find it impossible to believe that, in the true timeway, Thrall was meant to die at the hands of a Blackmoore from a completely *different* timeway. Thrall is a critical component of his timeway's future. To eliminate him means far too much would unravel. Not only would our time-way fall apart, I believe that all timeways would."

"And the other way around?" Taretha queried.

"Considering that this timeway is, frankly, something that should never have been—an illusion, as it were—it could potentially restore the balance." Krasus lifted a hand. "I am not a bronze dragon; I urge you to remember that. I only speak of what sounds logical, based on the little I know."

"I've got to get out of here," Thrall growled. His hands clenched and unclenched. "I've got to find Nozdormu and stop this. But I don't know *how*."

He sat back down and put his head in his hands. He was utterly and completely at a loss. He was failing the dragonflights and Ysera, failing Aggra and the Earthen Ring, failing his world. When a small hand dropped on his shoulder and squeezed gently, he covered it with his own. He was failing Taretha, too: dear, ill-treated Taretha, who should not even be alive.

He thought of the glitter of scales, seducing him into trying another timeway, taking another chance. He had found an answer, at least; he knew who was hunting him. And that knowledge had shaken him more badly than he wanted to admit.

"Ysera's worldview is . . . different from most," Krasus said quietly. "Yet it has a truth to it deeper than waking knowledge has. I do not think she would have felt you so vital to these tasks, Thrall, if you were not able to assist her."

Thrall was too disheartened to argue. Nothing was real. The glittering scales that lured him from timeway to timeway, an assassin who shouldn't exist, some deep draconic mystery—his head was swimming, trying to keep track of it. Taretha's hand on his shoulder wasn't real, yet it was. What was dream? What was reality? What was—

And then suddenly, with the gentleness of breeze and the force of an explosion, Thrall understood.

He saw again the black bird Medivh speaking to him: *This place is full of illusions. There is only one way you can find what you truly seek—only one way you can find yourself.*

And Krasus's words: *Though you must be very careful. It is easy to be trapped by illusions. . . . This timeway is, frankly, something that should never have been . . . an illusion, as it were. . . .*

The timeways were not full of illusions. This timeway was not an illusion.

It was *time itself* that was the illusion.

Historians and prophets made much of the past and future. There were tomes aplenty written about old battles, strategies, historical events, and how they had changed the world. And there were prophecies and predictions, hopes and wonderments and speculations about the next five hundred years, or the next five minutes.

But the only true reality was now.

Scholars would have debates raging over what he was wrestling with now, but in his mind it suddenly seemed so simple, so obvious. There was only ever one moment.

This one.

Every past moment was a memory. It was gone. Every future moment was a hope, or a fear. It had not yet manifested.

There was only now, *this moment,* and even it slipped away into the past, and the future moment became *this moment.*

It was so elegant, so peaceful and tranquil, and Thrall found himself letting go of so many things he could barely understand them all. They slid from his shoulders like a pack dropped to the earth. The obsession over past actions. The worry about future ones.

And still the need to plan, the need for regret—wisdom dictated that even in *this moment* such things were necessary. To understand the past was to be the best one could be in *this moment*. To anticipate the future could shape the next *this moment*.

But all that became so much easier—became light as a feather and magical and innocent—once he finally understood.

He was trapped in time, yes. In this seemingly endless path of revisiting his past—or, most recently, in glimpsing a possible future.

But all he needed to do was step out of the cycle by truly being in this moment. And Nozdormu—

Thrall blinked and trembled with the vastness of the understanding that broke upon him. Now he understood both how it was that he was so mired in these timeways that felt so personal, yet he saw Nozdormu in each one of them. Thrall had been trapped in a single moment—a vital moment of his own past. The mighty Timeless One was trapped *in all moments of time*.

But with his newfound ease, Thrall knew that he now could find the great leviathan.

Krasus was smiling at him. Thrall knew that the red dragon was dead in the real timeway, but that was not truth; that was not reality. This was. And Taretha, too, was real, and alive. He could almost feel her breath slipping into her lungs, hear each sweet heartbeat as if it were the only heartbeat ever to exist.

Which it was.

"You have figured it out," Krasus said, a slight smile curving his lips.

"I have," Thrall said. He turned to Taretha and smiled into her eyes. "I am glad to be with you."

Not glad to have been. To be.

He closed his eyes.

* * *

When he opened them, he knew he was in a place completely and utterly out of time. He was floating, unanchored even by gravity, the darkness around him illuminated only by the soft glow of a truly infinite number of portals. And through each one, Thrall could glimpse the glitter of golden scales.

It was a startling, unsettling image, yet Thrall felt complete peace in his heart as he drifted in a nothingness surrounded by everything. His mind was calm and open, holding something that it should not be able to hold for more than a moment—but he knew a moment was all that was needed. All that was *ever* needed.

And then his body fell with a gentle thump onto the cradling embrace of soft sand, and he realized he was once again in the Caverns of Time. He opened his eyes and gazed upon the Timeless One.

But not only upon a single being, however magnificent. On each of those scales, those glittering things that had taken him on so amazing a journey, Thrall saw moments.

His moments.

All the great deeds of Thrall's life were playing out on the scales of the Timeless One. There, he donned the armor of Orgrim Doomhammer. Here, he fought alongside Cairne Bloodhoof, protecting that great tauren's village. Over there, he called the elements for the first time; over there, he stood alongside Grom Hellscream. Countless moments, moments that had made a hero, a legend. Moments that had truly changed his world.

"Do you sssee?"

The voice was a deep rumble, deeper than any Thrall had heard from a dragon before. It thrummed along his blood, sang in his soul.

"I—see," he whispered.

"*What . . .* do you sssee?"

"The most important moments of my life," Thrall said, his eyes darting from one to another. So much, he could hardly take it in. But the moment could hold it, and it did.

"The deedsss that changed the course of hissstory," agreed Nozdormu. "I hold them all. All the great deedsss, of all beingsss who have lived. But that is not all there is."

Thrall was enraptured by the scenes, dancing and beautiful, and felt himself yearning to be swept up in them. Gently, with compassion for his yearning, he nonetheless rooted himself on the sand, Thrall-in-the-now, regarding Nozdormu-in-the-now.

He turned his head to regard the dragon's face. The wisdom in the gleaming, sun-colored eyes was almost unimaginably ancient, and yet oddly youthful. Powerful, beyond Thrall's comprehension. Beautiful.

"There is more to a life than the great moments, the ones the world sssees," Nozdormu continued. "You must sssee those for yourself."

And Thrall did. The discovery of Taretha's first enthusiastic note, and the glimpse of her waving to him when she was just a girl. The quiet evenings in camps after battles, drinking and laughing and telling stories around a fire. Running as a ghost wolf, working with the elements.

"This strong hand in mine," he murmured, the memory of Aggra's brown fingers clasping his.

"It is there that we are receptive, and learn. Where we take in. Glory, battle, great momentsss, are where we give to the world. But we cannot give without receiving. We cannot share what we do not have inside. It is this quiet, the pause between breathsss, that makes us what we truly are. Gives us ssstrength for all our journeys."

Aggra.

The moments shimmered, ceased, and Thrall was looking at nothing more—or less—than the beautiful golden scales of the minder of time. He realized, too, that he and Nozdormu were not alone in the Caverns. They were surrounded by several silent but happy members of the bronze flight who had come to sit quietly beside them.

Nozdormu looked at each of them, including his son Anachronos, then back to Thrall. "I owe you a debt I do not think I can repay," Nozdormu said. "You brought me back. I wasss everywhere, and nowhere at once. I had forgotten the Firssst Lessson. I, the Timelesss One." He made a rumbling noise, part self-deprecating amusement, part annoyance. "One would think that, surrounded by the grainsss of the sssands of time, I would remember the small thingsss more."

This strong hand in yours.

"I know why you have come," Nozdormu continued. Thrall suddenly felt sheepish. "Or rather . . . all the reasons you have come, some of which are not necessarily ssso. Speak, my friend."

Thrall did, starting with the visit from Ysera, and all that had occurred since then. Nozdormu's nostrils flared and his great eyes narrowed at the description of the ancients.

"They, too, are keepersss of time, in their own way," he said, but would not elaborate further.

Thrall continued, speaking of the mysterious assassin and his experience with the various manifestations of the timeways. "I learned that my pursuer was none other than possibly my greatest enemy," he said quietly. "Aedelas Blackmoore—an Aedelas Blackmoore who was strong, and cunning, and determined."

"And," Nozdormu sighed, "an agent of the infinite dragonflight."

"How do you—?"

Nozdormu held up a commanding forepaw. "In a moment. I have listened to your ssstory, and knowing what else I know . . . I have come to a very disturbing conclusion. A conclusion," he said, addressing not just Thrall but the gathered bronzes, "that will be difficult to accept. But accept it we must. My children . . . everything is connected."

The bronzes exchanged glances. "What do you mean, Father?" asked Anachronos. "We know that meddling in the timeways can have dire repercussions."

"No, no, it isss far bigger than that . . . farther reaching . . . almost inconceivably so. And this connection concerns usss. The dragonsss. Good, at least, has come of my being trapped in each moment. I have been held captive by the illusion of time. And in that captivity, I bore witnesss. I have ssseen things germinate, gain strength, and manifest. And I tell you, it is no accident." He took a deep breath and regarded them steadily.

"All the events that have occurred to harm the Aspectsss and their flights over the millennia—they are not coincidence, or simply random happenssssstance. This altering of the timewaysss, the construction of a monster out of Blackmoore. The Emerald Nightmare, which harmed so many. The attack of the twilight dragonflight, the madness of Malygosss and even Neltharion—they are *all intertwined*. Perhaps even entirely orchestrated by the same dark handsss."

For a moment, no one spoke. So many events—connected? Part of a far-reaching conspiracy so vast, it had taken aeons to manifest?

It was Thrall who broke the silence. "To what end?" he asked. Some of these incidents he hadn't even known about. It was almost too huge for him to even comprehend.

"To destroy the Aspects and the flights forever. To eliminate all chance of order and stability."

He turned to Thrall, bringing his great head down to the orc's level. Sorrow was in those amazing eyes as he spoke.

"I had become lost in the timeways, Thrall. Trapped in every moment. Do you know why I was there in the first place?"

Thrall shook his head.

"I was there to try to understand how sssomething dark came to be. How to prevent that. You asked me how I knew that the infinite dragonflight was behind Blackmoore'sss creation and liberation."

He hesitated, then looked away, unable to meet Thrall's blue-eyed gaze.

"I know this because . . . I sssent him after you."

Twelve

"What?" Thrall at first thought this was some kind of joke, a draconic attempt at mortal humor. But Nozdormu seemed very serious. Thrall was both furious and completely confused. Even the other bronzes drew back and murmured among themselves.

Nozdormu heaved a great sigh. "It was given unto me to know the very hour and method of my own death," he said. "I would never sssubvert it. But only one of the pathwaysss to my destiny can be correct. And in one unfolding future, I became the leader of the infinite dragonflight. That was why I became lost in the time-waysss, Thrall. I was ssseeking understanding of how such a thing came to be. How I, who have always striven to honor the great duty the titans charged me with, could have fallen so far astray."

Thrall nodded, though he was still shocked and more than a little wary.

"Did . . . you discover how to prevent such a thing from happening?" he asked.

Slowly, Nozdormu shook his massive head. "Unfortunately, not yet. One thing I do know, and that isss that all the flightsss must

unite against this current menace. Ysera was right: you have certain abilities, waysss of thinking, waysss of ssspeaking, that move
others. You have helped so much already, yet I must ask you to help
more."

Help the future leader of the infinite dragonflight? Thrall hesitated. And yet, he could sense nothing of evil in Nozdormu. Not
yet anyway. He sensed only worry and chagrin.

"For Ysera, and especially for Desharin, who gave his life that I
might find you, Timeless One, I will help. But I will need to know
more. I fear I have been operating in the dark most of this time."

"Considering Ysera sought you out, that does not sssurprise
me," Nozdormu said, dryly but with affection. "She is ssseldom
clear. Thrall, son of Durotan and Draka, you have my deepest
thanksss. We will share with you what we can . . . but you must
undertake this alone. This theory, this conviction—I must know
more if I am to truly know what we must do. Do not worry: I will
not forget that which you have reminded me to remember. I will
not get lost in the timeways a sssecond time. It is a difficult task I
ssset before you, but one that could sssave everything. You must
find Alexstrasza the Life-Binder, and rouse her from her grief."

"What happened?" Thrall inquired.

"I was not present, yet I know," said Nozdormu. Thrall nodded. If Nozdormu had been trapped in every moment, of course
he would know. "There was a meeting of the various flightsss at
Wyrmrest Temple not very long ago. It was the first sssuch since
the death of Malygosss, and the end of the Nexus War.

"Alexstrasza's mate, Korialstrasz, whom you knew as Krasus, lingered behind in the Ruby Sanctum. Each flight has a sssanctum, a sort
of . . . dimension that is jussst for them. The meeting was interrupted
by an attack from a flight known as the twilight dragonflight—who
ssserve Deathwing and the Twilight's Hammer cult."

Thrall frowned. "I know of this cult," he said.

"During the battle, there was a terrible implosion. Every one of the sssanctums was destroyed. With them went Krasus . . . and all the eggs in every sssanctum. He killed them all."

Thrall stared at the bronze dragon. He thought of what he had seen of Krasus: calm, intelligent, caring. "He . . . he murdered them? All of them?"

"So it would seem," growled Anachronos. His tail lashed and his eyes were narrowed.

Thrall shook his head firmly. "No. I don't believe it. There must be some reason, some explanation—"

"The Life-Binder is devastated," Nozdormu interrupted. "Imagine how she mussst feel. To think that her dearest love had either gone mad, or been in league with the cult—it has shattered her. Without their Aspect, the reds will not lend their aid to fight the Twilight Cult. And without the redsss, there is no chance of victory. All will be lossst."

He turned his great eyes upon Thrall and said intently, "You must remind her of her duties—of her heart's ability to care for othersss, even when it is wounded. Can you do this, Thrall?"

Thrall had no idea. It was a daunting task. Could no dragon accomplish it? He had no personal connection with her. How in the world could he convince her to put aside such powerful grief and rejoin a battle?

"I will try," was all Thrall could answer.

Alexstrasza did not remember where she had been for most of the last several days. Nor did she have any thought as to where she would go. She simply flew, blinded by pain and a desire to escape from it, and let her wings take her where they would.

She had flown over empty gray expanses of ocean, over elven lands and corrupted forests and winterscapes, until she reached this place which seemed as lonely and broken and empty as she was. Her final destination, she had decided, would be in Desolace—a fitting name, she thought bitterly.

She transformed and walked on two feet south from the Stonetalon Mountains. She passed a battle between Horde and Alliance, and gave it no heed; let the short-lived races destroy themselves. It was no concern of hers any longer. She passed a scarred vale pulsing with lava and temperatures only a black dragon could endure, and spared it only a dull glance. Let the world destroy itself. Her love was gone—her love, who had, perhaps, betrayed her and all she had fought for.

Alexstrasza cursed herself, her flight, the other flights; she cursed the titans, who had bequeathed such a burden upon her. She had not asked for it and now realized that she could not bear it.

She removed her boots, wanting to feel the hard, dead earth beneath her feet, and paid no mind to the blisters that formed. The rocky path grew no less rocky, but the land surrendered any memory of grass and became dull and gray. It was oddly powdery beneath her sore feet, comforting in a way the rock had not been. She sensed fel energies here, but merely acknowledged this and moved forward, step by step, leaving smeared bloody prints as she walked.

The dead were here. She saw countless bones of kodos and other creatures, bleached white with age. The skeletons dotted the landscapes as trees did in other places. What living creatures she did see seemed to feast on death—hyenas, vultures. Alexstrasza watched dully as a vulture wheeled over her. She wondered if it had ever tasted dragon before.

It would, soon. This place suited her. She would not leave it.

Slowly, the dragoness once known as the Life-Binder ascended a jutting peak to look down upon the wasteland. She would not eat, nor drink, nor sleep. She would sit atop the peak and wait for death to claim her, and then her suffering would, at last, be over.

Thrall almost missed her.

Even atop the back of one of the great bronze dragons, he could not see everything. He was looking for a red dragon, presumably easy to spot in this empty place. He was not looking for a slender elven female, huddled alone atop a stone peak.

"I will set you down a short distance away," Tick said. One of the dragons who had guarded the Caverns of Time, she had volunteered to bear Thrall wherever he needed to go—starting with this forsaken place. "I think my presence here will not be welcome."

She spoke this not in hostility but in deep regret. Thrall imagined that all the dragonflights mourned for what had happened to the Life-Binder. If they had any sense, Thrall thought, every sentient being would mourn it.

"I think that best," Thrall said. As they came closer, he could see the small form better. He could not see her face, but her body was huddled tight, legs clasped to chest, red head bent over them. Every line of her screamed pain and devastation.

The bronze dragon landed some distance away, crouching so that Thrall could dismount.

"Come here when you are ready to depart," she told Thrall.

"My hope is that Alexstrasza and I will be departing together," Thrall reminded her.

Tick looked at him somberly. "Come here when you are ready to depart," she repeated, and leaped skyward.

Thrall sighed, and glanced up at the peak, and began to climb.

"I hear you, orc," she said before he had gotten halfway to where she sat alone. Her voice was beautiful but shattered, like a precious glass sculpture smashed by a careless hand: still glittering, still lovely, but in pieces.

"It was not my intention to sneak up on you," Thrall replied.

She said nothing further. He finished the climb and sat down beside her on the hard stone. She did not even favor him with a glance, much less a word.

After a while, he said, "I know who you are, Life-Binder. I—"

She whirled on him then, her tanned, exquisite face furious, her teeth bared in a snarl. "You will not call me that! Ever! I bind no life, not anymore."

Her outburst startled but did not surprise him. He nodded. "As you wish. I am Thrall, once the warchief of the Horde, now a member of the Earthen Ring."

"I know who you are."

Thrall was slightly taken aback, but continued. "And whatever name I call you by, it is you I have been sent to find."

"By whom?" she said, her voice and face becoming dull again as she turned away to regard the empty, ugly landscape.

"By Ysera, in part, and by Nozdormu."

The barest flicker of interest crossed her features, like something half glimpsed in deep water. "He has returned?"

"I sought and found him, as I sought and found you," Thrall said. "There is much he has learned—much that he believes you need to hear."

She didn't reply. Hot air lifted her dark red locks and toyed with them. Thrall wasn't certain how to proceed. He had been prepared for grief and anger, but this dull, deathly despair—

He told her what had happened until this point, trying to make it sound like a story. If he could rouse some interest, some curiosity—

anything other than that horrible stone-still, pallid death mask expression she bore—he would feel heartened. He spoke of Ysera, and the fire elemental who had tried to destroy the ancients. The wind blew, hot and cruel, and still Alexstrasza sat as unmoving as if she had been carved from stone.

"The ancients spoke," Thrall continued. "Their memories are becoming confused. Someone was damaging the timeways."

"I know this," she replied bluntly. "I know the bronzes are concerned about it, and they are enlisting the aid of mortals to correct it. You tell me nothing new, Thrall, and certainly nothing to inspire me to return."

Her words and voice both were venomous. There was hate in them—but hate, Thrall knew, that wasn't directed at him. It was directed at Alexstrasza herself.

He pressed on. "Nozdormu believes that many things are connected. They are not separate occurrences. All the terrible events the Aspects have suffered—the mysterious attacks of the infinite dragonflight, the Emerald Nightmare, even the madness of Deathwing and Malygos—Nozdormu senses a pattern in it all, a pattern of attack hammering at the Aspects and their flights. An attack designed to wear them down and defeat them—perhaps even cause them to turn on one another."

A soft murmur. "Who would wish such a thing, even if it were true?"

Thrall was encouraged by even this faint sign of curiosity. "Nozdormu needs more time to figure it all out," he answered. "For now, he suspects the infinite dragonflight is at least somewhat involved."

A silence. "I see."

"He asked me to find you. To—to help you. Help you heal." It was difficult, and humbling, to believe that he, a simple orcish shaman, was in a position to heal the Life-Binder herself—perhaps the greatest healer there had ever been. He half expected her to scorn the offer and dismiss it, but she remained silent. He continued.

"If you can recover, many other things will be healed as well. Together we can go to the Nexus, speak with the blues, and help them find clarity. Then—"

"Why?"

The question, asked simply and bluntly, left him without words for a moment.

"Because . . . it will help them."

"I ask again: Why?"

"If they are helped, then they can join with us, and we can find out what's going on. And once we understand that, we can set it right. We can fight the Twilight's Hammer cultists and defeat them. Figure out what the infinite dragonflight's motives are. Stop Deathwing once and for all . . . and save this world, which even now is being ripped to pieces."

She stared at him, her eyes boring right through him. For a long time she said nothing.

"You do not see," she said at last.

"What don't I see, Alexstrasza?" he asked very gently.

"That none of this matters."

"What do you mean? We have information; we know this is part of a huge, complex plan that has been going on perhaps for millennia! We might be able to stop it!"

Alexstrasza shook her head slowly. "No. It doesn't matter. None of it. It doesn't matter if everything is interconnected. It doesn't matter how long this has been going on. It doesn't even matter if we can stop it."

He stared at her, uncomprehending.

"The children," she said flatly, "are *dead*. Korialstrasz is *dead*. I am dead in all ways but one, and that will soon happen. There is no hope. There is nothing. Nothing matters."

Thrall suddenly felt the heat of anger. He still felt the loss of Taretha as a quiet ache in his heart. Her loss was a necessary one, if all was to be as it should be. But he would miss her, now and always. He thought of how she burned to make a difference, to matter. She had felt there was little she could do, but she had done all she could. The Life-Binder could make differences on a scale that Taretha could not even comprehend, yet she preferred to stay here and insist that nothing mattered.

Things did matter. Taretha mattered. Azeroth mattered. Despite what she endured, Alexstrasza did not have the luxury to wallow in her pain.

He pushed back his anger and tempered it with the compassion he truly did feel for her. "I am sorry for the loss of the eggs," he said. "To have lost most of a generation—truly, I cannot imagine your pain. And I am sorry for the loss of your mate, especially in such a manner. But . . . I cannot believe that you would turn your back on those who need you," he said, anger creeping into his voice. "You are an Aspect, for ancestors' sake. This is what you were made for. You—"

She sprang from a sitting position straight up into the air with a speed that was almost faster than his eye could follow. A heartbeat later, a giant red dragon hovered over him. The fine gray dust of the dead land was stirred up and covered Thrall's skin and robe, causing his eyes to water. He leaped to his feet and stepped back quickly, wondering what would happen next.

"Yes, I was made," Alexstrasza said, her voice deeper, harsher, and full of anger and a blistering bitterness. "Made into the Life-Binder without truly understanding what was being asked of me. And what is being asked of me is no longer bearable. I have sacrificed, and given, and aided, and fought, and my reward is more pain, more demands, and the death of all I hold dear. I do not wish to kill, but I will, orc, if you trouble me further. Nothing matters! *Nothing! GO!*"

He tried one more time. "Please," he said, "please consider the innocents who—"

"*GO!*"

Alexstrasza reared back, beating her wings to keep herself aloft and opening her enormous, sharp-toothed maw, and Thrall fled. A sheet of billowing orange-red flame charred the stone where he had been sitting. He heard her drawing breath again and half ran, half fell down the side of the jutting peak.

A roar filled the heavy air. It was a mixture of anger and anguish, and Thrall's heart ached for the grieving Aspect. He wished he had been able to find some way to reach her. The thought of her dying here, alone, from lack of food and water and most of all from a broken heart, pained him. He regretfully imagined travelers one day coming across her bones, bleached and old like the other skeletons that dotted this landscape.

He slipped and slid the rest of the way and, bruised and with a heavy spirit, trudged to where Tick had said to meet her. The dragon wheeled above him for a moment, then landed and regarded him sadly.

"Where shall I bear you, Thrall?" she asked quietly.

"We go to the Nexus, just as we planned," Thrall said, his voice ragged. "We go to convince the blues to unite with the other flights, as Nozdormu asked."

"And . . . we go alone."

Thrall nodded. "Alone." He glanced back at the shape of a great red dragon, her wings beating erratically, her body contorted as she threw back her horned head. Perhaps, if she saw what the others were doing, her heart might yet be moved. "For now."

Yet even as they flew northward, over the sound of Tick's beating wings, Thrall could hear the bitter, roaring grief of a broken Life-Binder.

Like a shadow stretching out across the land at twilight, something dark lifted up from the hollow in which he had concealed himself. Far enough away so that he would likely not be seen, but close enough to keep the quarry within range, King Aedelas Blackmoore, perched atop a twilight dragon, followed.

The wind blew back his long, black hair. His face was, if cruel, not unhandsome. A neatly trimmed black goatee framed thin lips, and his blue eyes snapped beneath elegant black brows.

After the first effort, Blackmoore had decided not to follow Thrall through the timeways. It was too tricky; the odds of his prey eluding him and leading him on a futile chase were too high.

Better to wait, and bide his time, and be where he knew Thrall would eventually have to appear.

Thrall. He had heard enough about Thrall to want to dismember the orc with a paring knife. Thrall, who had slain him, whose mere existence had caused Blackmoore to continue down the path of a pathetic, drunken coward. Thrall, who had led an army of orcs against Durnholde. No, it was quite the joy that lay before him. The victory would be even sweeter, given what a challenge the greenskin actually was.

Fly away, orc, he mused, his thin lips curling in a smile. *Fly, but you cannot flee.*

I will find you, and I will slay you. And then I will help destroy your world.

Thirteen

Thrall had to admit to himself that he was uneasy about approaching the blue dragonflight in its own lair. Exposure to the great leviathans had in no way lessened their majesty in his eyes. Indeed, the more he learned of dragons, the more impressed he became. Green, bronze, the mighty yet heartbroken Life-Binder, who was arguably the most powerful dragon in all of Azeroth—even the least of them could destroy him with a single tail swipe or crush him beneath a clawed foot.

They had impressed him more than physically as well. Their minds were not those of the "shorter-lived" races, as they termed them. They thought on a larger scale, and no matter how long he lived, Thrall knew he could only grasp the merest fraction of their complexity: Ysera's dreaminess even as the Awakened, seeing things no other being had or ever could; the weaving of a life in Nozdormu's scales; the aching pain of one who held the world's compassion in her heart. . . .

Now Thrall and Tick were heading directly for the dragonflight that had recently caused so much harm—whose Aspect had been chosen to be the guardian of arcane magic in the world. Malygos had gone mad, and then, fearfully sane, had done worse things than he had ever done in the grasp of his insanity. Thrall had not walked in the Emerald Dream, but he had exchanged jokes with Desharin. He had done his best to help Alexstrasza, huddled and broken. He had been able to enlighten the Timeless One.

But the blues . . .

No love of the "lesser races" had they, this flight—masters of arcane magic, living in climates as blue and white and cold as they themselves were said to be.

He chuckled ruefully as he anticipated the meeting. "Perhaps I should have just stayed home," he said to Tick.

"Had you done so," Tick mused, "then this timeway would have been altered even more, and you would have created yet more work for my brethren."

It took Thrall a moment to realize that while in a way the bronze was serious, she was also attempting humor. Thrall laughed.

The blue-gray of the frigid ocean beneath them, which was all Thrall had been able to see for much of the journey, gave way to white and gray cliffs. Thrall had seen many impressive sights in his day, but the Nexus came close to topping them all.

Blue, it was all blue, with shades of silver and white here and there. Several flat disks hovered in the air, spaced around the Nexus itself. As Tick flew closer, Thrall could see that these disks were platforms. Their flooring was ornamented with glowing, inlaid sigils, and on a few of them were beautiful crystalline trees, their branches seemingly made of ice and leafed with frost.

The Nexus itself seemed to comprise many levels, each one connected to the one above by magical strands of arcane energy. It was, all in all, one of the most beautiful things Thrall had seen. Several dragons were lazily circling, their bodies in all shades of cerulean, aquamarine, or cobalt.

Thrall and Tick were spotted almost at once, of course, and four blue dragons broke away from their brethren and approached. Their challenge was not issued to the orc but rather to the mighty bronze dragon. Thrall was, for the moment, utterly ignored.

"We greet our bronze sister," one of them said as they flew in an apparently casual but nonetheless intimidating loose circle around Tick. "But the Nexus is not a timeway for you to explore. Why have you come to our sanctuary? No one invited you here."

"It is not I who come to you but this orc whom I bear," Tick said. "Nor is it I who send him this way. He was sent first by Ysera the Awakened, and then by Nozdormu the Timeless One, to this place. His name is Thrall."

The blues exchanged glances. "For a short-lived being, he comes heralded," one said.

"Thrall," another said, as if trying to recall. "The warchief of the Horde."

"No longer," Thrall said. "I am but a shaman working with the Earthen Ring now, in an attempt to help heal a world brutally wounded by Deathwing."

For an instant he wondered if that was the wrong thing to say. Instantly the blues looked angry, and one of them darted off and wheeled before returning, visibly needing to calm himself.

"That traitor would have seen all of our flight destroyed," one of them growled, his voice as cold as the blue ice he so resembled. "We will bring word of your coming to the others. Tarry here until we bid you approach closer or order you to leave."

The blues dove off, azure shapes against a dark blue and lavender sky. To Thrall's surprise, they did not alight on one of the floating tiers of the Nexus but instead flew downward, to the ice and snow below.

* * *

Kalecgos sighed. *Here we go again,* he thought, gazing at the icy ceiling that arched above this cavernous meeting hall.

The blue flight had done a great deal of talking, and more arrived daily at the Nexus to augment their meager number, but he did not feel that any solid conclusion had been reached.

Most agreed that the timing of the conjunction between the two moons was auspicious, if nothing else. One or two had dug up ancient spells they had wanted to try that, upon further investigation, had been proved inadequate. So far, it did seem that the blues were more than content with "anointing" one of their number during what was sure to be a visually stirring astronomical moment, but there was no real emotion behind it, no real sense that this was the single right thing to do.

Arygos was holding forth on his bloodline and how being the son of Malygos really did mean that, all things considered, he was the best choice. Kalec had heard this before, and was too disheartened to interrupt. He glanced out as two more blues approached, and frowned, his interest piqued.

These were not more newcomers to the Nexus but rather two of the Nexus's protectors. They landed beside Arygos, interrupting that dragon in his speech, and spoke quietly to him.

Arygos looked angry. "Under no circumstances!" he said harshly.

"Narygos," Kalec called, "what is it?"

"Stay out of this," Arygos said quickly. To Narygos he said bluntly, "Kill him."

"Kill whom?" demanded Kalec, ignoring the implied warning and moving quickly to Arygos and the others. "Narygos, what has happened?"

Narygos glanced from Arygos to Kalec, then said, "There is a stranger who comes to speak with us. He is one of the lesser races. An orc, once warchief of what is known as the Horde: Thrall. He and the bronze dragon who bears him insist that both Ysera and Nozdormu have sent him to us."

Kalec's ears pricked up. "Nozdormu? He has returned?"

"So it would seem," said Narygos. Kalec turned a stunned gaze to Arygos.

"*Kill* him?" Kalecgos repeated, loudly and disbelievingly. "One whom two Aspects have sent to us? Borne atop a willing dragon?"

They were attracting attention from others now, and Arygos scowled.

"Very well, then, do not harm him," said Arygos. "But a member of the lesser races has no purpose here. I will not see him."

Angry, Kalec turned to Narygos. "*I* will," he said. "Bring him."

"I would not care if the titans themselves brought him to us. I will see no short-lived being in our private refuge!"

Arygos was livid. He stalked back and forth, his huge tail twitching, his wings furling and unfurling in his agitation. Others had overheard the argument between the two and began to chime in.

"But . . . Ysera, and Nozdormu!" Narygos protested. "This is a far from common incident. Ysera has seen much in her dreaming, and finding Nozdormu is something the Timeless One's own flight could not manage on its own. Surely it would do no harm to listen to him!"

"The lesser races, as some have dubbed them, have proven themselves to be surprising at times. There is more to them than we often give them credit for. The fact that two Aspects have urged him toward us tells me all I need to know," said Kalec. "I say we bring him and find out what he has to tell us."

"You would," sneered Arygos. "You like to play in the mud with the lesser beings. I've never understood that about you, Kalecgos."

Kalec regarded Arygos sadly. "And I never understood your refusal to take help or information when it came from any source other than our own flight," he replied. "Why do you scorn them so? It was the short-lived races who freed you from your thousand-year imprisonment in Ahn'Qiraj! I would think you would be grateful."

Before Arygos could sputter out an angry and embarrassed reply, another, older dragon, Teralygos, snapped, "Surely no one knows the business of our flight better than we do!"

"Indeed! We have our own business to mind, Kalecgos, or have you forgotten?" Arygos continued. "The ceremony to choose a new Aspect is but a few days away. We should be preparing for that, not letting ourselves become distracted by the prattling of an orc!"

"Kill him and be done with it," muttered Teralygos.

Kalec turned. "No. We are not butchers. Besides, do you want to look Ysera and Nozdormu in the face and tell them you murdered one they specifically sent to us? *I* don't. No matter how disoriented the awakened Ysera might be."

There was some murmuring among the dragons, and Kalec saw some heads nodding.

"Let the orc come before us and state his reasons for being here," Kalec continued. "If we do not like what he has to say, we can send him away. But at least we should hear him out."

Arygos glowered, but he, too, could see that more were in agreement with Kalecgos than with him. "Ysera and Nozdormu, it seems, have more influence on the blue dragonflight than we ourselves do," he muttered.

"You are not Aspect yet, Arygos," Kalec said sharply. "If you are chosen, then you will have final say. Until then, with no leader, the majority's will shall be followed on this."

Arygos turned toward Narygos. "Bring him," he said. Narygos nodded and leaped skyward. When Arygos turned back, he frowned. Kalecgos had assumed his half-elven form. Some other dragons had also taken on the less threatening forms of human or elf, in an unspoken effort to show courtesy to their guest. Arygos did not emulate them, retaining his dragon form.

Kalecgos looked around. The chamber was hardly inviting to anyone other than the blues. He concentrated and waved his hands.

In one area of the cavern two braziers appeared. Dozens of furs now covered the floor for several feet. A thick fur cloak was draped over the curving arm of a chair made of mammoth tusks and hide. Food and drink sat on a short table: haunches of meat, cactus apples, mugs of foaming beer. Animal heads and weapons—axes and swords and wicked-looking daggers—were now mounted on the stone walls.

Kalec smiled. He was more accustomed to interacting with the Alliance races, but he had seen something of this world, and felt that he had created a fairly comfortable Horde enclave here in the heart of blue dragon territory.

A few moments later a bronze dragon came into sight, escorted by four blues. She flew low, but the spaces here were vast—they were, after all, meant to accommodate dragons. Kalecgos recognized her. It was Tick, one of the dragons who regularly patrolled the entrance to the Caverns of Time. It was a testament to Thrall's importance that so notable a bronze would be willing to serve as a mere method of transportation. Their eyes met, and Kalec nodded acknowledgment. Tick landed gracefully, lowering herself so that the orc atop her back could dismount.

Kalec gazed intently at their orcish guest. He wore only a brown, nondescript robe, and he bowed with proper courtesy to the assembled flight. Even so, when he straightened, there was a set to his shoulders and a calm alertness in his blue eyes that revealed his past as a thoughtful and powerful leader. Kalec smiled warmly and opened his mouth to speak.

"You are permitted here only because two Aspects have sent you, Thrall," said Arygos before Kalec could get a word out. "I suggest you speak quickly. You are not among friends."

The orc smiled slightly. "I did not expect to be," he said. "But I am here because I believe in my mission. I will speak as quickly as I may, but it might take longer than you think."

"Then start," said Arygos bluntly.

Thrall took a deep breath and began to speak, telling the dragons about Ysera's request, the confused ancients, becoming lost in the timeways and finding himself, finding Nozdormu. Despite Arygos's rudeness, they all listened attentively. These were dragons of magic, of intellect. Knowledge, even one brought by an orc, was meat and drink to them.

"Nozdormu believes that all the events—the tragedies—that have challenged the dragonflights are interconnected," Thrall finished. "He suspects the infinite dragonflight, and has lingered behind to gather more information before he comes to you with what he knows. He bade me find the Life-Binder and bring her with me, but . . . she has suffered a grave loss, and remains too shaken by it to come. So Tick agreed to bear me here. That is all I know, but if there is anything else you wish to ask, I will answer as best I can. I stand more than ready to help."

Kalec stared at the orc, shaken to his very core. "This is all . . . extraordinary news," he said, seeing his own concern and apprehension reflected on the faces of many of the other blues.

But not all of them. Arygos and his contingent seemed unaffected. "With all due respect to Ysera, she has much to sort out after thousands of years of abiding almost entirely in the Emerald Dream. She has admitted to being . . . confused. She does not know what is true, what is a dream, and what might be her own imagination. As for Nozdormu, you said he had been . . . caught?

In his own timeways? And *you* were able to help him escape? Please enlighten us as to how."

Thrall's cheeks darkened slightly at the obvious skepticism in Arygos's voice, but his expression didn't change, and when he spoke, it was in calm tones.

"I understand your doubt, Arygos. I myself had very serious doubts. But it does seem that Ysera was correct. I have already been able to be of some use to two dragonflights—if not to Alexstrasza herself. If you are perhaps implying that Nozdormu has been somehow addled by his experiences in the timeways, then I urge you to talk to Tick and see what she thinks. I for one think not. You ask how I, a mere orc, was able to pull the Timeless One out? It . . . was simple."

There was angry and offended murmuring at that, but Thrall held up his hand. "Know that I do not belittle anyone when I say this. 'Simple' does not mean 'easy.' I have learned that the things that seem the simplest are often the most powerful of all. They are the things that matter, in the end. Regarding Nozdormu: to free one trapped in all moments of time, I had to learn to be truly in one moment—*the* moment."

Arygos's disapproval deepened. "Anyone can do that!"

"Anyone *can*," Thrall agreed readily. "But no one *had*. It is a simple thought, to be in the moment—but one that I had to learn myself." He smiled a bit self-deprecatingly as some of the dragons began to look less annoyed and more thoughtful. "While the lesson itself was simple, the learning of it was most certainly not. We best teach what we ourselves have learned. If I could help two Aspects . . . perhaps I can help you."

"We are without an Aspect for our flight," said Arygos. "I somehow think that if such a problem is new and confusing to us, then you will be unable to assist."

"It's new and confusing to me too. That makes us equals, in that at least."

Mirth rippled through the assembled blues, even those who were allied with Arygos.

"Orc, you are here as a guest of our flight," said Arygos, a hint of warning in his voice. "You would be well advised not to mock us."

Kalec sighed; before his madness, Malygos had been known for a sense of humor and playfulness, two attributes which seemed completely lacking in his son.

"Arygos, he's not mocking; he's making a serious point in a light manner. These are uncertain times. We are blazing new trails, making history in a way even the Aspects have never made history. Thrall comes with the approval of two Aspects. What is the harm in letting him listen and offer his opinion?" Kalec spread his hands. "He is not one of us, and he's very well aware of it. He therefore can have no influence other than what we ourselves give him. He might notice things we miss. I think it would be a grave error if we do not let him stay, and observe, and speak his piece."

Arygos shook himself and lifted his head, peering down imperiously at the smaller half-elven form.

"You would give every member of the lesser races a soft bed and plenty of food if you could," he said, sneering.

Kalec smiled, gently. "And I fail to see the harm in that manner of thinking. He is but one orc. I can't believe that you are afraid of him."

That got to Arygos. He slammed his tail down, and the others who tended to think as he did looked offended as well. "Afraid? I? Not of a puny orc I could crush with one talon!"

"Well, then," Kalec said, continuing to smile, "there should be no problem with his staying, should there?"

Arygos suddenly froze. His eyes narrowed to slits, and he stared at Kalecgos for a long time.

"I fear nothing from this lesser being. But what we do here is of deep meaning to the blue dragonflight. I do not know that it is appropriate for a lesser being to witness these events, let alone be part of them."

Kalec folded his arms and gazed for a long, searching moment at the orc. Something inside him was saying that Thrall needed to be here. Something more than the simple respect all dragons should have for the opinion of an Aspect. If the world was indeed facing the sort of danger that Nozdormu implied, the blues could not afford to ignore any wise thought, regardless of the source. Moreover, they could not afford to isolate themselves under a false sense of superiority born of ignorance and arrogance. He turned his piercing eyes to Tick, lifting an eyebrow in a question. The bronze met Kalec's gaze evenly. In those eyes, Kalec read an unshakable certainty that echoed his own.

He made his decision. It was a calculated gamble, but one he knew, bone deep, that he had to take.

"Thrall stays," Kalecgos said quietly, "or I go."

An unhappy murmur arose. Arygos said nothing, but his tail twitched.

"I honored and respected your father, Malygos—for himself, and for the Aspect he embodied. But his choices were the wrong ones—not just for others, but for us. It may be that we, too, end up stumbling down the wrong path. But as long as I have breath and life in my body, I will not go down that path knowingly. Thrall should be here; he has done nearly as much for the dragonflights as most dragons themselves have done. I repeat: if he goes, I go. And others with me."

It was not an idle threat. If Arygos was going to force a schism, then let it happen here and now. Kalecgos would not depart the Nexus alone. And Arygos could not afford for that to happen. Too much was uncertain as it was.

Arygos was silent for several heartbeats. Then, moving swiftly, he went to Thrall and dropped his head down until it was within inches of the orc's.

"You are here as a guest," Arygos rumbled, repeating his earlier words. "You will deport yourself with respect and courtesy and obey our wishes."

"I am an ambassador," Thrall said. "I understand that. I have dealt with many ambassadors in my time, Arygos. I understand respect and courtesy."

There was almost, but not quite, an overemphasis on the word "I." Arygos's nostrils flared, and then he turned to the bronze dragon visitor. "Tick, you are no longer needed here. Thrall is now our responsibility."

Tick bridled, ever so slightly, then gave a bow that was so low as to border on impudence.

"I will return to my flight, then. Take good care of this one, Arygos."

Arygos watched her depart, then turned back to the assembled blues. "It is my understanding that there might be new information as to how this . . . ritual . . . will work," the dragon said. "Let us hear from the magi newly returned."

As it turned out, very little was revealed by the newcomers. Like many of those deeply focused on the minutiae of the arcane, they were excited about uncovering a few details that shed enlightenment on the possible process of determining a new Aspect, but there was nothing of great significance. After some discussion and several arguments—one of which erupted in shouting and a near-attack on one of Kalec's colleagues—an agreement was reached to continue to research and see if anything new came to light.

Thrall sat quietly in his small area, partaking of the fare provided and listening and watching. He said almost nothing, speaking only once to ask for clarification on something. The rest of the time he leaned back, arms folded across his barrel chest, simply observing.

When the meeting was over, there was some milling about, and many glances thrown in the orc's direction. At last, though, most of the blues left. Arygos was the final one to depart, pausing at the cavern's exit. He lifted his head and craned it over his shoulder, gazing balefully. He said nothing, and Thrall did not shrink from the angry stare. Finally, narrowing his eyes, Arygos turned and left.

Kalecgos exhaled, conjured a second crude chair, and plopped down into it. He propped his elbows on the table and rubbed his tired eyes.

"I sensed some tension at the gathering," Thrall said.

Kalec laughed. He waved a hand, created a goblet of wine, and took a sip.

"You have a gift for understatement, friend Thrall. I anticipated out-and-out violence on at least three separate occasions this afternoon alone. Perhaps it is your presence that keeps Arygos civil. After what happened to his father, he wouldn't want to appear erratic in front of someone who has the ear of two Aspects. For that alone, I will buy you a drink one day in some tavern when you least expect it."

He grinned, his blue eyes dancing with mirth. Thrall found himself smiling back. He liked Kalec. The young blue seemed quite comfortable in his half-elven form. Thrall realized Kalec reminded him of Desharin, and the pleasure grew bittersweet. He felt the smile ebb from his face.

Kalec did not miss the expression. "Is something wrong?"

"There was another dragon I encountered on my journey. He was much like you. His name was Desharin. He was—"

"A green dragon," Kalec finished, his eyes somber. "Past tense."

Thrall nodded. "He helped me on my journey, taking me to the Caverns of Time. He was killed there, by the assassin who ambushed us both while we were falling into a meditative state."

He could not keep the anger from his voice, and Kalec nodded. "Effective . . . but a coward's way to fight."

Thrall was silent for a moment. "Yes," he said. "I discovered who he was in the final timeway in which I was trapped. You likely do not know the name Aedelas Blackmoore, and for that I am glad. He amounted to very little in this timeway, fortunately. He found me when I was an infant and trained me to be a gladiator. His goal was to put me at the head of an army of orcs and overthrow the Alliance."

"Obviously he did not succeed," said Kalec.

"Not in this timeway. In that one . . . I died in infancy, and Blackmoore rose himself to lead that army."

"A chilling scenario," Kalec said, "but you said he attacked you *outside* the timeways. How—?" His eyes widened as comprehension dawned. "The infinite dragonflight must have pulled him out of the timeway to hunt you down." Thrall nodded. "That is . . . disturbing that they can do so."

"Everything I have learned since I began this journey is disturbing," Thrall said. He peered at his mug. "Except for the fact that conjured beer tastes delicious." He toasted his host, smiling slightly.

Kalecgos threw back his blue head and laughed.

The moons were close to full tonight, but that couldn't be helped. Arygos could not wait for another evening to conduct his business. Like all blues, he did not feel the cold as his wings beat steadily, carrying him through the freezing night that was so clear, the stars looked like chips of ice in the sky.

He took the utmost care to make sure he was not followed, wheeling back often. He flew due east, his wings beating rapidly. The jagged teeth of Coldarra gave way to slightly more temperate landscapes. Pools of scalding water, gushing straight from Azeroth's core, spat and hissed. Geysers, steam springs, floodplains—he ignored them, obsessed with his destination.

The spires of Wyrmrest Temple appeared ghostly in the moonslight. They were damaged, but they were not uninhabited. Shapes like shadows, black and purple and indigo, wheeled about slowly while others slept in various nooks of the temple. Two lounged about, sprawled like giant winged lizards, right on the mosaic floor of the highest level.

He was spotted.

Several of the twilight dragons assigned to guard the temple veered from their regular circuits, heading right for Arygos, and a voice seemed to come from everywhere and nowhere.

"Arygos, son of Malygos," came a familiar voice—the same voice that had taunted Alexstrasza and the rest of the dragons on that fateful day not so long ago.

"It is I," Arygos cried in response. He landed on the topmost level.

And bowed humbly before the Twilight Father.

FOURTEEN

K irygosa had been asleep, curled up tightly, her dreams erratic and alarming. When she heard her brother's voice, for a moment she thought she was in the grip of another nightmare. This time, and not for the first time, she discovered that reality was worse than her dreams.

She propped herself up as far as the chain tied to her neck and driven into the floor would permit, lifted her head, and stared as her brother Arygos made obeisance to the bastard who had attacked them all. Her fists clenched.

He lifted his head and his gaze fell upon her. "Kirygosa," he said. "How pleasant . . . and surprising . . . to find you still alive."

"If I could take my true form, I would rake your eyes out," she snarled.

"Now, now," interrupted the Twilight Father, amusement in his voice, "I do so hate to see bickering between siblings."

Kiry gritted her teeth. It had been Arygos who had betrayed her into the hands of this . . . this . . .

How could she have been so naive? She had known her brother all their lives. She knew he had idolized their father. And yet, when he had come to her privately one night, telling her of his change of heart and asking for her aid, she had willingly given it.

"Come with me," he had said. "You and I . . . surely we can form some sort of plan. I love Father, Kiry. Whatever he's done. We can find a way to end this war without killing him."

So many had died by that point already, including their mother, Saragosa, who had chosen to side with Malygos. Her death had hurt all of them, but Kiry had been adamant that Malygos needed to be stopped.

"Do you really think so?" Kiry had asked. She had so wanted to believe her brother.

"I do. I see now that you were right. Let's go and see what we can come up with. Maybe if we have a sound enough plan, the Life-Binder will listen to us."

So she had gone, willingly and trustingly with hope and love in her heart, with the future in her body. And he had delivered her and her unborn children, like prized beasts, to the Twilight Father.

Words boiled in her throat, crowding each other out so that she couldn't even speak. *What sort of power did he grant you? What sort of lies did he promise? Did you know what he would do to me? Did you have a moment's hesitation?*

But she would not give him the satisfaction, and so swallowed her bitter words.

Having addressed her and assured himself that the Twilight Father was still happy with his prisoner, Arygos turned his attention fully upon his master.

"How go the discussions?" the Twilight Father inquired. "The sooner you can determine what is required, the better for us all."

"It is . . . awkward," confessed Arygos. "We are, none of us, certain of how to proceed. This has never been done before."

He sounded unsure of himself—something Kirygosa had never heard in his voice before. *He wants reassurance,* she realized. *He wants to know he has done well, that he has pleased this monster.* The thought made her sick, but she kept her silence. What she learned could be valuable to Kalecgos—if she could ever figure out how to free herself.

"You assured me that you would find a way—and that the flight would select you as the new Aspect," the Twilight Father reminded him. "How else will you be able to deliver them to me as you promised?"

"I am certain that I will be chosen, however it turns out to work," Arygos said quickly.

Of course, Kirygosa thought. With their father dead, the blues alone among the dragonflights were without an Aspect. But choosing another? How was such a thing possible? The titans had charged the Aspects. Could lesser beings even do such a thing?

"We have need of you. Our champion must be awakened, and he must have an army if the flights are to be defeated."

"They will, I swear it!" Arygos's voice was rapt with desire. "We will defeat them, and destroy this world. All will perish as the Twilight's Hammer falls!"

An army. An army comprising her own dragonflight . . .

Kirygosa closed her eyes, fighting back tears. Arygos was as lost as his father had been.

"They shall be delivered to you. Chromatus shall live." His eyes gleamed in the darkness, his body taut with anticipation.

The Twilight Father smiled.

"You shall have their energy and my own devoted to this task, Twilight Father. But . . . I need them to be mine before I can give them unto you."

"But . . . ?"

The Twilight Father had picked up on the uncertainty, as had Kiry. Hope blossomed painfully in her heart. Things were not going smoothly.

"The orc you warned me about. He has come, as you feared he might."

Thrall! In the shadows, keeping her head turned away, Kirygosa found she could not suppress a smile.

The Twilight Father swore. "This will not make our master happy," he said. "I was told that Blackmoore would stop Thrall. Tell me what harm he has done so far . . . and why you have not slain him yourself."

Arygos bridled. "I attempted to do so, but Kalecgos would not let me, and the scene was public."

"Thrall is but an orc!" snapped the Twilight Father. "You could have easily killed him before anyone protested!"

"Two Aspects sent him to us! I could not dispatch him without either arousing suspicion or alienating many of my flight—and I need every one of them if I am to become the Aspect!"

"Must I walk you through this like an infant, Arygos?" The mighty dragon actually cringed at the criticism. "Arrange an accident!"

"You are safe here, with no prying eyes watching you for weakness," spat Arygos angrily. "It is easy for you to talk of accidents when you are not in the heart of the situation! If anything happens, suspicion will fall upon me!"

"Do you think I know nothing of concealing one's true nature?" The Twilight Father threw back his head and laughed. "I move among my kind as you move among yours, and no one is the wiser as to my true plans. It is a skill you need to master, young blue."

"There are enough whom Kalec is swaying that I cannot afford anyone wondering why I was so insistent that a simple orc meet his death!"

"He is no simple orc!" the Twilight Father shot back. "Do you not understand? Thrall will destroy you if you do not destroy him first! This is what I will, and what Lord Deathwing wills! Will you defy our master simply because you are afraid of being accused? I think you choose the wrong fear to feed!"

"Kalec has taken him under his wing," muttered Arygos, but his head was lowering. "I cannot do anything. But at least we know where he is. We can watch him. And perhaps there will be a chance. Soon none of this will matter, because I will become the new Aspect. Then I will be able to do as I please."

"Did you see him?"

The Twilight Father's question and apparent change of topic confused both blue dragons, the one to whom it was addressed and the one who was eavesdropping.

"See whom?" Arygos asked.

"Take flight again," the Twilight Father said, his voice suddenly calm. "Fly to the northwest. Look upon him and return to me. Go."

Arygos nodded and flew off again into the night. The Twilight Father strode to the edge of the floor and watched, the cold turning his breath to small puffs of air.

Kirygosa swallowed hard. She now knew whom Arygos was being sent to observe.

Chromatus. He of the multiple heads, he who should never draw breath. This was the sort of grotesquery that her blood brother had allied himself with. She felt a prickling as the Twilight Father's gaze fell upon her.

"He will die," he said conversationally. "I know you must know that."

"Arygos? Certainly," she retorted.

"I do not feel like crossing the floor to torment you," he said.

"Kalec will die, and so will you. No one can stand against both Chromatus and Deathwing. Even the world cries out in pain from his torture of it."

"Kalec might indeed die," Kirygosa agreed. "And so might I. But someone will stand against Deathwing and this *thing* his son created."

Kiry was fiercely proud of Kalec. She did not know if he yet suspected that Arygos had betrayed them, or if he simply wanted to make sure Thrall was safe from any who might wish him harm for any reason. Surely there were enough of those in the blue dragonflight to warrant caution.

One hand went to the deceptively simple chain that kept her a prisoner. The other went to her abdomen. A wave of remembered torment and sorrow rose inside her. She permitted it to wash over and through her, breathing out quietly. She had not broken under their treatment of her yet. She would not falter now, no matter how terrifying the thought of fighting both Chromatus and his multiple heads and Deathwing himself. Not when there seemed to actually be hope again.

There was the song of wings beating in the still night air, and a greatly subdued Arygos returned. The Twilight Father regarded the dragon steadily.

"You will do as you promised," the Twilight Father said very, very softly.

And the great blue dragon in front of him trembled.

"Tell me more about this celestial event," Thrall said.

"Azeroth, of course, has two moons," Kalec said. "Various cultures may have different names for them, but usually they play on a mother-and-child theme, as the white moon is much larger than the blue one."

Thrall nodded. "My people call them the White Lady and the Blue Child," he said.

"Exactly. The event is when the two come into perfect alignment with one another. It is often referred to as the Embrace, as it appears that the white moon, the Mother, is holding the blue Child. It's an extremely rare occurrence—once in approximately four hundred and thirty years. I myself have never witnessed it. Would that I were doing so when all that is involved is the simple appreciation of the phenomenon."

"So you agree with those who think this is the way to do it?" Thrall asked. "That this event is going to invoke the power of the Aspect?"

"Legend has it that the moons were in this conjunction when the titans created the first Aspects," Kalecgos said. "If there is any time that would be favorable for our flight to bestow the title of an Aspect upon an ordinary dragon, it would be now."

"Title? You do not think that anything particularly exciting will happen?"

Kalec sighed and ran a hand through his hair. "There is so much left unknown. We will have to have an Aspect, Thrall, and if it is best done by counting votes and calling someone an Aspect, then that will have to do."

Thrall nodded. "It seems . . . like a quiet ending to a great piece of music," he said, groping for words. "An Aspect is such a powerful being . . . and you, the blues, are the keepers of magic, of so much that is dazzling and imaginative. And if it is up to the flight to simply vote . . ." He did not finish his thought. He did not have to.

Kalec said quietly, "I do not particularly have ambitions to leadership, Thrall, but I tell you this: I fear for my flight, and for this world, if Arygos becomes the blue Aspect."

Thrall smiled. "Not all who become leaders crave the power that goes with it," he said. "I did not. But I did burn to help my people. To free them. To find them a home where they could belong. To protect them so that our culture could flourish."

Kalec looked at him speculatively. "By all accounts, you have done so. Even some members of the Alliance speak well of you. It could be said that they need you now more than ever, with the world in such a state. And yet here you are, as a humble shaman."

"I had another calling," Thrall said. "As you say . . . the world was in need, even more than my people. I went to help my world. And by a very, very strange twist of fate and events, I am helping my world by being here. In the company of blue dragons about to determine which one of them becomes an Aspect. It is a vast responsibility, Kalec, but from the little I have seen, I at least believe you to be the best choice. I only hope the rest of your flight agrees."

"I would not do it if I did not have to," said Kalec. "In a way, I am not sure what to hope for: an Aspect in name only, or an Aspect with all the powers that one ought to have. For me, it would be hard to surrender to being something so different. It is something I never imagined having to consider. Something no one ever did. It . . . is a great burden."

Thrall watched Kalec carefully as he spoke, and he thought he understood.

Kalec was . . . afraid.

"You think it will change you, if it truly happens," Thrall said, and the words were not a question.

Silently, Kalec nodded. "I am already, by the reckoning of most of those in this old world, a very powerful being. It is all I have ever known, and so it is easy to bear that responsibility. But . . . an Aspect?"

He looked off to the side for a moment, his gaze unfocused.

"Thrall . . . an Aspect is not just a dragon with extra powers. It is something else again. Something . . ." He floundered for words. "It will change me. It has to. But . . . two of the five of them went mad. Alexstrasza may be walking that line herself, and Nozdormu nearly lost himself forever in his own realm of time. What will becoming an Aspect do to me?"

He was right to be afraid. Thrall had faced something similar the day that Orgrim Doomhammer had fallen and named Thrall his successor. He had not asked for the weight of the mantle, but he had taken it on. He had become something more than himself, more than simply Thrall, son of Durotan and Draka. He had become warchief. And for years he had borne the responsibility. He had, as Aggra had said in her annoying and beloved, honest fashion, become a "thrall" to the Horde.

Kalec would never be able to lay aside the title of Aspect. And he would live much, much longer than a mere orc.

It would change him, and he would never be able to change back. He might be Kalecgos, the blue Dragon Aspect, but he would never again be just Kalec. What *would* it do to him?

"That is a very important question, my friend," Thrall said quietly. "You *don't* know what it will do to you. But there will always be things that even a dragon cannot anticipate. You can only act on what you *do* know. What your heart and your head and your gut tell you is right. The question of what will it do to you is not the one you need to ask. You have already asked the right question."

"What will it do to my people if Arygos becomes Aspect?" Kalec said.

Thrall nodded. "See? You already know what to ask. And you do not know the answer to that question specifically, either. But you know enough so that you will choose to open yourself to the responsibility rather than subjecting them to Arygos's rule."

Kalec was silent. "Arygos makes much of his bloodline," he said at last. "But what he doesn't understand is our entire flight, our entire *race*, should be a family. Be united. Arygos's way of thinking will no longer help us—if it ever did. And if the flight follows him, yes, they will be independent blues, separate unto themselves. But they will also be dead, or worse." He smiled gently. "My head, heart, and gut tell me that."

"Then your choice is already made."

"I am still afraid. And I cannot shake the feeling that this makes me a coward."

"No," Thrall said. "It simply makes you wise."

It was time.

Thrall pulled the heavy furred cloak more tightly around him. He was at the very uppermost of the levitating platforms of the Nexus, where he had a perfect view of the open sky. Some dragons in humanoid forms stood beside him, while others simply hovered in the air to wait. The night was bitterer than usual because it was so clear, the stars glittering against their ebony background. Thrall was glad of the clarity, although it meant for a colder experience. He wanted to be able to witness this remarkable, rare occurrence, although the blues assured him that the power of the event would not be mitigated if there was cloud cover.

They were already very close, the White Lady and the Blue Child, and soon the Embrace would happen. The blues were silent and still, which Thrall did not ever recall seeing before. For all their affinity with the cold, they struck him as a very vibrant, alive flight. The bronzes were more thoughtful in speaking and action; doubtless, on some level, the import of every word or deed on the timeway weighed upon them. The greens, too, seemed calmer, after millennia spent dreaming. But the blues seemed as alive to him as the crackle and spark of the magic that was such an inherent part of them. Their wit was razor-sharp and swift; their moods mercurial; their movements quick and lively. To see them all either standing still or simply hovering, their eyes raptly fastened on the sky—it was unnerving.

Even Kalecgos was unusually somber. He, like all the others, was in his dragon form now. While Thrall had initially found him easier to approach and converse with when Kalec opted for his half-elven form, he had grown comfortable enough with the young blue so that Kalec was now simply Kalec to him, whatever form he chose to assume. Thrall stepped closer and put a reassuring hand on the mighty dragon's lower foreleg, which was as high as he could reach. It was the equivalent of a squeeze on the shoulder, and Kalec glanced down at him, his eyes crinkling in a smile of appreciation before he again lifted his mighty blue head to regard the celestial phenomenon.

Thrall thought about what he was seeing, and the metaphor of it all. The Embrace. A mother's love for her child. He thought about Malygos. From all he had observed and heard, before the madness had descended upon him, Malygos had been as cheerful and greathearted as Kalec. What Deathwing had done to him—to the blues, to all the dragonflights, to the very world . . . Thrall shook his head sadly at the grim fortune that made this event a dire necessity.

The Child was moving toward the Mother now. Thrall smiled a little, even as he shivered in the brutal yet clean cold. An embrace. A moment to pause and think about love, and magic, and how the two were not so very different.

It was too late to sway any individual's opinion, to come up with a reasoned argument regarding why Arygos was dangerous and

Kalec was the better choice. All that could be said had been said. Each dragon was an individual. Each would choose as he or she would. Thrall thought about Nozdormu, and the nature of time, and how this decision had already been made. There was no point in hoping or fearing any longer.

There was only this moment. Standing in the cold, in the company of dragons, watching something beautiful and rare transpiring before his eyes. The moment would turn, and become another moment, and this moment would be the past and forever gone save in memory. But, for now, it *was*.

Slowly the Blue Child moved—and then there it was: after so long waiting and watching what had seemed so slow, it was happening. The larger white moon "held" the smaller. And Thrall felt a swelling of quiet joy and utter peace, and simply watched.

The icy, cold tranquillity of the moment was suddenly shattered as Arygos leaped upward into the sky. His powerful wings beat hard, keeping him hovering in position. He lifted his head and cried, "Let me lead my people! Give to me the blessing of the Aspect! I am my father's son, and this should be mine!"

Beside Thrall, Kalec gasped. "No," he whispered. "He will destroy us all. . . ."

Arygos's bold move had certainly attracted attention. The dragons turned, almost startled by the outburst, to regard him instead of the event unfolding in the skies.

Heartened, Arygos continued to attempt to rally his flight. "Yes! I stand for what we truly are: the real masters of magic. The ones who should be directing the forces of the arcane! You know my skills: I am not an Aspect yet, but I am my father's true son. I believe in what he fought for; I believe in the control of our own destinies! Of using arcane magic as the tool that it is for *our* ends, *our* benefit! For the blues! That is what magic is made for!"

The moons, the Mother and Child, did not care what was transpiring at the Nexus. They continued to glow softly, their blue-white radiance reflected back to them by the gleam of snow, the smooth surface of blue scales. It was beautiful, and haunting, and Thrall found his eyes held not by the shouting dragon, wings beating in the wind, but by the still quietude of the moment.

And slowly other heads turned as well. Turned away from Arygos and his promise of magic as a tool. Turned toward the breathtaking sight of celestial bodies in perfect alignment, in the wonder of their breaths freezing on the cold air.

And Thrall realized that in the choice between two ways of being—between Arygos and his invocation of the glory of the past and promise of the future, and simply beholding the Embrace—the blue dragonflight had chosen the stillness . . . the *magic* . . . of the moment.

Arygos kept shouting, bragging, begging. And yet the blues did not seem to want to listen. Like statues, which they looked like under the blue and white light of the two moons, they continued to focus their attention on the Embrace. They seemed . . . surprised by how beautiful it was.

Thrall thought that the combined blue-white radiance seemed to cast a magical illusion of its own on the still leviathans themselves. They seemed to glow with an exquisite illumination, and so compelling was that illusion that Thrall turned from observing the two moons to watching the dragons.

And then the light shifted. It seemed to diminish, passing from Arygos to the entirety of the assembled dragonflight. Even Thrall knew he was included in the generous radiance. And then, slowly, it faded from them as well.

It did not fade from Kalecgos.

And then Thrall understood.

This ritual was not an intellectual exercise. Nor was it about a vote among the blues for who they thought would be the best candidate. It was not about the "title" of Aspect, given to one who would use it as a tool only for himself and his flight.

The celestial phenomenon was called the Embrace. This was about the heart of the blue dragonflight, not its brain. The new Aspect could never be granted powers by thought alone. The titans had done what they *felt* was right. And so now, in this moment, had the blue dragonflight.

They had listened not just with their minds but with their hearts, when Thrall and Kalec had spoken. They had watched Thrall watch them, and noticed his reactions. It would seem they had heard him, about living in the moment, about the wonder with which they should regard their own lives, their own abilities, their own selves. Even more, when something truly beautiful and magical—with a strength that came only from its grace and rarity, and that offered no dominance or power—had come their way, they had turned toward it as a flower turns its face to the sun. And their hearts had been moved from fear to hope, from shutting out to letting in.

The glow around Kalecgos increased, even as the glow faded from the other dragons and then from the sky as the Blue Child moved out of its mother's loving embrace.

Kalec's breath was coming quickly, his eyes wide with wonder. Suddenly he leaped into the sky. Thrall lifted a hand to shield himself from the brilliance emanating from the newly born Aspect. Kalecgos was almost unbearable to look upon now, so bright was he, like a star—no, a sun—radiant and beautiful and terrible. His was now the ultimate mastery of arcane magic, given willingly, with hope and love and trust, by his flight, by the Mother and Child, by the echo of what the titans had willed, long ago.

And then suddenly, as his wings seemed to almost tear the sky as they beat, something unexpected happened.

Kalecgos laughed.

The joyous sound tumbled from him, bright and crystalline as the snow, light as a feather, pure as a mother's love. It was not the sneering sound of a victor laughing in triumph. It was delight that could not be contained, something so strong and alive and truly *magical* that it must be shared.

Thrall realized that he, too, was laughing in delight. He could not tear his gaze from the figure of a blue-white dragon dancing in the night sky. Dragon laughter, bell-like and oddly sweet, rose around him. Thrall's heart was unspeakably full, and as he looked around, feeling a kinship with the great dragons in this enchanted moment, he saw tears of joy glistening in their eyes as well. His heart felt light and settled at the same time, and he thought if he jumped up, he, too, might be able to fly.

"You *fools!*"

The fury and affront and shock in Arygos's voice shattered the moment into a thousand pieces. "You stupid *fools!* You are the ones who have betrayed the flight, not I!"

Before Thrall had the wherewithal to even digest the words, Arygos threw back his head and let out a terrible cry. Thrall felt it buffet him almost physically. There was more than air and voice to the cry; there was magic to it as well, and it thrummed along Thrall's blood and bones and brought him to his knees.

You are the ones who have betrayed the flight, not I. . . .

He glanced upward to where Kalecgos, the new blue Dragon Aspect, still bright with arcane magic, hovered. Kalecgos was now visibly larger than his former rival, who looked less like a magnificent being and more like an ugly smudge against the night sky. Still radiant, still glorious, Kalecgos was no longer a joyful thing but an avenging god. He folded his wings and dove toward Arygos.

"No, Arygos! I will not let you destroy us!"

At that moment the air was full of a dreadful sound: the sound of dozens of powerfully beating wings. Thrall's eyes widened at the approach of the twilight dragons—for although Thrall had never seen one, he knew it must be they. They were like dark ghosts, living shadows in the shape of dragons, bearing down upon the blues' stronghold.

The blues exploded into action with startling speed for such gargantuan creatures. Before Thrall even realized it, they were leaping skyward and rushing to meet the enemy, and the night sky was brightening with white and pale blue tendrils and eruptions of arcane energy. Thrall glanced up to where Kalec and Arygos were engaged in combat.

"Kalec!" Thrall cried, thinking that it was impossible for the new Aspect to hear him over the sounds of battle but knowing he had to try anyway. "Look out!"

For a terrible moment, it did not appear as if Kalecgos had heard. Then, at the last minute, he released Arygos and hurled himself to the left. Three of the twilight dragons headed straight for Arygos. At the last instant, to Thrall's shock, all three turned incorporeal, passing harmlessly through their blue ally, then wheeled to join the fray.

Thrall felt rather than heard the dragon behind him. He whirled, pulling out the Doomhammer and gripping it with both hands, his teeth clenched. He would swing with his whole heart, protecting the dragonflight he had come to like and respect. Had come to help heal.

He would defend it with his life.

The twilight dragon was beautiful, and terrifying. She opened her mouth, revealing teeth almost as large as Thrall's entire body. Her forelegs were extended, claws open, to capture and rend and tear, if the gaping maw did not do the job first.

Thrall's battle cry of *For the Horde!* came to his lips, but he did not utter it. He did not fight only for the Horde, not anymore. He fought for so much more: for the Alliance, and the Earthen Ring, and the Cenarion Circle, and the broken and scattered dragonflights.

He fought for Azeroth.

He raised his hammer. The twilight dragon was almost upon him.

And then suddenly Thrall was fifty feet up in the air, something strong and implacable and secure folding around his torso. He glanced down to see talons encircling him. Kalec's voice came to him: "On my back, quickly! You will be safer there!"

And Thrall knew he would be. As Kalec moved the orc to his massive winged shoulders, he opened his claw. Thrall leaped, flying through the air for a few seconds before landing on Kalec's broad back.

Despite the blue dragons' affinity with cold magic, Kalecgos felt warm to Thrall. Warmer than either Desharin or Tick had felt when he had ridden atop them. If what Thrall had experienced flying atop the other two dragons had been a whisper, sitting on the back of the blue Aspect was a joyful shout. Energy, the crackle of magic, flowed through Thrall, and he held on as Kalecgos darted and dove. Kalec swooped down on a pair of twilight dragons, breathing a deadly, icy breath. They bellowed in pain and turned translucent—everywhere save where Kalec's breath had touched them, freezing the flesh solid. Kalec turned and struck one with his tail, shattering her frozen foreleg. The other's wing had been frozen, and now the twilight dragon fell frantically, her useless wing unable to bear her.

The orc and the Aspect were in beautiful synchronicity. Thrall stayed atop Kalec as if he were welded on, feeling no fear as the great being dove and banked and swerved. Kalec attacked with magic, illusions that lured one twilight dragon one way while Kalec dove toward another, moving almost close enough to touch a third so that Thrall could make his own attack.

"The back of the skull!" shouted Kalecgos.

Thrall sprang, in such perfect sync with Kalecgos that he did not give it a second thought. He landed on the neck of one of the twilight dragons and brought the Doomhammer crashing down where Kalec had told him to strike. So surprised was the beast that she didn't even have a chance to shift, instead dying instantly and plummeting toward the earth. And there was Kalec, swooping in smoothly, and again Thrall leaped from the back of one dragon to another. The Aspect's wings beat, and up they climbed, ready to continue the battle. The orc glanced about, barely winded, senses at peak alert, and permitted himself a small smile.

The blues were winning.

FIFTEEN

*T*he blues were winning!

They were outnumbered, but they were unquestionably winning this battle. They had been heartened with the appearance of a new Aspect. The ritual had worked; the blessing of the titans had been humbly requested and granted; and the upwelling of joy and relief had given the dragons new energy and strength of will to fight to protect themselves.

This was not how it was supposed to happen!

Bleeding, part of him frozen, one wing damaged from the targeted attack by Kalecgos, Arygos maintained himself in flight with an effort. He felt weak, and frightened, and was accustomed to neither sensation.

How had things gone so terribly wrong?

All Arygos could think about—like any trapped animal, he thought with a mixture of panic and disgust—was safety. A den. A place to recover and rest and think. There was one such place, where he could be calm and shake this terror that seemed to clamp down on his brain like a dark fog.

He glanced about wildly for Kalecgos. There he was, huge and luminous and proud, radiant with all the power that he, Arygos, should have been chosen to embody. And atop his back, adding insult to injury, was Kalec's beloved orc clinging like a burr, swinging his hammer and smashing the skulls of Arygos's twilight dragons.

The Eye. He had to go to the Eye of Eternity, to think, to rally, to come up with some plan. It was the heart of the Nexus, his father's place of refuge and retreat, and it called to him now in his moment of panic. Just the thought sent at least some manner of steadiness through him. Whimpering, as ill befit a dragon, he spread his wings and flew. He dove from the pinnacle of the Nexus, where the aerial battle was going so impossibly poorly, like a stone. He fell more than flew, at the last moment opening his wings and gliding into the entrance of the Nexus. Through its labyrinthine passages he bolted, his heart racing as panic dug its icy claws into his heart.

And there it was: a swirling, misty portal. On the other side was the Eye of Eternity. Arygos flew swiftly through it, emerging into the night sky of this small dimension complete unto itself. Once, there had been a blue and gray magical platform on which one could perch and rest while contemplating the mysteries that swirled past. Magic runes had danced, appearing and disappearing like softly flowing snowflakes. The black night sky, dotted with cold stars, had turned and twisted, and in one part a blue-white nebula had whirled.

Now there was no platform. It had been shattered into drifting pieces in the battle that had claimed his father's life; one such still held the closed magical orb known as the Focusing Iris. Malygos had used his own blood to activate and control this orb, which had lain dormant for millennia. With the open Focusing Iris, Malygos had been able to direct powerful surge needles, using them to pull arcane magic from Azeroth's ley lines and channeling that magic into the Nexus. And it had been the opening of the Focusing Iris a slender crack with a long-forgotten key that had lured Malygos to what had been his final battle.

Even though it reminded him of a grim moment in his life, this place was comforting and familiar, and Arygos felt himself relax. He perched atop one of the slowly moving pieces, folded his wings against his great body, and opened his jaw to take great, gulping breaths.

"Arygos?"

The dragon opened his eyes and unfurled his wings, instantly on the alert. Who had dared—?

"Blackmoore!" He breathed a sigh of relief. "I am glad to see you."

"I wish I could say the same," the human said, striding forward. He stood on another one of the platform pieces and peered up boldly at the hovering dragon. He lifted off his helm, and his long black hair spilled out. His blue eyes flickered over Arygos. "What has happened? I don't know much about all this Aspect business, but . . . I'm guessing that it's not you."

Arygos winced. "No. They chose . . . *Kalecgossss.*" He hissed the name, deeply angry, deeply wronged. "That stupid orc—he turned the heart of the dragonflight away from me. From what was right-fully mine!"

Blackmoore frowned. "This is not good," he muttered.

"Don't you think I know that?" Angrily, Arygos slammed his tail on the piece of the platform, tilting it precariously. "It is all Thrall's fault. If you had just killed him as you were supposed to—"

The human's eyes narrowed. "Yes, and if you had become As-pect as *you* were supposed to, we would not be having this pleasant conversation." His voice cracked like a whip. "But neither of us has what we want right now, so we had best put aside our anger and figure out how to get it."

The human was correct. Arygos calmed himself. He needed to focus; it was why he had come here.

"Perhaps together we can accomplish both our goals," Arygos said. "And please our Twilight Father and Deathwing at the same time."

Blackmoore eyed him. "Go on."

"We both want Thrall dead. And we both want me to become Aspect. Come with me back to the battle, King Blackmoore. Take your revenge. If you kill the orc, Kalec will see that not all works out as he wishes. And if Kalec falters, the faith of the rest of the flight will be shaken, the miserable wyrms. Then Kalecgos will be vulnerable, and I can destroy him."

He grew more excited as he spoke, working it out, visualizing each step. "Once Kalecgos is slain, the blues, desperate for someone to guide them, will turn to me—and so I will gain the powers of the Aspect as I should have done in the first place! All will be as it should have been."

"You know this for a fact?" challenged Blackmoore.

"No . . . not exactly. But whom else could the power possibly pass to? I was the only one who challenged Kalec. Surely they will turn to me when I reveal him for the weakling he is."

Blackmoore stroked his goatee with a mailed hand, considering. "I don't like the odds. I am but a human. Against one or even a few dragons, maybe—but an entire flight?"

"Trust me. Thrall will be completely undone when he sees you again," urged Arygos. He did not like to beg, but he needed this human. "And when Thrall is dead, the blues will be stricken. There are still many twilight dragons in the air. We can do this if we are together on it!"

The human nodded. "Very well," he said. "A risky plan, but what is life without risk, eh?" He grinned suddenly, white teeth flashing, the smile of a predator.

"Only a little risk," said Arygos, "for such a great reward." He was more relieved than he had anticipated. He knew the history of this human, knew his hatred for Thrall. Blackmoore wanted the orc dead. Just as Arygos wanted Kalec dead. Arygos flew toward the platform bearing the human, positioning himself next to and slightly below it so that Blackmoore could easily climb atop him.

They could do this. He knew they could. Then the obstacles would finally be cut down. He would be Aspect, as he had always yearned to be.

His heart lifted with each wing beat as he rounded toward the whirling portal. Below him, the pieces of the platform turned almost lazily. Arygos looked down in time to see one of them roll over, revealing the Focusing Iris directly below him.

The pain was sudden, shocking, and brutal: a white-hot needle piercing the base of his skull. As Blackmoore's sword thrust down, down, Arygos clung to life long enough to see a drop of his red blood splash on the Focusing Iris, to watch it snap wide open. And as he hurtled downward, watching Blackmoore make a daring leap from his back to land on a slowly turning piece of platform, Arygos, son of Malygos, understood that he would die betrayed.

Holding the Doomhammer in one hand, Thrall lifted the other. Lightning crackled, zagging in a chain of scorching death between no fewer than four twilight dragons. The strike stunned them momentarily, blackening their sides and searing their leathery wings. They shrieked in pain, staying in their corporeal forms long enough for Thrall to again leap from Kalec's back onto a twilight drake, lift the Doomhammer, and bring it smashing down on the drake's skull. It was a glancing blow, though, and the drake had the wherewithal to turn incorporeal. Thrall abruptly started to fall. He glanced downward at the snow rushing up to meet him, but then suddenly he saw the broad, shining blue back of Kalecgos. Thrall landed hard, but safely.

Thrall was just about to lift his gaze to meet the next foe when the Nexus was suddenly rocked. Light seemed to explode from everywhere, and even the mighty Aspect wheeled and dove away from it, with Thrall clinging tightly to Kalec's back.

"What happened?" Thrall shouted.

"An explosion of arcane magic!" Kalec shouted back. His long, sinuous neck was lowered as he stared down below at the Nexus, which was still spurting magical energies like dying fireworks. "I am not sure what—"

"The twilight dragons!" Thrall was looking around as Kalec was looking down. "They're fleeing back to the temple!"

"Blues! To me!" Kalec cried, his voice sounding amplified and deeper and trembling through Thrall's very sinews. "Our enemy is escaping—we have the advantage! Destroy them before they can reach their lord!"

If Thrall had thought Kalec was swift before, now he found himself barely able to breathe, so fast did the Dragon Aspect fly. The twilight dragons were giving their best to their frantic, abrupt escape. They were too busy fleeing to fight, all of them in their incorporeal forms. The blues responded with solely magical attacks. The air crackled and sparked with white arcane energy, shimmered with icy frost and the sudden squalls of an isolated blizzard. Several fell, but more escaped.

The blues followed, grimly determined.

Kirygosa stared, horrified, willing with all her heart that what she was watching would not succeed.

She'd felt her brother die, felt his life energy, the blood of a scion of Malygos, being harnessed and channeled in a way that was disturbingly familiar to her. The Twilight Father, no doubt thanks to information supplied to him by Deathwing, seemed to know exactly what he was doing.

Seconds after her brother's death, a storm appeared in the skies above Wyrmrest Temple. Purple-black clouds swirled angrily, like a whirlpool, and then with a mighty crack that made Kirygosa cry out and clap her hands over her poor human ears, the skies opened.

Blinding white light shot both upward and downward, a lance that pierced the heavens beyond where the eye could follow and also struck deep into the earth. She recognized it as a surge needle, a tool composed of arcane energy, a tool of rich, flooding power. Once, Malygos had used such needles to draw arcane magic from the ley lines of Azeroth and transfer it to the Nexus.

Now that process was being reversed. This surge needle was drawing power *from* the Nexus.

And caught by that needle between heavens and earth was Chromatus.

The spike of almost inconceivable magical energy was now boring into the enormous, mottled, lifeless body of the monstrosity. Kirygosa shivered as she watched, wrapping her arms around herself, dimly aware of the needle marks and scars on her pale flesh. She knew sickly that she was part of the reason the ghastly display before her was occurring. They had used her for their experiments. But they had kept her alive for two reasons: her bloodline and her gender.

"You are lucky, my dear," said the Twilight Father beside her. "Fortunate among dragons are you to witness this . . . and to have helped contribute."

"It looks as if my brother contributed more," Kiry said, angry that her voice sounded raw and broken. "So this is how the Twilight's Hammer rewards service and fidelity. Arygos betrayed his whole flight—indeed, an entire race—to your cause, and you killed him!"

"I killed him because he failed, not because he served," the Twilight Father said mildly. "And yes, this is how the Twilight's Hammer rewards failure."

"Deathwing did not seem altogether pleased with the sort of progress *you* were making," Kirygosa snapped recklessly. "You might be next after my poor deluded broth—"

He jerked on the chain. Her words turned into an agonized whimper as the chain burned her throat. "I would choose my words with more care, little one."

She had her breath back now, and for a despairing moment the death he threatened her with seemed sweeter than continuing to exist solely to be used as a tool to harm her own flight. She opened her mouth for a scathing retort when a wild, giddy roar from an excited crowd of cultists below made the words die in her throat.

Chromatus was *moving*.

It was subtle, hard to see, but one claw was opening and closing. The rest of him lay still as death. And then the mighty tail twitched, ever so slightly. A head—the black one—jerked.

The Twilight Father rushed to the side of the circular floor. "He lives! *He lives!*"

He made fists of his gloved hands and raised them in the air. The crowds below increased their cheering.

The surge needle pulsed, its energy drilling into the now-animated corpse. With each moment that passed, it seemed to Kirygosa that the monster grew stronger. His other limbs began to twitch. One by one, each hideous head lifted. Like the tentacles of a great sea creature, they dipped and moved, gazed about, opened their jaws. Ten eyes were opened now, and their color displayed a uniformity the rest of him lacked. Every pair of eyes gleamed a brilliant, glowing purple. Alive, moving, speaking he might be, but Chromatus was hideously not whole. In some places, bones were visible. Scales had fallen off, showing skin that was healthy and skin that was decayed. Each of the heads seemed to have *something* amiss with it: a missing ear, an oozing eye . . .

"Chromatus!" cried the Twilight Father. "To me, my son whom I have birthed. Look to me!"

A red ear twitched. Green nostrils flared. The bronze head moved slowly on its neck. One by one, awkward, unused, each head followed, until all five of them regarded the Twilight Father.

"Our . . . father," the bronze head said in a stately voice, though the words seemed to come awkwardly at first. The purple eyes of the blue head narrowed, then that gaze fell upon Kirygosa. Dark laughter rumbled through the blue head. When it spoke, its voice was oddly mellifluous, though the words came hesitantly.

"Fear not, little blue. Your brother lives—within me. We feel our kinship." The other heads turned, mildly interested in what the blue head was saying. "You will serve too."

"Never!" screamed Kirygosa, her mind almost unraveling at the horrors she had been forced to behold. "The blues will never serve you! Not with Kalecgos leading them!"

She expected a hard jerk on the chain and steeled herself for the sharp, bright pain. Instead, the Twilight Father laughed. "Do you not yet understand? And I thought the blues were intelligent!"

She didn't want to hear. She didn't want to understand. But she found her lips moving in the question: "Understand what?"

"What he was made for!"

Kirygosa forced herself to behold Chromatus. She saw a hideous chromatic dragon, more horrible than others because of his five heads, which—

"No," she whispered, as comprehension struck her like a physical blow. "No. . . ."

"Now . . . now you see," purred the Twilight Father, his voice gleeful. "Glorious, isn't it, this coming doom in all its inevitability? It doesn't matter if the blues now have an Aspect. It doesn't matter if Ysera is awakened, or if Nozdormu is found, or even if the Life-Binder herself returns." He pressed his lips to her ear and whispered, as if sharing the most intimate of secrets, "Chromatus lives . . . so that the Aspects will die."

Kirygosa lost whatever grip she might have had on control. She launched herself at the Twilight Father, screaming and clawing and biting, her simple, human attack no match for his magic—or the power of the chain. She kept screaming a single, futile word, as if that could avert the coming catastrophe.

"No! . . . No! . . . No. . . !"

"Silence!" cried the Twilight Father, violently jerking on the silver chain. Kiry fell hard, convulsing in agony.

"Nay, nay," continued the black head of Chromatus. This one's voice was silky, sibilant, cold. Chromatus rose slowly, but his movements were starting to become more and more graceful as he discovered how to control his body. "Let the little blue prattle. It will be all the sweeter later. She will—"

The red head interrupted the black, turning toward the west. He shifted, still slightly uncomfortable with his body. "They come," the head cried in a clear, strong voice. "I am not fully recovered! What have you done, Father?"

And Kirygosa started laughing. She heard it in her own ears, knew it to be hysterical, but it kept coming, bubbling out of her like a suddenly uncapped spring. She lifted a shaking finger, pointing at the twilight dragons flying full tilt toward the temple, with her own brave blue flight not far behind them.

"You miscalculated!" she cried. "The great Twilight Father, with all his wonderful plans! But your dragons turned tail too soon, and my flight comes to destroy them, your abomination, and you! What plan do you have now, O wise man?" The Twilight Father was so enraged he didn't even bother using the chain. One gloved hand cracked her cheek hard, jerking her head to one side. Still, Kirygosa laughed, waving her arms.

"Kalecgos! Kalec!"

And there he was!

Her heart soared. His wisdom and compassion had prevailed. He flew, the Aspect of Magic, larger than any of the others, limned in a shining light with a small figure atop his back. All that power, after far, far too long, was being wielded not by a mad mind, nor by one bent on revenge or betrayal. Tears filled her eyes, and she sobbed with joy.

He would not fall, nor would any of the other Aspects. They were striking now, before Chromatus had reached his full devastating potential.

Below her, Chromatus threw back his heads and bellowed, all the voices—hissing, strong, melodic—blended into a terrifying symphony. Then the monster leaped into the sky. He faltered, but just for a moment; then his wing beats grew stronger, and he began his attack.

Kirygosa had had nightmares, particularly in the last several months when she had been held prisoner, tormented daily, locked into a human form and thinking that the only respite would come with death. Yes, she had had nightmares aplenty.

But nothing like the dreadful reality she beheld now.

He moved jerkily, like a puppet, a thing that ought never to have existed. Bigger than any of them, even the Aspect Kalecgos, Chromatus's awkward movements somehow were faster, and his blunt strikes more deadly, than those of the living dragons who fought with and against him.

He brought to bear more than physical strength and agility. The white hue of arcane magic and the sickly purple of the twilights' attacks were augmented by other colors—the scarlet of the red's fire, the emerald poison cloud of the green—as Chromatus fought with the skills of all of the ancient dragonflights.

She could hear the bellows of triumph from the twilight dragons as they fought with renewed enthusiasm. They might have been turning tail a few moments ago, but now they were all deadly purpose and implacable intent.

Too, the simple sight of the obscenity was unsettling. It ought not to *be,* and yet here it was, breathing fire, using illusions, dealing death in an awkward manner that somehow was brutally and lethally efficient.

Several of Kirygosa's flight were killed by Chromatus alone. Others, horrified by and fixated on the sight of the chromatic dragon, were careless of the twilight dragons still filling the air. Even as she watched, a blue tried to approach Chromatus from behind, only to have his neck broken with a single, almost careless strike of the monster's powerful tail. The blue, dead instantly, fell to join his brethren. Anguished, Kirygosa turned away, hiding her face. A hard hand grasped her hands and jerked them away. She turned her tear-filled eyes up toward the Twilight Father, almost but not quite able to make out features beneath the dark cowl.

"Who is laughing now, little blue girl?" he cackled. "Your precious flight—he is barely animated, and look what he is doing! Look!"

He hauled her to the edge of the platform, one hand gripping her chin and the other like iron, binding her arms to her side. *"Look!"*

At least, Kirygosa thought, her heart breaking, *he cannot force me to keep my eyes open.*

Thrall could feel the sense of defeat ripple through the blue dragonflight. And he felt it along with them.

It was a dragon, but such a dragon as might have been conjured by a Forsaken's worst nightmare. No fewer than five heads, each one seeming to be a different color, sprouted from massive shoulders. It seemed jerky, rotten, like Scourge stumbling to the attack. Yet it was alive, not undead. Alive, each of the monstrous heads attacking with such furor that an entire flight, with victory clenched in its claws, had become rattled and panicky.

"What is it?" he shouted to Kalec.

The Aspect did not reply at once; he was too busy fending off a pair of attacks. Then Kalec cried, "A chromatic dragon!"

Thrall recalled what Desharin had told him of such creatures— patchwork monstrosities, bits and pieces of the other five flights. Desharin had said they were all dead.

But this one certainly was alive enough.

Thrall stared for a second at the beast, trying to wrap his mind around what it was and what it was doing to the blue dragonflight— even to Kalecgos, the flight's new Aspect. It was only an instant of inattention, of shock—but it was an instant too long.

The thing charged at them, five heads gaping. The stench of rotting flesh that emanated from him was almost overwhelming. Kalec dove out of his way. Thrall held on with all his strength. He thought he had made it safely until something slammed into his midsection, swatting at him as if he were no more than a flea riding on a wolf's back, and he realized that although Kalec's skill-ful flying had saved him from a direct attack from the many-headed chromatic dragon, it had not saved Thrall from the power of even this casual brush of the monster's tail as he dove past.

So this is death at last, he thought, *falling from the back of an Aspect to be crushed on jagged rocks.*

He closed his eyes, clutching the Doomhammer to his heart, glad that he would die with a weapon in his hand. He wondered if he would even feel the impact that would shatter his spine or smash his skull.

He had not seen, not then. He had been filled with hope after freeing Nozdormu. Kalec, too, with his cheerful optimism and great heart, had encouraged Thrall to keep fighting, to keep struggling, to stand against the encroaching twilight.

But Alexstrasza was right. None of it mattered.

Kalecgos had likely been defeated by the appalling creature, which had managed to repel the blues' attack as if it were the sting of so many angry insects. The Twilight's Hammer cultists would prevail. They would first enslave and then destroy.

What did it matter, if he continued to draw breath? What did it matter, all the hard work and concern and study that the Earthen Ring was putting into its understanding of how to heal the world? It was for nothing.

Except . . .

The delicate face of the shattered Life-Binder gave way in his mind's eye to that of another. It was a harsher, more angular face, with tusks and dark skin. But his heart suddenly began to beat in a painful fashion, as if it were waking up.

Maybe the world would be destroyed by the cult. Maybe the shaman of the Earthen Ring were indeed fooling themselves, trying to heal a land, only to witness its doom.

But in the desolation, in the despair and darkness, Thrall knew one thing.

Korialstrasz is dead, Alexstrasza had said. She would never again behold her mate, her companion and friend and champion, never touch his face in love, never see his smile.

But Aggra was not dead. Nor, surprisingly, after his fall, was Thrall.

He gasped with the pain of returning feelings. His chilled lips moved to whisper her name. *"Aggra . . ."*

She had encouraged him to go—the blunt encouragement of

Sixteen

Thrall did not feel either. What he did feel was an impa
softer than stone that slowed but did not stop his fa
instant later, when he finally did come to a stop, he
ized that a cold wetness enveloped him. He could not see,
barely breathe. And then he understood: he had fallen not or
but on snow, which had broken his fall. He was alive. His
was shaken, rattled, and his lungs were laboring . . . but h
alive.

He closed his eyes against the reality.

The image that filled his mind was that of him sitting a
stone peak next to a beautiful, broken form. Alexstrasza lool
him, her body radiating a violent grief and dull despair.

You do not see, she had told him.

What don't I see, Alexstrasza?

It doesn't matter. None of it. It doesn't matter if everything is int
nected. It doesn't matter how long this has been going on. It doesn'
matter if we can stop it.

The children are dead. *Korialstrasz is* dead. *I am dead in all*
but one, and that will soon happen. There is no hope. There is no
Nothing matters.

practically ordering him, admittedly, but with a depth of love behind that "order" that he only now could fully appreciate. It had not been for her own sake that she had wanted Thrall to leave. She had wanted him to go for himself, and for his world, not merely for her. He recalled how irritated she had made him, with her quick wit and sharp tongue. She spoke what she thought and felt, when she thought and felt it. He remembered the unlooked-for tenderness of her protection and guidance on his vision quest, and the sweet combination of gentleness and wildness in their joinings.

He wanted to see her again. Before the end of all things.

And unlike Alexstrasza, broken and alone in Desolace, surrounding herself with an ashy emptiness reflective of her own devastated heart . . . he *could* see his beloved again.

He was cold, his body rapidly growing numb, but the thought of being with Aggra—so vibrant and alive and warm and real—began to push that lethargy aside. Thrall forced his lungs to work, to breathe the frigid air as deeply as he could, and tried to tap into the Spirit of Life that he felt was now dormant inside him.

This was what gave the shaman his connection to the elements, to others, and to himself. All beings had this; shaman, though, understood it and could work with it. For a moment Thrall was terrified of failure. This was the part he could not work with before, back at the Maelstrom. This was where he had failed the other members of the Earthen Ring: he had been too distracted to focus, to drop deeply into himself and bring forth that deep, rich knowing.

But this time he was not scattered or unfocused. He held Aggra's face before him, like a torch in the darkness of the unknown future. With his eyes closed, he saw her, smiling with a hint of playfulness in her gold eyes, holding out her hand.

This strong hand in yours—

Oh, how he wanted that. How right that seemed to him now. A

little thing, yet greater in his heart now than any fear of death or destruction could be.

And even as he opened his heart to both her and the Spirit of Life within him, another vision came to him.

This vision was not of Aggra, nor of his own life. Like a scene in a stage play, it unfolded in his mind: hero, villain, a shocking twist, tragedy, and misunderstanding. His heart, full with wanting and missing Aggra, now ached not with sympathy but with the empathy of sharing an experience.

This knowledge . . . Alexstrasza . . .

"She must know," he whispered. "I must find her and tell her."

In the end, these connections were what mattered most. In the end, they were truly all that mattered. They were what inspired songs and art, what drove those in battle to fight: love of country, or culture, an ideal, or an individual. It was this feeling that kept hearts beating, that moved mountains, that shaped the world. And Thrall knew, through both visions, that he and another who also grieved were loved truly and deeply—loved for who they *were*, not what they could do. Not what title or power they wielded.

Aggra loved Thrall for who he was at his core, and he loved her the same way.

Alexstrasza was loved so, and she needed to be reminded of it. Thrall knew, knew deep in his bones and blood, that he was the only one who could let her know that.

The Spirit of Life opened to him. It flowed through him, warming and soothing and strong. Energy surged through nearly frozen limbs, and he began to claw his way upward through the snow that had caved in upon him. He worked with the rhythm of his own breath, resting upon inhaling, moving snow with his exhalation. He was calm, clear, focused as he had never been, his heart full with the new revelations that needed to be shared.

It was not easy, but the Spirit of Life buoyed him. Its energy was strong but gentle, and at last he pulled himself out of the hole and sat, catching his breath. Slowly he got to his feet and began to think about his next move.

His robes were soaked. He needed warmth, a fire, and to remove his saturated clothing before it killed him—and in this weather, it would, and quickly. He looked about for any dragons who might be searching for him, but saw nothing in the skies save clouds and the occasional bird. He did not know how long he had been unconscious; the battle was clearly over—one way or another.

Shelter first, then fire. He looked about for any likely spot. Over there—there seemed to be a cave or at least a hollow in the stone, a darker smudge against the gray.

And it was his focus, his clarity, not his senses, that a heartbeat later saved his life.

He whirled, the Doomhammer at the ready, and was barely in time to block the blow from the shadow that had been haunting him for so long.

Blackmoore!

Wearing pieces of plate that Thrall now completely recognized, swinging the massive, glowing broadsword that was almost bigger than the one who wielded it, Blackmoore pushed the attack with what seemed like more than human strength.

But it wasn't.

The first time the dark assassin had sprung out of the shadows, to attack so completely unexpectedly and slice Desharin's head from his body, Thrall had been taken by surprise. When Blackmoore had followed him through the timeway, manifesting with his brutal solution of slaying the infant Thrall, the orc had been unsettled. And when he had discovered the mysterious assassin's true identity, he had been dismayed.

The fact that Blackmoore had not only lived but grown to such power had shaken Thrall's faith in everything he had done. It had cast shadows on the inevitability of who Thrall was, all he had achieved, become.

But now Thrall set his jaw, refusing to let fear weaken him. His body was healed but still deeply chilled, and he knew his movements would be too slow to defend himself without aid.

Spirit of Life, help me, that I may defeat this foe who should not live and that I may carry your visions to those who must know of them!

Warmth flooded through him, gentle yet powerful, granting vigor and suppleness to his limbs. Dimly, Thrall was aware that even his clothing had somehow dried. Energy, sharp and soothing both, strengthened him. He did not question, merely accepted gratefully. Thrall attacked without even needing to think about it, letting years of battle guide his hand and landing blow after blow on the purloined armor Blackmoore dared wear. The human was startled and sprang back, crouching into a defensive stance, mammoth sword at the ready.

"I see why I wanted to train you," Blackmoore sneered, and now Thrall recognized the voice even though Blackmoore wore his helm. "You're very good . . . for a greenskin."

"Your decision to train me was your death once before, Aedelas Blackmoore, and will be again. You cannot outwit destiny."

Blackmoore laughed, a loud boom of genuine mirth. "You fell from a nearly impossible height, orc. You're wounded and barely alive. I think it's your destiny to die here in the frozen north, not mine to be slain by you. Though your spirit is admirable. I'd have enjoyed crushing it, but I fear I have other business to attend to. Fleshrender hasn't claimed a life for a while. I'll make it quick."

He emphasized the name, as if to strike fear into Thrall's heart.

Instead, the orc laughed. Blackmoore frowned. "What amuses you at the moment of your death?"

"*You* do," Thrall said. "The name you have chosen for your sword makes me laugh."

"Makes you laugh? You should not. It has indeed rent the flesh of the corpses I make!"

"Oh, of course," Thrall said. "But it's so blunt—so brutal and unsophisticated. Just like you are, at your core. Just like you tried so hard not to be."

Blackmoore's frown deepened as he growled, "I am a king, orc. Remember that."

"Only of a stolen kingdom. And you will make no corpse of me!"

Furious, Blackmoore again charged, and again Thrall, despite his injuries and near-death fall, parried and went on the offensive.

Blackmoore had said, at the moment of his death, that Thrall was what he, Blackmoore, had made him. It was a statement that had sickened the orc—to think that anything of this man was a part of him was appalling. Drek'Thar had helped put some of it into perspective, but now, as weapons clanged together and struck sparks, Thrall realized that he had never truly shaken Blackmoore's vile grip on his spirit.

The man before him, swinging the broadsword with powerful arms and a deadly determination, was his shadow side. Under him, at one point, Thrall had tasted utter powerlessness, and he had spent most of his life determined to never again feel so helpless. Too, Thrall realized, with the clarity and insight that still lingered from the twin visions, that Blackmoore represented everything Thrall was fighting against—in himself.

"I feared you once," Thrall grunted. He held the Doomhammer in one strong green hand, lifted the other, and spread his fingers.

He opened his mouth, and a cry of righteous anger ripped through the frigid air. A whirlwind came to his call, swirling and picking up frozen snow like a cyclone made of ice. With a swift, precise motion, it descended upon Blackmoore. It lifted him up, higher and higher, then with another hand motion Thrall hurled the human down. He lay where he had fallen, one arm curled up to his chest, and swiftly Thrall closed the distance between them.

He stared at the limp form, his eyes narrowing. As he spoke, he slowly lifted the Doomhammer over his head in preparation for the killing blow.

"You were everything I hate . . . weakness lucky enough to be in a position of power. You made me see myself in a way I loathed, in a way—"

Blackmoore surged upward onto his knees, thrusting Fleshrender toward Thrall's exposed torso. Thrall threw himself backward, but the very tip struck home. Thrall hissed as two inches of steel pierced his belly and he fell into the snow.

"Say whatever makes you feel better, orc," said Blackmoore, "but you are still about to join your ancestors."

The voice was slightly fainter, and the blow was weaker than earlier ones had been. Thrall must have wounded Blackmoore more than he had initially thought.

Thrall snarled and swung the Doomhammer, targeting his adversary's legs. Blackmoore had been expecting him to struggle to rise, not attack from a fallen position, and cried out as the Doomhammer slammed into him. The armor took much of the impact, but the blow was powerful enough to knock Blackmoore completely off his feet.

This was no giant among men. Just as Taretha had still been her true self even in the corrupted timeway, so was Blackmoore. He might not have succumbed to drinking, or misspent his energy leaning on another's strengths. But he was still Aedelas Blackmoore—a small-spirited man, a bully who thrived on treachery and manipulation.

And Thrall was still who *he* was.

Blackmoore might have intimidated Thrall as a youth, might have unnerved him when he reappeared as a seemingly stronger individual. But although Thrall wore only robes, he had new armor; though he wielded the familiar Doomhammer, he had new weapons. He felt his love for Aggra burning within his soul. It was not a distraction but a steady, calming ember, constant and true—truer than the hatred offered by the man who thrashed frantically in the snow, trying to rise on two wounded legs, wielding a sword with an arm that was weakened and rapidly becoming useless. Aggra's love was like armor and weapon both, protecting him, shielding him, enabling him to bring the very best of who he was to this battle, which was as much about spirit as it was about the body.

Thrall understood, in a way he had never known before, that those moments when Blackmoore had won, when he had intimidated Thrall and undercut his resolve and made him feel less than who he was—those moments were in the past.

And that made them powerless over him. Thrall was in *this moment,* and in *this moment* he was unafraid.

In this moment Blackmoore would not win.

It was time to end this. To send Blackmoore to his destined fate: death at Thrall's hands. To send all those doubts and insecurities and fears where they belonged: truly, forever, in the past.

His wound was bleeding freely, the warmth of his own red-black blood saturating his robes. The pain helped him to focus. Thrall began to swing the Doomhammer like the master of weapons he truly was as Blackmoore somehow managed to get unsteadily to his feet. The hammer knocked Fleshrender aside, Blackmoore's weakened arm unable to effectively wield a two-handed sword. In the same movement, following through on the swing of the great weapon, Thrall lifted one hand from the shaft and up to the skies. There was a sudden cracking sound.

A huge icicle had broken free from its place beneath a rock overhang. It flew, like a dagger hurled by a skilled hand, toward Blackmoore. It was only frozen water; it could not pierce armor.

But it could—and did—knock the human down like a giant fist. A cry of pain and alarm escaped Blackmoore as he fell to his knees in the snow. Weaponless, nearly knocked unconscious, Blackmoore raised his hands imploringly to Thrall.

"Please . . ." The voice was rasping and faint, but on the clear air Thrall could hear him. "Please, spare me. . . ."

Thrall was not without compassion. But greater than compassion in his heart was the need for balance and justice—both in the twisted timeway that had birthed this Aedelas Blackmoore, and in Thrall's own timeway, where the human did not belong.

Thrall raised the weapon, lifting it high above his head. His gaze was caught and held not by the begging gesture but by the gleam of plate armor that Orgrim Doomhammer had once worn. That he, Thrall, had once worn and since had reverently discarded.

The snake shedding its skin. The spirit growing ever purer and stronger. It would seem that such a discarding of one's old self was a lifelong process. Now Thrall was prepared to discard any lingering remnants of power this human held over him.

He shook his head. His heart felt calm. It was not joy or vengeance that filled it, for there was no delight in the act. But there was a sense of freedom, of release.

"No," Thrall said. "You should not be here, Blackmoore. You should not be anywhere. With this blow, I make things right."

He brought the Doomhammer crashing down. It crushed the metal helm and the head inside it. Blackmoore fell beneath it, dead from the first instant.

Thrall had slain his shadow.

SEVENTEEN

Blackmoore was silent as he died. The snow beneath his corpse turned slushy and red. Thrall took a deep breath, exhaled, and then stumbled to the side before sitting down heavily. The pain of the battle and the fall surged forward, and Thrall felt a small smile creep across his face as he realized, in this moment, that he hurt very badly indeed. He closed his eyes, asked for healing, and felt an answering warmth seep through his body. He was exhausted and still hurting, but he had tended to the worst, and he would survive.

Still, there was no question in his mind about giving up. After a moment to steel himself for the pain, he rose. He still needed to find shelter. He still needed to start a fire and find sustenance. He was not going to die here, not when he had to return to Aggra—and to another being who needed Thrall's help.

He had been trudging slowly for some time before the shadow fell on the snow. Thrall looked up, eyelashes crusted with ice, to see a huge reptilian shape hovering above him. It was between him and the sun, and he could not see its color. His body almost numb, barely able to move, he nonetheless lifted the Doomhammer. He was not about to let something as trivial as a twilight dragon stand between him and Aggra.

"Hold, friend orc," came a slightly amused voice. "I've come to bear you back to warmth and food. I confess, I thought I would bear you back for a hero's funeral, but instead I will gain the gratitude of my Aspect."

It was a blue! The relief that swept through Thrall was so profound, he felt his legs give way. The last thing he felt before unconsciousness claimed him was powerful talons closing gently around him.

An hour later, Thrall found himself back in the now-familiar conjured space in the Nexus. He sat in the chair, wrapped in a warm blanket, holding a steaming cup of some beverage that was both sweet and spicy and seemed to restore his strength with each sip.

The brazier burned brightly, and Thrall extended his hands to it. He had come close to death today more than once—the death of more than the body. But he had refused to die and now was here, alive and glad of it, grateful for the warmth of the fire and the friendship of the blues, who had continued to look for him long past the time when they should have abandoned hope.

"Thrall."

The orc rose to greet his friend Kalecgos. A relieved smile was on the dragon's half-elven face, and both hands clasped Thrall's upper arms.

"You are a sight for sore eyes," said Kalecgos. "Discovering you was a blessing on an otherwise dark day. Tell me how it is we came across you. My heart was wounded when you fell: I could not find you."

Thrall smiled a little, though his eyes were somber. "The snow broke my fall, but also hid me from your sight. It would seem the ancestors are not ready for me to join their numbers yet."

"Narygos, the one who found you, told me there was a body not far away," Kalec said.

"Blackmoore," Thrall said. He had expected to spit the word angrily, and was more than a little surprised to find no more anger or hate in his heart as he spoke the name. Blackmoore was well and truly defeated. Not only was he gone from this timeway, where he never should have been, but his influence was gone as well. Any power he had held over Thrall had died with him.

Kalec nodded. "I suspected as much when the body was described to me. I am glad you were victorious—and surprised, if I may say so. To have suffered such a fall, and such cold, and then have to fight—well, it seems you orcs are even tougher than I thought."

"I was not alone in my fight," Thrall said quietly. "But I know one who is."

Kalec looked at him curiously, and Thrall explained. "There is one I left behind in order to do as Ysera asked. I would see her again, whatever happens in this world."

Now the blue dragon nodded. "I understand," he said. "I hope you will, Thrall."

"I know I will. I am certain of it." He eyed Kalec. "But I think . . . you are not so certain."

Kalec frowned and turned away, pacing. "You fell partway through the fight, Thrall," he said quietly. "You did not see what followed." He fell silent, and Thrall waited patiently.

"This being, this—Chromatus, as I heard the Twilight Father call him . . . do you understand what he is?" Kalec asked.

"You called him a chromatic dragon. Desharin told me of such creatures. He said they were all dead."

Kalec nodded his bright blue head. "So we thought. They are

nothing natural, Thrall. They are creations. Made things. And this one—I have never heard of him before, but he was clearly Nefarian's success, and his greatest one. Never have I seen a beast with five heads."

"Five heads," mused Thrall. "Each one the color of a different flight." It was a hideous image, one he could not seem to banish, hard as he tried.

"Five heads," repeated Kalecgos in growing horror. "That's it. Thrall, chromatic dragons never lived very long. But maybe that was the secret Nefarian learned: five heads, five brains. Perhaps this is what makes Chromatus so powerful, even though . . . even though he seemed weak."

Now Thrall could not hide his astonishment. "Weak?"

Kalec turned and locked gazes with him. "Weak," he repeated. "He stumbled; he faltered. Sometimes his wings would not bear him. And yet my flight was unable to stand against him and the twilight dragons. He defeated me, Thrall. I am an Aspect now, and I am not being arrogant to say that, barring other Aspects, no single dragon should be able to defeat me. But I had to order retreat, or he would have killed me and my entire dragonflight. We brought everything we had to bear against him. And he was *weak*."

Kalec was, Thrall knew by now, someone who attempted to think positively. He did not give in easily to negative emotions such as anger or despair. And still Thrall noted resignation and worry and, yes, hopelessness in his mien and voice.

Thrall understood why. "He was not at full strength for some reason," he said. "And when he is finally healed . . ."

Kalec's blue eyes held a universe of pain. "It does not seem as if anything will stop him," he said quietly.

"No," Thrall agreed thoughtfully, "not any *one* thing."

"We are scattered at a time when we most need unity," Kalec

said. "This Chromatus at the head of the twilight dragons . . . he will defeat—he will *obliterate*—both me and my flight if we approach him a second time without reinforcements."

"Ysera and Nozdormu will come," Thrall said confidently. "They and their flights will join you."

"It won't be enough," Kalec said dully. "We need the reds. No . . . more than that, we need the Life-Binder herself. My flight was frightened, Thrall, and I admit it: I was too. To see such a thing, to know you cannot win . . ." He shook his head. "We need the hope she could bring us, but she has none even for herself. And without her, I truly believe we will fall."

"I will speak to her again," Thrall said.

"She did not listen to you the last time," Kalec said, uncharacteristic bitterness poisoning his pleasant voice. "She will not listen this time. We are lost, Thrall, and . . . I do not know what to do. I am an Aspect. I have . . . new insights, new ways of understanding things. It is hard to explain. I am more than I ever was, and yet in so many ways I feel that I have not changed. I feel that I am simply Kalecgos, and I do not know what to do."

Thrall walked over to his friend and placed a large green hand on Kalec's shoulder. "It is that humility in your heart that turned the hearts of your flight to you. You may have all the power of the Aspect of Magic, but it has not changed who you are at your core. I know you have courage, Kalec. And I know that this seems almost impossible. But . . . while I was lying in the snow, halfway between living and dying . . ." He hesitated. ". . . I had a vision. One I know in my own heart is true, not the last gasp of a dying orc's hope."

Kalecgos nodded, believing him completely. "What was this vision?"

Thrall shook his head. "It is not to be shared with you, not yet. It is for Alexstrasza's hearing before any others'. And this is why I think perhaps I may be able to bring her back to herself. And with the Life-Binder and her reds at your side—well, I think Chromatus might just start to feel a bit uneasy."

And they grinned at one another.

The Twilight's Hammer cultists were being kept busy.

Chromatus had been given the spark of life, although his body remained abhorrent and decaying. He had fought fiercely and triumphantly even while still weak and new to this life. Now he lay on the snow outside the temple, ravenous and demanding, and they brought in flesh for him to feed upon, each set of jaws feasting greedily.

The Twilight Father stood beside him, almost giddy with victory. Deathwing surely could find no fault with what had transpired this day. Blackmoore had destroyed the disappointment that was Arygos, utilizing that dragon's rare blood to serve the cause in a way the blue dragon had failed to do in life. Additionally, one of the twilight dragons had reported that Thrall had fallen from atop Kalecgos's back, and Blackmoore had set after him in case he had somehow survived. The twilight dragons had rebuffed the blues, and most importantly of all, Chromatus had been given life. And even newborn, as it were, he had defeated the best the blue dragonflight, led by its new Aspect, Kalecgos, had to throw at them.

Chromatus had been largely silent for the last hour as he fed upon the carcasses of snowfall elk that had been hunted and brought to him. But now he paused and lifted his enormous black head.

"I will need more," he said perfunctorily.

"You shall have all you need, Chromatus," the Twilight Father assured him. "We will bring you flesh until and unless you prefer to hunt it yourself."

"I will, soon," the black head said in its deep voice, more felt than heard. "The closer to living it is when my jaws crunch upon it, the sweeter the taste."

"Such a thing is always true," the Twilight Father agreed.

Chromatus dropped the black head to resume feeding, but lifted the red one. He kept the head in profile but rolled one massive eye to stare down upon the human.

"The dragons are not turning up their throats for me to crunch upon quite yet," he said. "They will try again."

The Twilight Father did not quite catch the warning in the voice. "They would be fools to do so, and I think them too broken even to be foolish," he said. "Ysera is missing, and her flight is at a loss. Nozdormu might have been found, but he has yet to stir himself or his flight to come to the aid of his fellows. Alexstrasza is sobbing her heart out like some human girl, and her flight apparently cannot even perform basic functions without her. You have shown the blues how powerful you are, and their Aspect is too softhearted to lead them well. Their supposed hero Thrall is either dead in a snowbank or will soon be speared on Blackmoore's broadsword. I think you may recover at your leisure, my friend."

The dragon's red head glared at him balefully with glowing purple eyes. "I am not your friend, Twilight Father," he said softly, but with an edge that made the human's heart stop beating for a moment. "Nor am I your child or your servant. We both serve the mighty Deathwing, whom my father made me to serve, and that is our only commonality."

The Twilight Father did not show fear, though he suspected the dragon smelled it. He took a moment to make sure his voice did not quiver.

"Of course, Chromatus. We both serve with perfect loyalty."

The great eyes narrowed, but Chromatus did not pursue the point. "You are not a dragon. You do not understand them as I do. Scattered and despairing they may be, but they will come again. They will come until there are no more of them to come."

"Which," added the blue head, chuckling slightly, "might be after the next battle. Regardless, it is you who are foolish if you let down your guard. I am still recovering my full strength. I cannot be at less than that when the next attack comes." He paused, lowering his blue head and opening its jaws wide to devour an adult female elk in one gulp. "Malygos's daughter still lives, does she not?"

The Twilight Father was confused. "Yes, she does, but we have already used the blood of a scion of Malygos to activate the needle."

The black head gave the human a withering look. "It is her bloodline, not her blood, that matters now."

"Oh," said the Twilight Father, then, as comprehension dawned: "*Oh*. Shall I, uh, bring her to you now, then?"

"Time passes," said the bronze head. "I am the only success of my father's experimentation. Perhaps a more stable—a more . . . *traditional*—method of creating chromatic whelps will ensure that they are strong enough to survive. I the father, and the mother the last child of Malygos? Yes . . . our children will be stronger. But I must rest first. Bring her to me in a few hours. Do not worry about the necklace: I will free her when I am ready. Even in dragon form, she will be no match for me."

The Twilight Father turned to one of his assistants. "In three hours, bring the blue dragon prisoner to Chromatus. I must speak with our master and inform him of our success."

"Your command is my life," said the assistant, and hastened away to obey. Chromatus's green head ate another elk, crunching the bones as he watched the assistant hurry off. Then, with a great sigh of breath that reeked of raw meat, he lowered himself to the snowy earth and closed his ten eyes. But before he surrendered to a deep sleep, the black head had a final word.

"And my command," he said to the Twilight Father, "is *yours.*"

The Twilight Father knelt before the orb, which was filled with darkness and danger.

"My lord Deathwing," he said humbly.

The orb cracked open, releasing night-dark smoke that formed the image of a glowing-eyed, monstrous dragon. "You had best have good news for me," rumbled the black Dragon Aspect.

"I do," the Twilight Father said quickly. "The best possible news. Chromatus lives!"

A low, pleased chuckle rumbled, and in either answer or echo, the Twilight Father felt the very earth rumble ever so faintly as well. "That *is* good news. I am delighted that you succeeded! Tell me more good news."

The Twilight Father hesitated. There was, unfortunately, bad news along with the good, but even that had its bright spot. "Arygos failed us, but he was able to be of use to us at the end, as you predicted the female might be. His blood activated the Focusing Iris, and with the Iris we were able to harness all of the Nexus's arcane energy! We created a surge needle to transfer all that glorious power directly into Chromatus."

There was a stillness almost more terrible than Deathwing's anger; for a long moment, it seemed to last for centuries.

"Arygos was not chosen as the Aspect, then. He did not deliver me the blues." The voice was quiet, almost calm. But nothing, really, was ever truly calm about the insane Aspect.

"No, my lord. I do not understand how such things work—it seemed as though no one truly did—but somehow the powers of the Aspect were transferred to another."

"Kalecgos," said Deathwing, drawing out the word and infusing it with hatred.

"Yes, my lord. Arygos called in the twilight dragonflight as soon as he realized what had happened. He then fled to the Eye, where Blackmoore slew him and harnessed his blood. The blue flight, led by Kalecgos, attacked us immediately. But, my lord, Chromatus, although newly born and weak, still was able to send them fleeing! Once he is at full strength and power, nothing and no one will be able to stand against him. So you see, it doesn't matter if Kalecgos is the new Aspect. We will triumph even so!"

He waited, sweat gathering beneath his armpits, for his master's response. It was a long time coming.

"I was beginning to think I needed to come and get the job done myself," said Deathwing, his voice a warning.

The Twilight Father had to make a great effort not to visibly sag in relief. "No, Great One. You see that I can serve you well."

"It is . . . reassuring. I am at a delicate juncture in my current plans. It would have made me angry indeed to be called away from them. What you say has merit. But what of Thrall? Is he dead?"

"He fell to the earth from the back of Kalecgos during the battle," the Twilight Father said. "Even if he survived the fall, which is unlikely, Blackmoore went after him."

"You think him dead, then?"

"Certainly."

"I do not," said Deathwing. "I want the body. Search for as long as you must to bring it before me. I will see it before I discount him."

"As my lord wills, it shall be done."

"Chromatus still needs a watchful eye until he has fully recovered. No harm must befall him."

"It shall not. In fact, Chromatus has an eye to the future. He has demanded that Kirygosa be brought to him. With the promise her eggs showed before, I believe we may have solved the problem of short-lived chromatic dragons."

"Chromatus is wise. Good, good. She should be honored to be the mother of the future." His grotesque metallic jaw dropped slightly in an approximation of a grin. "This pleases me. You have done well despite the setbacks you have had to face, Father. Continue to do well, and you shall be rewarded."

The smoke that had formed Deathwing's image once again became swirling black mist, drifting to the floor to coalesce into a black, solid orb that cleared to assume its original appearance. The Twilight Father sagged and wiped at his damp brow.

They had managed to bring a fairly complete laboratory with them. And Kirygosa had come to know it intimately. She knew every bubbling beaker, every small burner, every vial and needle and "specimen" in neatly labeled jars. She knew the scents and the sound of the place, and she knew the tools with which the apothecaries did their jobs.

Here she had known agony, and humiliation, and racking grief. But she had always known that, even as she sometimes silently wished for death, she did not truly desire it. And she had known that they would not kill her . . . until they no longer had need of her.

And once they had done to her what they had brought her here to do, they would, indeed, no longer have need of her.

Her heart was racing. They were watching her closely. In the past she had fought them tooth and nail, extracting what little satisfaction she could by harming them before they began tormenting her. They were no doubt expecting an even fiercer struggle. Instead she put on a bleak face. Exhausted as she was, it was not difficult to even coax tears into her eyes.

"The blue dragoness no longer protests?" said one, half goading her and half surprised.

"What point is there?" Kirygosa said dully. "It has availed me nothing before. And before, I had the hope of rescue." She lifted her tear-filled eyes to his. "But this time I will not be dragged off and forgotten until you need me again, will I?"

The other one, a female troll named Zuuzuu, shook her head and cackled wildly. "I guess nobody told you where you going dis time."

Horror coiled coldly in Kirygosa's belly. "I . . . thought you were taking me to the laboratory again."

The two cultists exchanged cruel smiles. "No, you cute little dragon girl," said Zuuzuu. "You be catchin' da eye of Chromatus."

"Wh-what?" Kiry stammered. Surely they couldn't mean what she thought they meant . . . not with that five-headed, decaying monster. . . .

"He figures that you two might produce stable chromatic offspring," said Josah, a large, stockily built human with reddish blond hair. "A word of warning: Don't expect a nice candlelit dinner beforehand."

The two of them laughed, Zuuzuu with her awful cackling and Josah with his smug, hearty bellow.

Kirygosa wanted to kill them. She wanted to shred them to pieces, to flee, to fly, to be killed by the twilight dragons, to be tortured to death, to endure any fate other than the one they were leading her to.

At the same moment, she realized that this was a chance that had never before come her way. Stifling the gorge that rose in her throat, forcing herself not to tremble with fury and horror, she frowned as if thinking.

"If we did produce offspring," she said, "I would have value."

"Dat you would," Zuuzuu said. "With your bloodline, you jest might be da only one who can give Chromatus the kind of babies he wants."

Kiry forced herself not to cringe at the thought of other females of all flights being subjected to Chromatus's desire. Instead, she nodded. "I could be queen."

"For a time, maybe," said Josah. He had moved ahead of Kiry and Zuuzuu a little as they walked. "But the end of all things will come. Even for you."

Zuuzuu was holding the silver chain, but Kirygosa had noticed that as she spoke, the troll had loosened her grip. She made note of their weapons: two daggers in sheaths at their hips. They were approaching a circular stairway, which would take them to the ground level. And Chromatus. Josah had already started to descend, and they would soon need to go single file.

Now.

With her right hand, Kiry yanked the chain out of the troll's careless grasp. Her left arm came up to wrap around Zuuzuu's neck. Zuuzuu's fingers flew up to pry the choking arm off, scratching long furrows in Kiry's arm. The dragon ignored the pain, squeezing tightly and quickly, until the troll's eyes rolled back in her head and her body went limp. Kiry lowered the body to the floor and seized Zuuzuu's dagger in the same quick motion.

She had been silent. Josah had noticed nothing and was still carrying on his now one-sided conversation. "I hope I live long enough to see it," he was saying, almost wistfully. "The end, you know.

Though it is our fate to die as the Twilight Father commands. Perhaps he would be pleased if—"

His words ended in a confused gurgle as Kirygosa plunged Zuuzuu's blade into his throat. She covered his mouth so that the ugly sounds would not carry, then lowered him to the floor as she had done with Zuuzuu.

Her hands came away covered with blood. Her heart was racing and her breath came swiftly. She wiped them and the dagger on Josah's robes as best she could, her ears straining for any sign that she had been discovered. All was still.

One hand closed briefly on the chain. It still held her prisoner in this weaker human form, but at least no enemy was clutching the other end.

There was no place to drag the bodies and hide them; the temple was open and airy, with very few nooks or compartmentalized places. Very soon, when she did not show up as she was supposed to, they would come looking for her and find the bodies on the ramp.

But with any luck, Kirygosa would be long gone by then.

She moved quickly but quietly, booted feet making only the barest whisper as she raced down the ramp. Fortunately, it was after sunset; she could at least hope to move in the shadows.

Even after dark, though, the Twilight Father kept his minions busy. There were torches stuck in the snow, their orange-red glow chasing away the purple-blue shadows. Kirygosa reached the bottom level and flattened herself against one of the archway walls, looking about.

If only she could simply change into her true shape and fly away! But they had seen to it that she could not. She fingered the chain on her neck that kept her locked in this form. She would need some kind of mount. They used all kinds here, but mostly as pack animals—just like those that, until recently, had drawn the wagon that had borne the inanimate body of the nightmare who now lay drowsing not too far from where Kirygosa hid in the shadows.

But there were some that were personal mounts. A few of the higher-ranking members of the cult owned them. They had not been forced to slog across Northrend on foot, as most of the others had during the brutal trek to the temple. Over there, several of them were tethered a fair distance from the light provided by the torches. She saw a few wolves, thicker-coated horses, nightsabers, and even a few elk and one or two wyverns. Some of them would not permit anyone other than their riders to mount them.

But some of them would.

There was just one catch: in order to get to a wyvern, she would have to walk right past the sleeping Chromatus.

She hesitated, the horror resurfacing. . . . If he awoke—

Then you would be no better off than if you had gone to him docilely. But if you get past him—

It was the only way. If she didn't get past him, she yet had the dagger. She would use it on herself rather than submit to such an abomination.

She tucked the dangling chain into her linen shirt, gripped the dagger—pitiful weapon though it would be against so great a creature—and stepped slowly forward.

His breathing sounded like a small wind as it moved in and out of enormous, unnaturally animated lungs. In her human form, Kirygosa was as a mouse to a tiger, and yet somehow she thought the sound of her snow-muffled footfalls and rapidly beating heart would awaken him. He was not curled up but lay with his heads stretched out before him, his body moving slowly up and down with each breath.

Kiry wanted to break into a run but did not. Instead, step by quiet step, she moved down the length of his enormous, mottle-hued form. He smelled musky and rank, as if the stench of rot that had clung to him for so long could not be dispersed merely by the spark of life. Hatred suddenly formed in her belly, its heat warming her, giving her renewed determination.

More than her life was at stake here. She had been kept prisoner by the Twilight Father long enough to learn things—things he was not aware that she knew. If she could reach Kalec and the blues with that information, she might be able to tell them something that could help them in their attack.

Because they would, indeed, attack again. Kirygosa knew her people. And she wanted to be with them this time, not kept help-less and weak by a chain around her neck.

Chromatus stirred.

Kirygosa froze in mid-step, not breathing. Had he somehow sensed her sudden flush of hatred? Smelled it on her, perhaps? Or had she been careless and crunched a twig hidden beneath the snow?

He shifted, lifting his massive bronze head and resettling it, heav-ing a great sigh. His tail lifted, thumped down. Then he was again still and the heavy breathing that denoted deep slumber renewed.

Kirygosa closed her eyes briefly in relief and resumed her slow, careful movements past the sleeping chromatic dragon toward where the mounts were tethered. Her eyes flicked from the hulk-ing, ugly form of Chromatus to the wyvern who would bear her to freedom.

The wolves and nightsabers were too bonded to their riders for her to steal. The elk were not sufficiently tamed to carry riders, though they were native to this land and would have borne her swiftly if they had been. Besides, they and the other herbivores would be skittish at the smell of blood that still clung to her. The wyverns that the Horde used as its primary beasts for flying were surprisingly calm, she had found, and as there were so few of them gathered here at the temple, they were trained to accept anyone atop their backs.

Anyone, that is, who knew how to manage them. Kirygosa once again chased away her fear, telling herself that she was lucky that there were still two available.

She approached the one she had chosen, murmuring softly. The lionlike head turned to her, eyes blinking with bored inquiry while his bat-like wings stretched and flexed. He was not saddled, and she could not spare the time. Any moment now, the alarm would be raised, and she needed to put as much space between her and the temple as possible before then.

Kirygosa had watched wyverns being ridden but had never mounted atop one herself. Cautiously, she slipped a leg over the great beast. He grunted, turning to look back at her, obviously sensing at once that she was a novice rider.

Kiry stroked him in what she hoped was a reassuring fashion, grasped the reins, and turned the wyvern's head skyward. Obedient and well trained, he leaped up—and she gasped, draping her body atop him and clinging tightly. He evened out quickly, hovering, awaiting a command. She took the reins and guided him to the west, to Coldarra and the Nexus, and desperately hoped that that was where Kalecgos and her flight would still be gathered.

She leaned close to the wyvern's ear, summoning what faint magic of persuasion she could with the chain still about her neck, and he calmed.

"We both know how to fly," she whispered. "Teach me how to be a wind rider, my friend."

It was probably her imagination, but she thought he gave her an approving *whuff*.

Eighteen

Thrall had not imagined he would be returning here again, especially so soon. But as he flew on the back of Narygos, Thrall felt that he was an entirely different person from who he had been the last time he had approached the Life-Binder.

The thought of Aggra burned warm in his heart, a quiet, ember-fueled fire that both buoyed and calmed him. He had watched—and indeed, had played a vital role in—the blues' rediscovering the true depths of their own hearts and spirits. They had received the Aspect they deserved: one of strength, and compassion, and wisdom, who truly had the best interest of the flight in mind.

"The last time I saw her, she was there," Thrall said, pointing. The dragon dove smoothly and flew toward the stone peak. As they drew closer Thrall saw, with more than a twinge of concern, that Alexstrasza was still here. She was as she had been then, sitting with her legs clasped to her chest, the image of pain. He wondered if she had moved at all since his last visit.

"Set me down a distance away," Thrall said. "I don't think she wants to see anyone right now, and seeing me by myself might be easier."

"As you wish," said Narygos, landing gracefully and lowering himself so that Thrall might dismount with more ease. Thrall turned and looked up at him. "I thank you for bearing me here," he said, "but . . . perhaps you should not wait for me."

Narygos cocked his head. "If you do not succeed in convincing her—"

"If I do not succeed in convincing her," Thrall said with quiet earnestness, "then there is little point to my returning at all."

Narygos nodded, understanding. "Good luck, then, for all our sakes." He gave Thrall a gentle, affectionate nudge with his huge head, then gathered himself and leaped skyward. Thrall watched him fade into the distance, then went to the Life-Binder.

She heard him approach, as she had before. Her voice was raspy, almost unused-sounding.

"You are either the bravest or the most foolish orc I have ever seen, to dare return to me a second time," she said.

He smiled a little. "Others have said similar things, my lady," he said.

"Others," she said, lifting her head and piercing him with the intensity of her gaze, "are not me."

Despite all he had seen and fought in this life, Thrall felt himself tremble at the quiet threat in that voice. He knew she was right. Should she decide to end him, he would not stand a chance.

"You have come for more torment?" she said, and he wasn't sure if she meant that he would torment her or vice versa. Probably both.

"I hope to bring an end, or at least a mitigation, to yours, my lady," he said quietly.

Her anger held for another moment, then she looked away, once again resembling more a broken child than the most powerful of the Aspects.

"Only death will do so, and perhaps not even then," Alexstrasza said, her voice breaking.

"I do not know enough to say yes or no to you," Thrall said, "but I must try."

She sighed deeply. He looked at her carefully. She was thinner than she had been the last time he was here. Her cheekbones, angular to begin with, seemed to jut through her skin. Her eyes had dark hollows around them, and she looked as if a good wind would blow her away.

Thrall knew better.

He sat down beside her on the stone. She did not move. "When last we spoke," he continued, "I asked you to come with me to the Nexus. To speak with the blues. To help them."

"I have not forgotten. Nor have I forgotten my response."

It doesn't matter. None of it. It doesn't matter if everything is interconnected. It doesn't matter how long this has been going on. It doesn't even matter if we can stop it.

The children are dead. *Korialstrasz is dead. I am dead in all ways but one, and that will soon happen. There is no hope. There is nothing. Nothing matters.*

"I have not forgotten it, either," Thrall said. "But others do not know, or believe, that it does not matter, and stubbornly persist in continuing. Such as the blue dragons. They have chosen their new Aspect: Kalecgos. And they have a new foe: a chromatic dragon named Chromatus."

The faintest flicker of surprise had crossed her face at the mention of Kalecgos, but her eyes dulled again at the name of Chromatus.

"For each victory, a defeat," she murmured.

"I fell during that battle," Thrall said bluntly. "Quite literally. I tumbled off Kalec's back and landed in the snow. I nearly gave in to death and despair. But something happened. Something that made me want to move my frozen limbs, claw my way out of the snow—and survive a surprise attack by an old, old enemy."

She didn't move. She appeared to be ignoring him completely. But at least she had not roused to anger and attempted to kill him, as she had last time. And that meant that she just might be listening.

Ancestors, I pray I am doing the right thing. I act with my heart, and that is the best I can do.

He extended a hand. She turned her head slightly at the movement and gazed at it dully. He moved it toward her, indicating she should take it. She slowly turned her head back to staring at the horizon.

Gently, Thrall reached down and took her hand himself. Her fingers were limp and unresponsive. He folded his strong green hand about them carefully.

"I had a vision," he said, keeping his voice soft, almost as if he were trying not to startle a shy forest animal. "Two, actually. It is . . . such a gift to be granted one such. To be blessed with two, especially one entrusted to share with another . . . was an honor unlooked for."

The words were spoken with true modesty. Even though he knew his powers were growing, his connections to the elements deepening, he was still humbled by the grace that was being bestowed upon him. "One was for me. And this one . . . was for me to share with you."

He closed his eyes.

The egg was hatching.

It was a dispassionate environment in which to witness a birth, a makeshift laboratory set up under a huge tent. Outside, the storm raged as the little whelp struggled against its confining shell.

It had many to watch its arrival. One appeared to be a human, wrapped in a hooded cloak that concealed his face. The others wore robes that marked them instantly as members of the Twilight's Hammer cult. They all looked on gleefully, their gazes locked on the emerging infant.

Standing beside the human, a slender chain trailing from his hand to her throat, was an attractive human female with blue-black hair. Unlike the others, she watched with a stricken expression on her face, one hand on her abdomen, the other curled tightly into a fist.

"Kirygosa!"

The name was whispered sharply by Alexstrasza. Her voice intruded, but only to Thrall's ears. The vision unfolded exactly as it had the first time. He felt a pang at the name. So—this was what had truly happened to Arygos's sister, who had been thought lost. Lost indeed, but not dead, not yet. Her face told him everything he needed to know.

The tiny being heaved and shoved, and a piece of the egg fell away. Its mouth opened as it gasped for breath.

It was hideous.

It was blue and black and purple, with grotesque splotches here and there of bronze, red, and green. One of its forelegs ended in a stump. It only had one eye, mottle-hued and bruised-looking, with which to regard its audience.

Kirygosa let out a single harsh sob, then turned away.

"No, no, my dear, do not avert your eyes. Behold what we have made of your plain blue child," gloated the human. He extended a gloved hand and gathered the chromatic whelp into his palm. The thing lay limply, tiny chest heaving. One of its wings was fused to its side.

The cloaked man walked a few paces away and placed it on the earth. "Now, small one, let us see if you can grow bigger for us."

One of the cultists stepped forward, bowing obsequiously. The human extended his hands. One held an imperfectly glimpsed artifact glowing with pale violet energy. The fingers of the other hand fluttered in conjuration. He spoke an incantation, and a strand of white arcane energy shot out from the artifact. It wrapped itself around the whelp, a rope of magic, and began to pull golden life energy from the small dragon. It squeaked in pain.

"No!" screamed Kirygosa, lunging forward. The man jerked on the chain, hard. Kirygosa dropped to her knees, hissing in agony.

The whelp grew. It opened its mouth and let out a small, squeaking cry as its body spasmed. Thrall could almost hear bones creaking and skin stretching as the mage drained its life energy, aging it quickly. At one point, the squeak deepened into a croak, and then into a sharp cry. One wing beat frantically; the other, still fused to its side, simply quivered.

The chromatic whelp collapsed.

The human sighed. "It almost made it to drake size," he said thoughtfully. He stepped forward and nudged the corpse with a toe. "Better, Gahurg. Better. The Aspect blood in her does seem to render her children stronger than most, better able to withstand modification. But still, not perfect. Take it away. Dissect it, learn from it, and do even better next time."

"As you desire, Twilight Father," Gahurg said. Four other cultists stepped forward and began to haul the chromatic dragon away.

"What are you doing *to my children?*"

Kirygosa's voice had begun low, deep in her chest, but it built to a furious shout. Again, heedless of the pain she must have known would come, she launched herself at the man known as the Twilight Father.

"Oh, dear one," whispered Alexstrasza. Thrall knew she, too, now saw the marks on Kirygosa's body where she had been bled or experimented upon. Oddly enough, the pained empathy in Alexstrasza's voice gave Thrall hope. Better the hurt and the horror than the dull emptiness.

"I am making perfection," said the Twilight Father, again tugging on the chain.

She winced in torment, then found her breath. "I am glad I must watch only one clutch of my eggs sacrificed to your obscenity," Kirygosa spat. "My mate is dead. I will give you no more."

"Ah, but you are still a daughter of Malygos," said the Twilight Father, "and who is to say that fate—or I—might not find another mate for you, hmm?"

The scene shifted. Thrall's eyes were still closed, the vision still playing in his mind. He could feel Alexstrasza's hand, her fingers now winding around his, but the sensation was somehow distant, like a sound heard from far away. He knew what they would see next, and he knew that it would either destroy her, or enable her to save herself.

Either way, he would be there with her.

The place was a sanctuary. Thrall had known instantly what it needs must be, even though he had never beheld the Ruby Sanctum with his own eyes. It bore damage from what was obviously a recent attack, but the beautiful forest, with bright meadows and softly rustling trees crisscrossed by gently meandering rivulets, was already healing itself. As the Dragonqueen's true home, the heart of the red dragonflight, should do.

A large male dragon lay in the shade of one of the trees. He seemed awkward in his relaxation, as if he did not often permit himself to so indulge, and continued to watch the clusters of dragon eggs through half-closed eyes.

Her gasp was pure, raw, filled with longing and pain.

"Korialstrasz," whispered the Life-Binder. "Oh, my love . . . Thrall, must I see this?"

So distraught was she that she did not command or order, merely pleaded brokenly. For whatever reason—despair or hope, he did not know—the great Life-Binder, Alexstrasza, had seemingly placed herself firmly in Thrall's hands.

"Yes, my lady," he said, making his deep voice as gentle as possible. "Endure but a moment, and all will be revealed to you."

And then, in an instant, he was alert and on all four paws, sniffing the air, ears swiveling to catch the slightest sound. A heartbeat later Korialstrasz was airborne, moving swiftly and gracefully, eyes scanning the ground.

His eyes widened, then narrowed, and with a bellow of protective rage he folded his wings and dove. An instant later Thrall and Alexstrasza saw what Krasus had seen: several intruders of all races, uniform only in that they wore the dark maroon and black robes of the Twilight's Hammer cult.

Korialstrasz did not breathe fire or use magic. The violators of
the sanctuary were scattered among the precious eggs. Instead he
dove with massive claws outstretched, plucking up and crushing
the cultists as quickly and efficiently as Thrall might crush a bug.
There was no screaming in terror from them; Thrall watched,
angry and sickened, as they smiled while they embraced death.

The threat seemingly ended, Korialstrasz landed next to a cluster of eggs, lowering his scarlet scaly head and nuzzling them with
the utmost gentleness.

One of them cracked open. An ugly ochre mist wafted up from
the egg, and Krasus's eyes widened as he recoiled from the small,
deformed shape of a chromatic dragon.

*"No!" screamed Alexstrasza. Thrall felt for her. It had been painful enough
for the Life-Binder to watch Kirygosa's torment. To know that the same
horrible fate had been visited upon her own children—*

Horrified, Korialstrasz reached out with a tentative claw to touch
the tiny creature. There was a soft sound, and more and more of
the eggs began to crack open. All of them hatched squeaking, mal-
formed chromatic dragons.

And then Krasus gasped as he looked down at himself. The very
tip of his foreclaw was starting to turn black. Slowly but inexora-
bly, the contagion spread, climbing from his claws up his foreleg.

A low laughter, weak but triumphant, drew the red dragon's attention.

"And so, all of da chil'ren become da chil'ren of da mad one, da
great Deat'wing," murmured one of the cultists. He was a troll, his
skin dark blue. Korialstrasz had crushed his ribs, and blood trickled

from his mouth around his tusks, but he yet lived. "All of your p-people . . . will belong to him. . . ."

Krasus stared at his infected limb. He closed the paw tightly, into a fist, and brought it to his chest for a moment. Closing his eyes, he lowered his head.

"No," he said quietly. "I will not permit that to happen. I will destroy myself and . . . and my children, rather than see them so perverted."

The cultist laughed again, weakly. He began to cough, spitting up frothy blood tinged pink with air. "We s-still win," he rasped.

Krasus stared at him, then suddenly remembered the precise words he had spoken. "What did you mean when you said, 'all of the children'?" The cultist was silent, leering at him as he labored for breath. "How many were infected? *Tell me!*"

"*All* of dem!" the troll crowed triumphantly. His eyes gleamed and his smile was enormous. "*All* da eggs! *All* da sanctums! You be too late! Dey all be hatching now. You cannot stop it."

Krasus was very still. He narrowed his eyes and cocked his head, thinking.

"Yes," he said quietly. "Yes, I can."

"All of the eggs," whispered Alexstrasza. "All . . . of us . . ."

"It was a terrible choice," Thrall said quietly. "He knew that it was likely that no one would ever know what had really happened. That without knowing the truth, others would deem him a traitor. That perhaps even you would believe it."

He heard her gasp and whimper, and squeezed her hand.

"He saved us. . . . He never betrayed us; *he saved us . . . !*"

They stood in silence, eyes closed, as Korialstrasz gathered up all his energy and magic, folding in on himself. He took a deep, steadying breath, and whispered a single word:

"Beloved."

And then it went dark.

Thrall opened his eyes. Alexstrasza's were open as well. She stared out into nothing, all the blood drained from her face, her hand clamping down on Thrall's so hard it hurt.

"He . . . he used his life energy to link the portals," Alexstrasza whispered. "To destroy all the contaminated eggs before anyone else became infected. I couldn't understand why there was so much verdancy that remained. . . . Now I know. Somehow, I understand. He brought death with *life* . . . to preserve other lives."

"The Spirit of Life is telling you things it cannot show," Thrall said quietly. "This was why I had to come. Korialstrasz was not a traitor. He was a hero. And he died well and willingly, saving not just his own flight but all the flights, with you in his heart."

"He was the best of us," she whispered. "He never failed me, nor anyone else. I—I have failed, and faltered, but not him. Not my Korialstrasz." She lifted her face to Thrall's. "I am glad I know how brave he was. I am so proud of him. But now . . . knowing that, how can I possibly endure without him? Can you, so short-lived, possibly understand what it is I have lost?"

Thrall thought of Aggra. "I may have only a short life span, but yes. I know of love. And I know how I would feel if I had lost my beloved as you have lost yours."

"Then how could you continue on without this love? What is there to go on for?"

He stared at her, his mind suddenly blank. All the images, the ideas, the pat words and clichés that rose to his lips, seemed so empty and devoid of meaning. What reason, indeed, would there be for a sole survivor to continue, when one had had such a love?

And then he thought of it.

He continued to hold the Life-Binder's hand in his right one. With the left, he reached into his pouch and brought forth a small, seemingly humble object.

It was the acorn that the ancient had gifted him with. Desharin's words came back to him: *Take good care of it. That acorn holds all the knowledge of its parent tree, and all the knowledge of that parent's parent tree . . . and on and on, back toward the beginning of all things. You are to plant it where it seems right for it to grow.*

Krasus had known it was not for him, though he had longed for it. Thrall wondered if the red dragon had guessed that, perhaps, such a thing was meant for his mate. Thrall hoped so.

The orc turned over Alexstrasza's hand, placed the acorn in her palm, and gently closed her fingers over it.

"I told you of Dreamer's Rest, in Feralas," Thrall said softly. "Of the ancients who were in peril there. What I did not tell you was how truly magnificent they are. I did not tell you of their . . . presence. The simple power of age and wisdom pouring from them. How small and awestruck I felt surrounded by them."

"I . . . have known ancients," Alexstrasza said, her voice small. She kept her fist tightly closed over the acorn for an instant, then opened it.

It shifted in her hand, so subtly that Thrall thought it was simply rolling over the hills and valleys of her palm. Then a small crack appeared at its light brown base. The crack spread, and then a tiny green shoot, only a fraction of an inch long, extended from the tip.

Alexstrasza let out a sobbing gasp. Her other hand flew to her heart, pressing down hard on a slender chest that suddenly heaved once, twice, three times with racking, gulping sobs. She kept pressing on her heart as though it hurt her. For an instant Thrall was worried that all this was too much—that it was killing her.

And then he understood. The heart of the Life-Binder had been closed—closed against the pain that caring brought. Against the torment of losing someone dearly loved. Against the agony of compassion.

And now, like the shell of the acorn, like ice during the spring thaw, her heart was cracking open.

"I am who I am," she whispered, still staring at the germinating acorn. "Whether in joy or in pain. I am who I am."

Another sob racked her, and then another. Tears welled in her eyes as she grieved for her lost love, finally weeping the healing tears that had been locked inside her shuttered heart. Thrall put an arm around her shoulders, and she turned into his broad chest; she, who had once been tortured and enslaved by orcs to serve them, wept freely against him.

Her tears seemed endless, as the tears of the Life-Binder ought to be. It was more than the loss of Krasus, Thrall suspected. He sensed she wept for all the things that had fallen; for the innocent, and the guilty; for Malygos and Deathwing and for all they had harmed; for the corrupted children, who had never had a chance to truly live; for the dead and the living; for all those who had suffered and tasted the salty tang of their pain on their cheeks.

They came freely now, her weeping as natural and pure as breathing. Tears rolled down her face and dropped onto the acorn she held, onto the soil beneath where they sat.

And as the first one splashed gently down, a flower began to push its way through the crust of the soil.

Thrall looked about, disbelieving. Before his eyes, ten thousand times more swiftly than it should have happened, he saw plants appear: flowers of all shades, small shoots that stretched into saplings, thick, soft green grass. He could even hear the sound of growing things, a vibrant and joyful striving and crackling.

He recalled that the druids had been working hard to bring back life to this place. Their efforts were successful from time to time, but always temporarily. He knew deep in his bones, though, that the new, lush life he beheld would not fade with time. Not when it was born of the Life-Binder's tears of reawakening compassion and love.

Alexstrasza stirred against him, pulling back gently. He lifted his arm from around her shoulders. She took a deep, shuddering breath, and moved, slightly unsteady, to kneel on the earth. Thrall did not assist her; he sensed she did not want him to. Gently, Alexstrasza scraped at the newly verdant soil, pressed the acorn deep, then covered it reverently. She rose and turned to face him.

"I am . . . chastened," she said quietly. Her voice was still thick with hurt, but there was a calmness to it that had not been there before. "You have reminded me of things that, in my pain, I had forgotten. Things . . . *he* would not wish me to forget, ever." She smiled, and though it was a sad and haunted smile, it was sincere and sweet. Her eyes were red with weeping, but there was a clarity in their focus, and Thrall knew she was all right.

And indeed, when she stepped back and lifted her arms to the sky, her beautiful face was set in an expression of righteous fury. There was more grieving to be done for all that had been lost, and he knew she would do so.

But not now. Now the Life-Binder was using her pain to fuel action, not tears. And Thrall almost felt a twinge of pity for those who would feel the heat of her fury.

Almost.

As he had witnessed her doing once before, Thrall again watched as she leaped upward, transforming from slender elf-like maiden to the most powerful of the Aspects—arguably the most powerful being in the world. This time, though, he knew he had nothing to fear from her in this shape.

She looked down at him, her eyes kind, and then the Life-Binder lowered herself so that the orc could climb atop her broad back.

"We will go to join my brothers and sisters, if you wish to come with me," she said quietly.

"I am glad to be of service," Thrall said, yet again humbled and awed by the sheer magnificence of the crimson dragon before him. He carefully and respectfully climbed atop her, settling himself at the base of her neck. "With their defeat, I believe the blues will have retreated to the Nexus."

"Perhaps," she said. "We will either find them there, or else Kalec will have joined the other flights and be assembling near Wyrmrest."

"The twilight dragons will see them," Thrall said, thinking aloud.

"Yes," agreed Alexstrasza, gathering herself and leaping into the air. "They will. What of it?"

"The element of surprise will be gone," Thrall replied.

"We no longer need it," Alexstrasza said. Her voice was strong and calm, and Thrall found himself relaxing as she spoke. "Our success or failure depends upon something much more important than military strategies or advantages."

She craned her neck to look at him as her wings powerfully and rhythmically beat the air. "It is time for the dragonflights of Azeroth to put aside their quarrels and unite. Or else, I fear we are all lost."

NINETEEN

Alexstrasza had been right. Sure enough, when she and Thrall were a few miles from Wyrmrest Temple, they saw blue and green dragons in the air and on the ground. She was spotted, of course. Several flew out to her and darted about almost giddily.

"Life-Binder!" Narygos cried happily. "Dark is the hour and dark are our hearts, but to see you brings a lightness to both. Thrall—thank you for what you have done."

"Friend Narygos," said Alexstrasza warmly, "I see my sister, Ysera, and the new Aspect, Kalecgos, and their flights. My own reds will come as soon as they know I am here."

"Then I shall seek them out at once, Life-Binder," said one of the greens. Thrall wondered how it was that the green knew where the reds were. Perhaps Ysera knew and had told him. There was so very much about dragons he had yet to grasp.

"Have we heard nothing from Nozdormu, then?" Alexstrasza queried.

Narygos and the others dropped back, above and below her, escorting and guarding her as they flew toward the gathering place.

"Not yet," Narygos said, with a quick glance at Thrall. "We have heard no word from him. Have you?"

"I have not been contacted," Thrall replied. "I can only assume that he is still investigating and learning."

"Knowledge is power," a large green agreed, "but it will do us no good if he learns something useful and Chromatus has slain us all."

"Hush, Rothos," Alexstrasza said sternly. "It is not the orc's fault if the Timeless One is not present. We . . . all do what we must." The last phrase was said in a sweet, sad voice, and Thrall knew she was thinking of Korialstrasz. He had done what he had to do, at a terrible cost.

Rothos looked apologetically at Thrall. "I am sorry, my friend, but you have seen what we fight. I would have Nozdormu and his bronzes with us when we try again."

"No offense taken, and I agree," Thrall said sincerely.

They had almost reached the site. "Please—go ahead and gather everyone," Alexstrasza asked of Rothos. "I have . . . some information they must know."

"Information about Chromatus?" Rothos asked hopefully.

Alexstrasza shook her head. "No. But I hope it will give them courage, and fresh hope, and those are weapons indeed."

A few moments later they landed. Thrumming, musical dragon cheers filled the bitterly cold air. Thrall was smiling as he slipped off of Alexstrasza's back into calf-deep snow.

"Thrall!"

He turned to see Kalecgos beaming down at him. The Great Aspect reached out a paw and very gently gathered Thrall in it. Thrall felt not a twinge of worry, only pleasure at seeing his friend again.

"I must stop underestimating you," Kalec said, bringing the orc closer to his face. "You have done as you said you would. You brought us back our Life-Binder—in all senses of the word," he added, looking over to where Alexstrasza nuzzled maternally at both greens and blues who rushed up to her. "I know not what magic you used, but I am grateful for it."

"Only the magic of the heart," Thrall said. "She will tell you what I learned, and shared with her. We will all know."

Ysera craned her head at the sound of Thrall's voice and moved toward them. She dipped her head on its long, sinuous neck in a gesture of respect.

"You were part of my dreaming, and one of the best parts," she told him. "You have done so much to help us. I grieve for Desharin, but I am glad you escaped."

"Know that if I could have saved him, I would have."

She nodded. "The Hour of Twilight awaits us," she said. She lifted her head and looked around, her rainbow-hued eyes bright with pleasure. "I see green and blue dragons gathered together. It is well, son of Durotan. It is well. But, ah, our red brothers and sisters have come to join us!"

Thrall turned to follow her gaze, and a short moment later could both see and hear the approaching leviathans. Dozens of them, there must have been, bearing down upon this gathering place. Thrall gazed in wonder, then looked about. Three Dragon Aspects and their flights were assembled now. He recalled the fight against the twilight dragons, and began to feel hope rising inside him. Surely there were three times the number of dragons gathered here now as had been at that fight, and with the Life-Binder leading them . . .

Alexstrasza leaped into the air. The reds clustered and darted about her, moving in lightly to reverently nuzzle her, dropping back respectfully. There was joy in her that he had not seen before, joy at being with her flight after so much anguish and bitterness.

After a few moments of the aerial dance of this beautiful reunion, Alexstrasza landed lightly on one of the jutting peaks, positioning herself where everyone could see her. They fell silent, eagerly awaiting the words of the Dragonqueen. She looked at them all for a moment, her head moving slowly as her eyes scanned the crowd.

"My brothers and sisters," she said, "we stand on the brink of a dreadful battle, against a foe whose power is terrifying. But there is something you must know before we begin our planning. Something that will, I hope, give you yet more reason to fight for yourselves, your flight, and the whelps not yet hatched."

This was received in silence. Some of them shifted uneasily. It was as if they had suddenly remembered that Alexstrasza's mate had been the one to destroy so many eggs.

Kalecgos gently lifted Thrall up toward his shoulder. The orc made the now-familiar leap, landing securely atop the blue Dragon Aspect as Kalec rose and flew to stand beside Alexstrasza. He offered wordless solidarity as she began to tell the other dragons about the vision Thrall had shared with her. Ysera glided to land at Alexstrasza's left side, supporting her sister.

Some, probably those who knew Korialstrasz best, seemed to be more than willing to believe Alexstrasza, their own scaly faces and lambent eyes showing deep sympathy. Others, while not outright protesting—Thrall suspected that they were too glad to have the Life-Binder returned to them to challenge her story—seemed to be dubious or plainly skeptical.

Thrall was pleased, but not surprised, to see that Kalecgos was among those who believed at once. He felt for the blue, however, when Alexstrasza described what had been done to Kirygosa. Many of the blues muttered angrily, but Kalec simply looked away, pain on his face. When Alexstrasza had finished, it was Kalec who broke the silence.

"So much is clear now," he said. "We know that a chromatic dragon exists. And while I am horrified to learn that Kirygosa has been . . . tortured in so dreadful a fashion, I am deeply glad she yet lives. When the sanctums were destroyed, we were in ignorance. To our minds, there was no reason for Korialstrasz to behave as he had. But now we know. We understand."

"If all is indeed as was said," said one of the older blues. Thrall recognized him as Teralygos, one who had stood staunchly by Arygos. "All we have is a so-called vision. There is no proof that any of this happened."

"She is Alexstrasza," said Narygos. "She is an Aspect . . . the Life-Binder!"

"And it is very convenient that she happened to have a vision—no, wait, that an orc came along at just the right time to tell her of a vision that exonerates her mate," continued the older blue. "What say you if I have a vision that Alexstrasza is making this up? Or has gone mad? That perhaps the vanished Kirygosa, who—"

"Can verify all that the Life-Binder has said," came a thin, fragile voice. Another one of the blues alighted, and he bore on his back a human girl.

Thrall recognized her at once: it was Kirygosa, from his vision.

"Kiry!" cried Kalec. Thrall slid off his shoulder quickly, and Kalec transformed into his half-elven shape as Kirygosa unsteadily dismounted. He raced to her, catching her up in his arms and hugging her tightly. She smiled faintly at him and others who hurried up to her, looking weary and painfully thin, but clearly happy to be with her flight again.

"Are you all right?" Kalec asked, concerned. "After what they . . . did to you?"

"Now that I am free, I will be," Kirygosa said, leaning on

Kalecgos. "As I said . . . what Thrall saw about me in his vision is true. I believe the vision about Korialstrasz to be true as well." She looked up at the great red dragon smiling benevolently down at her. "My lady, I grieve for your loss."

"Thank you, Kirygosa," Alexstrasza said. Her voice was heavy with sorrow but not despair. Not anymore. "And I grieve for yours."

Kalec's worried frown deepened. "Do you know about Arygos?" he asked Kiry quietly.

Kirygosa nodded. "Yes. He was betrayed by the Twilight Father, and slain by a human assassin named Blackmoore. I understand this Blackmoore had also been sent to kill you, Thrall," she said, turning to the only orc present. "I am relieved to see he has not succeeded. The Twilight Father and Deathwing both fear you. I am glad you are on our side."

"Come, sit and rest," Kalecgos urged. "Eat something and tell us what you know."

"The chain . . ." Kiry reached with fumbling fingers and pulled out a slender silver chain that hung around her neck, a simple-looking thing. Kalec clearly understood at once what it was. "I tried so hard to break it—"

"I know," Kalec said gently. "Dar'Khan once placed such a collar on me. I well know your fear and frustration, dear sister. One I cared for freed me . . . and now I free you."

Gently, he grasped the necklace between his thumb and forefinger. With the faintest of tugs, the blue Dragon Aspect snapped the chain as if it were nothing more than an ordinary piece of jewelry. Kirygosa sobbed joyfully. The others backed up, smiling, to give her room as she shifted into her true form. Thrall smiled to himself as he watched her rise into the air, flying weakly but spiritedly, free once more.

* * *

Kirygosa was attended to. Thrall helped to heal her while Kalec-gos conjured meat and drink for her. Alexstrasza and Ysera stood beside her in their humanoid forms, offering what comfort they could. Thrall was surprised to see Ysera's preferred shape. She had first appeared to him in night elf form. She still had the dark-purple skin and long ears of the kaldorei, but the crown of fierce horns that adorned her green hair marked her true nature. A few other dragons, some in humanoid forms, others in their draconic shapes, gathered around as Kirygosa's brutal story unfolded.

"I will tell you all I know, and hope that something I say can help you," she told them. "There is much that . . . to be honest, does not give me cause for hope."

"You escaped, which should have been nearly impossible," Kalecgos said. "I, for one, find great hope in that fact."

She tried to smile, but something deeply worried her. "I thank you for that, but . . . well, you will understand what I mean."

"Start at the beginning," Alexstrasza said. "How were you captured?"

"After the loss of Jarygos . . . my mate . . . Arygos tricked me into accompanying him. He turned me over to the human—for I know he is human—known as the Twilight Father. The Twilight Father and Arygos were working with the twilight dragonflight—and with Deathwing."

The three Aspects exchanged glances. "The first attack," Alexstrasza said, "the one who taunted us—he named himself the Twilight Father."

"Go on, dear one," said Ysera gently.

"They kept me imprisoned in my dragon form until my eggs were safely laid, then they put that chain on me." Kiry winced, recalling it.

"Easier to control you in human form," said Kalec. "I know."

She nodded. "They began experiments—on me, on my children . . ." Her voice caught for a moment. Alexstrasza laid a reassuring hand on her shoulder. Kiry gave her a faint smile and continued.

"That, Life-Binder, was what Korialstrasz stumbled upon. They had improved the odds of creating healthy chromatic dragons by experimenting on my children. It seems that, as I am a child of Malygos, my children are stronger. Korialstrasz dealt them a serious blow by eliminating their prospective army. Another blow was dealt when Arygos failed to become the Aspect. He had promised to deliver all of the blue flight into the Twilight Father's hands."

"We will never know if Arygos was sane when he made that bargain," said Kalec with quiet fury. "But, for the sake of his memory, let us hope he was not."

Kirygosa nodded, composing herself with a visible effort. "He was certainly devoted to the cult, but beyond that, I cannot say."

"What he did to you—"

"It is done, and over," she said, and Thrall realized that she was trying to reassure Kalecgos, even after all she had endured. She was unspeakably brave.

"So two blows were dealt to their plans. But they still had Chromatus." Her voice broke, and she struggled visibly to regain her composure.

"I don't know where they found him. The cultists brought him all the way to Northrend, knowing that they needed vast stores of arcane energy to give him the spark of life. And for that, they needed a surge needle created from the blood of a child of Malygos."

"Then—forgive me," said Thrall, "but . . . why did they not use your blood for that purpose sooner?"

"I believe they wanted to wait until Arygos brought them the blues," she said. "Think of what a sight that would have made:

Chromatus would have first been beheld by his enemies at full strength, at the forefront of a vast dragon army. I do not think the Twilight Father originally intended to kill Arygos. But when my brother failed, the Twilight Father made sure he still had a use. He made sure I did, too. I escaped before they tried to—to *breed* me to that *thing*."

Thrall was appalled. The two female Aspects looked ill, and Thrall realized that if the Twilight Father were to suddenly appear right now, Kalec would likely cheerfully have ripped him apart. And Thrall would have joined in.

"It could have worked, too," Kiry continued. "I could have been the mother of an entire new flight of abominations. Chromatus was the final experiment of Nefarian—who, as I have learned, also lives. After a fashion. He has been reanimated, but not brought to life as Chromatus has been."

"Nefarian is an undead atrocity, then." While Kirygosa had spoken, other dragons had drawn close to listen, and now a large red moved his massive frame to stand protectively over Alexstrasza and Kirygosa—both with hearts and spirits terribly wounded, and yet both so strong. The red continued: "Is he here as well?"

Kiry shook her head. "No, I think Deathwing has other plans for him. Chromatus will be enough. Kalec—you surprised him last time. He was but newly born. And even so . . ." Her voice trailed off.

"Even so, my entire flight was defeated," Kalec finished for her.

"You do not stand alone now, Kalecgos," Alexstrasza reassured him. "Three full flights stand together. He may have been able to defeat one flight, but three? Long has it been since we fought so, and I do not think, monstrous as he is, one single dragon can stand against all of us!"

Kirygosa seemed agitated at the words and grasped Alexstrasza's hand. "Life-Binder," she said, "He—he was made . . . for you." She looked at Kalec and Ysera as well. "All of you. He is more than just an exceptionally powerful chromatic dragon. He was brought to life with a specific purpose: to destroy the Aspects!"

Thrall opened his mouth in an automatic denial, then closed it. He had seen Chromatus. He saw what the monster could do. At full health, with the abilities of each flight his own—

"So it is true," said Ysera, looking stricken. "My vision is true."

Alexstrasza reached out her other hand to Ysera. "Speak, Sister," she implored.

"I had hoped . . . I was wrong. . . ." Ysera closed her eyes and spoke in a dreamy, singsong voice. It was not a spell, not in the truest sense of the word, but the scene she described had an enchantment all its own. Thrall could almost see what she spoke of in his own mind: the death of all things, save the twilight dragonflight. No plants, no beasts, no beings, no living thing at all drew breath save them. And each of the Aspects lay dead and stiffening.

Even the darkest, cruelest one of all. The one who had helped make the monster that brought it about.

Deathwing.

Thrall trembled and felt cold sweat trickling over his skin. Panic threatened to seize his throat. Others around him lifted their voices in fear, in anger, in grim acceptance, but one voice rang out clearly.

"It is not our doom!"

The voice belonged to the Life-Binder. She stood, still in her humanoid form, still holding the hands of her sister and the traumatized Kirygosa. Her face was bright with resolve and passion. "We have already seen that we have disrupted this grandiose plan of Deathwing's. Arygos's failure. Kiry's escape. The blues attacking Chromatus before he was fully ready. No, this is not set in stone. Ysera's visions always have meaning, yes. But dreams always rely on interpretation. Sister—could this be a warning as to what might happen if we do not fight?"

Ysera cocked her horned head. "Yes," she said. "Only Nozdormu knows what will truly be. I only share what I saw."

"Then let us resolve now," Alexstrasza said, "that we will set to this fight with all we have. Every blue, every green, every red dragon—know that you fight not only for your lives but for *all* life. All things. We will take on this so-called Aspect slayer, and we will show the Twilight Father and Deathwing himself that we will not be cowed. No matter what we have lost—or stand to lose—the thing we will *not* lose is our world. Chromatus will fall!"

And the hope that Thrall felt swell about him was so real, so sincere, he could taste it, and he lifted his own orcish voice in the cry of determination and will that filled the air.

TWENTY

Despite her ordeal, Kirygosa was more than eager—and able—to help plan the attack. Thrall noticed that even those who had once supported Arygos gravitated to her. The process of winning the heart and soul of the blues, begun with Kalec and his joyous ascent to Aspect in the light of two moons, was cemented by bearing witness to Kirygosa's calm courage.

The three Aspects, Thrall, Kirygosa, and a few representatives from each flight, all in humanoid forms, gathered together to begin strategizing in earnest. All present knew the layout of Wyrmrest Temple, and Kirygosa was able to tell them exactly what was now where. Here was where Chromatus rested and recovered—"More with each passing hour," she warned them darkly. There was where the Twilight Father spent most of his time. All beasts of burden and mounts were in another area, and she was able to give a solid approximation of the number of cultists and dragons the three flights were likely to encounter.

"Are there any weaknesses we can exploit?" asked the red dragon Torastrasza.

"The Twilight Father is human," Kirygosa replied. "He is older, with a weathered face and a gray beard, and he is extremely arrogant. I know that he is powerful in his own right, and that those he leads know nothing about his true loyalties."

"He is a leader?" asked Thrall. "A military commander, perhaps?"

"He does strike me as a military man," Kirygosa said, "but I admit I know little about humans. One thing I do know: he fears Deathwing."

"As all sane beings should," murmured Ysera, and she ducked her head in sorrow.

"It may make him overconfident," mused Torastrasza. "He may make foolish errors."

"I am not certain that any amount of overconfidence will be detrimental to him with such an ally as Chromatus," said Thrall. "You did not witness the battle against the blues. We now have greater numbers and different methods of attacking. But we should not underestimate him."

"Too, the cultists will gladly die for him," said Kirygosa. "They will fight until they are slain."

"Is the Twilight Father relying solely on Chromatus and the twilight dragons, or is there other weaponry?" asked Alexstrasza.

"They do not have any truly devastating weapons for ground or air combat," Kirygosa said. "But I do not know that they will need them. They have an entire flight, and Chromatus with all his heads—each one with a brain that knows all the skills of its flight."

Everyone fell silent at that simple but powerful observation.

"It seems we know our foe," said Alexstrasza at last. "Kiry, is Chromatus under the Twilight Father's control in any way?"

The blue dragon shook her head. "No, he is his own self. He is very dear to Deathwing, who has great pride—and great plans—for him."

"Then we three Aspects will take him as our primary target," said Alexstrasza. "Whatever else they may send at us, we need to concentrate all our efforts on him. The rest of our flights need to keep us from being distracted by other attacks. If he is so prized by Deathwing, his death will be more than a tactical victory. We can always retreat and return later to deal with the Twilight Father and the cultists. But Chromatus *must* die."

All the assembled dragons nodded in agreement, as did Thrall.

Chromatus must indeed die. Or else the cultists, whose focus was the end of everything, might see their goal realized all too soon.

The Twilight Father had instructed that the bodies of Zuuzuu and Josah be unceremoniously removed, and had ordered all of the cultists to submit to a beating. They had done so with perfect obedience, of course, and he had taken rather petty solace in their cries of pain.

How could they have let this happen? Kirygosa was a single being, only as strong as a human in that form. She shouldn't have been able to overpower even one of them, let alone both. And who had been so stupid as to not be watching the wyverns? No one had admitted to such an egregious lack of observation.

"We have lost our chance to breed the future," Chromatus growled when the Twilight Father had come to give him the bad news. "And if she survives, she can reveal information that could possibly harm us."

The thought had already occurred to the Twilight Father. With a confidence he did not feel, he said, "What can she tell them? They know we are here; they already know about you. Perhaps this is a blessing in disguise. She knows that you were weak at the time they attacked, and yet you utterly defeated them. I think the news she brings them—if she survives—will only discourage them. And when we win, if she survives, you will still be able to father an entire flight of chromatic dragons."

Chromatus eyed the smaller figure. "That is possible. But any strategic advantage we give them is to be deplored. I am sure Deathwing will be most unhappy to hear of this."

To that comment, the Twilight Father had no response.

They came at dusk.

The already darkening sky was made black with their approach, and the sound of hundreds of beating wings vibrated through the air as the foolish dragonflights drew closer.

The Twilight Father was excited. Surely Chromatus's rumbled words of warning were overly conservative. In the rays of the dying sun, he could count three colors of dragons bearing down upon the temple. So, the bronzes were still hanging back, their leader nowhere in sight. Even better.

There was an answering beat of wings as his own army of twilight dragons lifted into the sky. Behind them, flying almost lazily, was Chromatus.

The Twilight Father could not suppress a grin. Let them come. Let them come to their destruction. Chromatus would vanquish them, and the Twilight Father would report the deaths of no fewer than three Aspects this night.

Thrall was not astride Kalecgos, not this time. Torastrasza, who he had learned was Alexstrasza's right hand—foreclaw?—in military matters, had agreed to bear Thrall upon her back. The Aspects needed to be free to concentrate their attack on Chromatus. They could not be even briefly distracted by worry about his fate—or, indeed, the fate of any of them.

Thrall completely understood. He would contribute as best he could, without causing any of the Aspects to waste a moment worrying about him.

He was still in the front line as they descended once again on Wyrmrest. They were met by the first wave of twilight dragons, the beautiful yet horrific beings heading straight for the three Aspects. At once, though, the twilight dragons came under attack. The dragons of the various flights harried them, drawing their attention away from the Aspects. The greens used poison breath or, even worse, their ability to direct nightmares. At least, that was what Thrall assumed when he saw two twilight dragons suddenly shriek and flee erratically, as if something unspeakably terrifying was after them.

The reds and blues worked in tandem, the blues using their skills with cold magic to freeze or slow their enemies, and the reds attacking the corporeal dragons with fire. This time, the combined dragonflights outnumbered the single twilight dragonflight four or five to one, and what the enemy had no doubt thought would be a damaging attack—or at least a distraction to the powerful Aspects—was little more than flies buzzing about them.

They heard Chromatus before they even saw him.

"Kalecgos, so you have come back for more torment!" The voice was issuing from the black head, deep, rumbling along the bones and in the blood. Thrall shivered once, then set his jaw. "Deathwing once tried to eradicate your flight," said the blue head. "You must be determined that they all die, to come challenge me again. And I see you've brought your little friends with you." The red head spoke in a mocking tone of voice, "Life-Binder, all done weeping?" while the green said, "And are you finally awake, little Ysera?"

The words were laced with venom and contempt, but they fell on deaf ears. The once-Dreamer was now truly Awakened, her wings as swift and sure as Kalec's or Alexstrasza's. The Life-Binder had returned to herself, and Thrall knew her beloved's sacrifice had only given her strength for this battle. He wanted to shout back to Chromatus, let him know how foolish he had been to try to taunt them, but he was no dragon, and his words would be lost in the wind.

The Aspects were so focused, the insults had as little effect as raindrops sliding off their scales. Smoothly, yet with determination, as they had practiced, they moved gracefully into their attack formation.

It was like watching a beautifully choreographed dance. Kalecgos, Ysera, and Alexstrasza each took up positions around Chromatus. Alexstrasza flew above him, bearing down on him and blasting him with orange-red flames. Kalecgos attacked from below, buffeting him with both icy-cold attacks and magical ones. Ysera darted about unexpectedly as openings occurred, her mercurial nature meaning that Chromatus would never know where she would be next.

Thrall had watched, openmouthed in awe, as they had practiced this attack. They had done so with red, blue, and green dragons, feigning attacks but encouraging each "Chromatus" to "attack" with his or her flight's tactics.

It seemed as if they would win.

After Ysera's grisly description of each one of the Aspects being slain by his or her own particular magic, they had decided that each of them would target a different head on the chromatic dragon. Ysera concentrated on the bronze head, attacking not just with her corrosive, sickly green breath but by suddenly creating an illusion of a massive bronze dragon. More than the others, Ysera was unpredictable, and seemed to be staying a step or two ahead of Chromatus's bronze-dragon brain. Kalec targeted the red head, countering blasts of fiery breath with ice and magic.

And Alexstrasza went for perhaps the most intelligent one of all: the blue. In her rage, she was without a doubt the most beautiful, dangerous thing Thrall had ever seen. The blue head looked taken aback at first, as she attacked ceaselessly, breathing fire and then darting out of the way, shaking off clusters of twilight dragons as though they were little more than a nuisance. Everything she held precious in this world had been taken from her by those responsible for Chromatus's unnatural life: the mysterious Twilight Father and, of course, Deathwing himself. She was determined that the five-headed monster would not live to continue the slaughter and destruction.

Chromatus was clearly stunned by the smoothness of the coordination.

For a few moments.

Then, as if he had only been toying with them, he suddenly began striking back with twice the speed and determination. He had five heads, and there were three foes. The blue and red heads continued to fight Alexstrasza and Kalecgos; the black and green ones suddenly turned on their long necks and joined the bronze head in the attack upon Ysera.

She was unprepared for the sudden switch in tactics, and one of her forelegs was engulfed in shadowy flame. The green head fixed her with an intense stare, and Thrall guessed it was probably attempting to send the green Dragon Aspect one of her own nightmares. But Thrall knew, from what Ysera herself had said, that she had witnessed such things as this creature could not even imagine. Ysera pulled the injured limb in close and dove out of the stare's path, shaking her head and closing her eyes, deliberately casting off the green dragon head's attempt to use her own magic on her.

The bronze head opened its mouth and breathed out sand, scouring her, while black jaws closed on a wing, bit down hard, and ripped. Ysera cried out and pulled free, leaving a chunk of wing in her attacker's mouth. Quickly she healed herself from both injuries, but in that precious moment the other two heads ceased struggling with Alexstrasza and Kalecgos, and all five converged on the green Aspect, who was now clearly fighting for her life.

Thrall held fast to Torastrasza as she dipped and dove. He continued to use the Doomhammer when he could, but the twilight dragons were now prepared for such attacks. When Torastrasza drew near them with the orc on her back, the twilights made certain they were not in corporeal form, fighting only with their ugly, purple-hued magic. Thrall realized that he needed to use his shamanic skills now, and opened himself to the elements.

He reached out with his mind. *I fight to save all of you, all the elementals. All of this wounded land. Come to my aid, that I may protect you!*

Erratic they were at first, but Thrall put all of his urgency into his plea. And finally they obeyed. A wind elemental took the shape of a cyclone, picking up enormous boulders and hurtling toward Thrall's foes. Gusts of air came to his call, microbursts that caught spread wings and sent their owners slamming into one another. Blinding snow swirled up to envelop them, only to turn to boiling water that targeted open eyes.

Together, he and Torastrasza slew several of the twilight dragons. Then suddenly the great red dragon dropped in a tightly controlled dive. Thrall wondered what she was doing, and then realized. She was flying close to land, targeting the cluster of Twilight's Hammer cultists, opening her mammoth jaws and spewing flame. Their robes caught quickly, and they screamed in torment. It would seem, Thrall thought darkly, that not all of the cultists were so willing to sacrifice themselves when actually faced with death in the form of a huge, angry red dragon.

Torastrasza wheeled and rose, almost lazily, curving around the temple to the other side. Again she flew low, breathing fire on the screaming cultists, then caught the wind as lithely as a sparrow and rose gracefully to rejoin the battle in the air.

Thrall glanced over at the battle with Chromatus, and his heart sank. He could see that all three of the Aspects had been wounded—burned, frozen, crippled, injured in some other way. And Chromatus seemed barely touched. Even as Thrall watched, the dragon threw back two of his heads and laughed.

"Life is sweet, to offer such entertainment!" he bellowed. "Come for me again! Let us play some more!"

Ysera veered erratically away. She flew close to Thrall before heading back—long enough for him to catch fear and despair in her brilliant eyes.

Kirygosa's words came back to him: *He was made . . . for you. All of you. He was brought to life with a specific purpose: to destroy the Aspects!*

They fell almost like raindrops, the reds and blues and greens. Wyrmrest Temple might now just as well have been called Wyrmrest Abattoir.

This couldn't be happening! Three Aspects and their flights—certainly the number of cultists and twilight dragons was dropping, but Chromatus seemed to be gaining strength the longer the battle continued.

Where were the bronzes? Nozdormu had said he would come. They were desperately needed now. With another Aspect, perhaps that would be enough to emerge victorious. Thrall looked around wildly, hoping against hope that—

There was a dark smudge against the evening sky now. More twilight dragons? And then Thrall realized that their scales were much, much lighter-hued than those of the twilights. Much lighter than any other dragonflight.

"There!" cried Thrall. "The bronzes! They have come!"

The reds, blues, and greens had spotted them as well, and a wave of joy rose in their throats. Now, with the bronze dragonflight added to the fight, they could turn the tide. Four Aspects—surely even Chromatus could not stand against them!

The bronzes scattered, joining their brethren in attacking the twilight dragons, while Nozdormu dove straight to his fellow Aspects. They broke off the attack, wheeling away to meet him partway. It was a beautiful sight: four Aspects, flying together, united in battle.

And then Nozdormu said something Thrall did not expect to hear.

"Retreat!" he called. "Retreat! Follow me!"

Thrall felt his heart sink in his chest like something physical, and he knew the other Aspects felt the same way. All eyes turned to the Life-Binder. For a long moment she hovered. Then Chromatus made the decision for her. He had flown off a slight distance, doubtless confused by their abrupt departure, and had waited for them to resume the attack. When they did not, he came after them, flying straight and true, with deadly intent.

"Retreat!" cried Alexstrasza in a broken voice. "Retreat, retreat!" Ysera and Kalecgos took up the cry, ordering their own flights to follow.

Those who could obey at once did so. Others were still locked in combat and came when they could—or not at all. They flew swiftly and steadily at top speed to the east. Thrall, perched atop Torastrasza's strong back, clung on as air created by the sheer speed threatened to dislodge him.

He craned his neck and looked over his shoulder. Chromatus was still following, and as Thrall watched, he opened his red mouth and bellowed a sheet of flame. Then he broke off the attack, veering back toward the temple. A few of the twilight dragons pursued, but soon they, too, turned back.

Why? They were winning; why would they break off the attack?

After a few moments of hard flying, making sure that they were not being followed by the nightmarish creature, the Aspects slowed. They alit upon a snowy peak, their flights landing close beside them.

Alexstrasza whirled on Nozdormu. Grief and anger were in every line of her crimson form. "Why? Why did you not join us in the attack, Nozdormu?" she cried. "We could have—"

"No," the Timeless One said, bluntly and brutally. "We would have all died if we had persisted in our attack."

"How could that be possible?" spat Torastrasza. Thrall could feel the coiled anger in her body. "You brought another full flight, and yourself—four Aspects! How could anything stand against that?"

Even Kalec, normally so calm, looked frustrated and upset, and mild Ysera appeared agitated. Thrall, too, was confused, but trusted Nozdormu. The others must as well, or else they would not have broken off the attack as they had.

"I have learned much, in my wandering of the timewaysss," Nozdormu said. "I asked this orc to tell you that I was ssstill searching for answers. I have found sssome, at least. We cannot defeat Chromatus without true union amongst ourselves."

The other dragons exchanged glances. "We are working together as seldom before," protested Kalec. "All four flights are united in this! You saw us: we worked cooperatively, none of us seeking glory!"

"Perhaps that was what the vision was trying to tell me," came the soft voice of Ysera. "We cannot defeat him by simply fighting together. We need to fight . . . *together*."

"Exactly!" said Nozdormu. The others simply stared at him, and Thrall knew what they were thinking. Had Nozdormu and Ysera, too, gone mad?

Nozdormu shook himself impatiently. "We are Aspectsss," he said. "We are not sssimply dragons with different skills and more power. We were changed when the titans gave us our abilities. We cannot defeat this monster by something so sssimple as coordinating an attack. We must think and act and fight as one. United. Share the essence of what it truly means to be each Aspect."

"I think I understand," said Alexstrasza, frowning slightly. "We were meant to join. Combine our skills, our knowledge. Is that what you are saying?"

"Yes, that is it exactly, Life-Binder! Do you remember what the titans sssaid as they departed?"

"'Unto each of you is given a gift; unto all of you is given the duty,'" said Alexstrasza, her eyes widening. "We . . . were parts of a whole. We were never meant to be separate."

"Will . . . we lose ourselves?" asked Kalec quietly. Thrall knew how important Kalec's individuality was to him. More than any of the other Aspects, he was used to simply being himself. Being an Aspect at all was still very new to him, and the thought of having to lose himself utterly was not a pleasant one. Still, Thrall knew his friend, and knew that if Kalec had to "die" as an individual in order to stop Chromatus, he would not hesitate to make the sacrifice.

"No," answered Nozdormu. "Not if we do so properly. We are partsss of a whole, but complete unto ourselves as well. *That* is the great myssstery."

Suddenly, Alexstrasza closed her eyes in pain. "Then . . . we are indeed doomed," she said, her voice breaking.

"What?" said Torastrasza. "Life-Binder, you have suffered and endured so much. Why do you give up now?"

And then Kalec realized it as well. "We are only four," he said. "We will never again be as we were intended to be. Neltharion is Deathwing now, and there is no Aspect of Earth."

The silence was almost unbearable, yet no one could think of anything to say. It was a crushing truth, but was the truth nonetheless. They could not even try to call a new Aspect, for Deathwing yet lived.

And Chromatus was Deathwing's tool.

Thrall slumped, almost numb with the realization. All that remained to them, then, was to throw their lives away fighting Chromatus, and fail. The world, and every living thing in it save the twilight dragons, would then fall. The cult would triumph, and Deathwing, insane and evil, would be victorious, living only long enough to be impaled on the very spire of Wyrmrest Temple. Thrall would never return to his Aggra, never be able to work with the Earthen Ring to—

He blinked. Was it possible? Could he . . . ?

His connection with the elements had only seemed to grow stronger with this unexpected journey he had undertaken. His renewed connection with the Spirit of Life seemed to make everything stronger. The knowledge of the importance of the moment made him feel . . . solid. Grounded. As long as he remembered that, nothing could uproot him again.

"Life-Binder," he said, his voice shaking with hope, "I . . . may have a solution."

TWENTY-ONE

They turned weary heads to him expectantly. He looked at them each in turn. "It might not work, but I think—I believe it's worth a try," he said. "This may sound—well, I simply ask that you hear me out."

"My friend, of course we will," Kalec said. "And I hope with all my being you have some option for us."

"I . . . may. We have four Aspects gathered here now: the Life-Binder, the Awakened Dreamer, the Steward of Magic, the Guardian of Time. You are only missing one . . . and that one happens to be the Earth-Warder. I am a shaman. I work with the elements. I could do nothing to aid you if it were any one of you who were missing. I could not step into the role that any of you four occupy.

"But you're not missing magic, or time guardianship, or the power of life, or the knowledge of the Dream of Creation. You are missing Earth. And that . . . I know how to work with."

He hoped they would not be angry with his presumption. He, a simple shaman, was offering to stand in the place of a Dragon Aspect.

Ysera brightened noticeably. Nozdormu eyed him speculatively, and Alexstrasza looked uncertainly at Kalecgos.

"I knew you would be important," Ysera said happily. "I just didn't know how."

"Please do not be offended, my friend," said Kalec, "but . . . you are not even a dragon, let alone an Aspect."

"I know," Thrall said. "But I have spent years working with the elements. And I have learned much over the course of my journey." He looked to Nozdormu. "You know this to be the truth."

The Timeless One nodded slowly. "You have been given insight you did not have before," he said, "the sssort of insight that calms a ssspirit, and does not agitate it. There is no harm in attempting such a thing."

"But how would you aid us, Thrall?" asked Alexstrasza. "You cannot fight alongside us."

"I sssay again, Life-Binder, this is not about individual acts in battle," Nozdormu said. "This is about combining our essences. Obviously Thrall cannot attack with us. But he can possibly offer us with his ssspirit what another Aspect could. I tell you truly, there is no hope otherwise. None. Each Aspect alone will fall, and it will be the end, first of the dragonflights, and then of Azeroth. I . . . have seen that end."

So had Ysera, who had told them of it. Nozdormu's voice was heavy and somber, and Thrall felt a shiver run down his spine.

Yet, strangely, Thrall did not second-guess his impulse. It felt right in his heart in a way he could not properly describe. It seemed ages ago that he had been so distracted and unfocused that he had faltered during the Earthen Ring's effort to calm the distraught elements. He knew, without knowing how he knew, that now he could hold in himself the peace, the solidity, to do what he needed to. His strengthened connection with the Spirit of Life made working with all the elements easier—even more joyful. The earth held life; it nourished the seeds and the roots that animals in turn fed upon. The Spirit of Earth and the Spirit of Life would welcome him back now; they would trust him to hold and gently direct and contain the Spirit of Earth, even while working with four Dragon Aspects. The earth was enormous; its spirit was great; and in his humility to accept that, Thrall knew he could, conversely, succeed with it.

"Let me try, at least," he said.

"My flight has done what we once thought impossible," Kalecgos said. "We have chosen a new Aspect. From what I have seen, in Thrall, in Chromatus, in my own flight, I believe this has a chance of working. I say, let us attempt it."

"Yes," said Ysera at once. "Thrall still has a role to play here. The puzzle pieces have not quite fit exactly in my head."

Alexstrasza regarded him kindly. "You have helped me open my heart when I thought it shattered beyond repair. If you think you can do this thing, then I, too, am more than willing to try. But please . . . let us hurry!"

"It is an old and formal ritual," Thrall said. He slipped off from Torastrasza's broad back. "I will go as quickly as I may. If the four of you could take your humanoid forms?"

Quickly they responded. Thrall looked at the high elven, half-elven, and night elven faces. Three he had already seen in these forms, but not Nozdormu, whose appearance was much different. The others had all selected shapes of beauty and physical grace, some opting to keep their horns, some not. Not so with the Timeless One. While he had a slender but strong, somewhat elven body, sand seemed to be drifting off it in a gentle fall. He wore simple white linen, and while he kept his golden horns and his eyes remained large, brilliant, and gemlike, his face was that of an owl—wise and calm.

"I have participated in circles similar to this," Thrall began, focusing now on the approaching ritual and not Nozdormu's startling appearance. "But never with such powerful participants."

"We trust you," said the Life-Binder, and she smiled. Thrall found himself deeply moved. He thought of Aggra, and smiled a little to himself. She certainly could not accuse him of lacking humility in his heart at this particular moment.

"I will cast the circle and acknowledge the elements," he said. "It sounds as if our task is to open to one another. Your hearts and minds, everything that makes you *you*—and makes you an Aspect. This is not a time for secrets, or even self-protection. I am honored you trust me. But you must also trust yourselves, and each other. Take one another's hands, to strengthen that connection. Are you ready?"

They looked at one another and nodded, doing as he requested. Thrall took a deep breath, in through the nose, out through the mouth, letting himself drop into a peaceful place. He began facing the east, long connected with the element of air.

"Blessed east," Thrall said, his voice strong and steady. "New beginnings, where the sun rises. The home of Air, who inspires, and rules the mind and thought. I honor and—"

"They come!"

The anguished cry filled the air. Thrall's eyes snapped open, his concentration shattered. Sure enough, he heard the familiar thrum of hundreds of leathery wings beating the air. The twilight dragons had come back for another round. And this time, they would win. Weakened as the Aspects were, once the revitalized Chromatus entered the fray, nothing they could do as separate beings could stop him.

Thrall tasted bitter despair. He had been so convinced it would work—so hopeful, and they had been so close. And now there was no time to complete the ritual.

Something flashed into his mind.

There is *time,* he remembered.

Pictures suddenly filled his mind's eye: the sun rising, strong and life-giving. The joy that came with new ideas, lively conversation, breakthroughs and achievements and beginnings.

To his surprise, he saw the Aspects glancing at one another, nodding and smiling, and knew that somehow, through him, they could see the pictographs too.

And this had all transpired in the time it took the eye to blink.

Now the pictures in his mind were of campfires, the jungle climate of Stranglethorn, the baking lands of Durotar. This was Fire, whose home was the south, who gave all living beings the passion to achieve their goals and dreams.

Dimly, Thrall could hear the sounds of dragon fighting dragon all around him: the cries of anger, the bellows of pain. He could smell burning flesh. He kept his eyes tightly shut. In a moment they could help.

In a moment—

Swiftly came the images of the west: the realm of the Spirit of Water, oceans, tears in this place of the heart, of deep emotions.

And then the north, realm of Earth. Thrall saw mountains, and caverns, and the sleepy, calm veil of winter upon the land.

In the dancing pictures in their shared vision, they were no longer seated on cold stone on the top of a mountain at the roof of the world. He saw each of the Aspects, but not as they appeared now, clasping hands; not even as they appeared in their draconic forms.

Thrall saw not just what they were but *who* they were, and their beauty was almost overwhelming.

Gentle Ysera, a glowing green mist, the very essence of creation, shifting and pulsing. *You are bound to the waking Dream of Creation.*

Nature is your realm, and all things have caught glimpses of the Emerald Dream when they sleep. You see them all, Ysera. And they see you, though they may not know it. Like the Life-Binder, you touch all living beings, and sing to them the songs of creation and interconnectedness.

The Aspects gasped softly, and Thrall understood that, somehow, he was hearing what one of the titans had said to Ysera so long ago, during that moment when she had received her powers. The voice in his head died away, but not the sense of awe and wonder it left in its wake.

Noble Kalec, a shard of gleaming ice, as beautiful as any gem, shimmering with the quintessence of arcane magic, the magic of power and spells and runes, even of the Sunwell, the magic of thought, of appreciation, of connection.

I believe that you will find that my gift to you is not just a profound duty—which it is—but also a delight—which it is! Magic must be regulated, managed, and controlled. But it must also be appreciated and valued and not hoarded. Such is the contradiction you must deal with. May you be dutiful . . . and joyous both.

The battle continued raging overhead. Thrall's heart ached, but he shut out the sounds, shut out the desire to shout his battle cry and join in the fight. There would be time for that when—

Time—

The sands of time trickled up, and down, and in all directions—past and future and this precious moment.

Unto you is charged the great task of keeping the purity of time. Know that there is only one true timeline, though there are those who would have it otherwise. You must protect it. Without the truth of time as it is meant to unfold, more will be lost than you can possibly imagine. The fabric of reality will unravel. It is a heavy task—the base of all tasks of this world, for nothing can transpire without time.

And Alexstrasza—

Thrall loved her. How could he not? How could anyone, any *thing*, not love this fiery, tender essence of pure heart energy? She was a brazier on a cold night, the life contained in a seed, or an egg, all things growing and bright and beautiful. No wonder flights of all colors adored her; no wonder she had been the last thought of Korialstrasz as he took action that would destroy so much, but preserve more.

This is my gift: compassion for all living things. A drive to protect and nurture them. And the ability to heal that which others cannot, birth what others may not, and love even the unlovable—who surely need such grace more than any other souls.

And himself—

He felt rooted, solid, deeply wise. Thrall well knew that it was not his own knowledge that he was experiencing but the knowledge of the earth. This was where the ancients dug their roots; this was where bones, over time, turned into stone. He felt bigger than he had ever been, expansive, for all this world was his to mind.

My blessing upon you will seem humble compared to those which have been bestowed upon the others: the managing of time, of life, of dreams and magic. I offer you the earth. The soil, the ground, the deep places. But know that the earth is the basis of all things. It is where we are rooted. Where you must come from, if you are to go to. Here is whence true strength comes. From deep places . . . within the world, and within oneself.

The blessing had not been intended for his ears originally. But it was now.

The energies of five Aspects stood together, as they had not done for millennia.

And then it happened.

The images that the Aspects and Thrall had become in this spiritual realm exploded. Not violently, or angrily, but as if the joy could no longer be contained in anything resembling structure or form. Like fireworks, the essence of who and what each Aspect truly *was* soared forth.

They met, hues of each one, bronze and green and blue and red and black, and twined about each other, weaving the colors together.

Like strands of thread on a loom.

. . . To unravel part of the piece, all you need to do is pull on a single loose thread.

No, Thrall suddenly thought as the words of Medivh, spoken to him in the timeways, rushed back to him. Not weaving. Threads could be pulled, or broken. They must not interweave; they must *blend. . . .*

Thrall visualized his color, a pure, peaceful black hue, merging with the other dancing plumes of the Aspects. They understood at once, and each yielded its boundaries. The colors began to blend, turning a single uniform hue of—

"He comes!"

The voices of the lookouts shattered the moment. Thrall struggled to stay in the sacred space, to detach calmly, but there was too much urgency. Even before he had opened his eyes, the four Aspects had all leaped upward, shifting back into their true forms and climbing skyward. For a moment, as the dragons sprang upward, wings beating fiercely, Thrall thought he would be left behind. An instant later he was snatched up by a giant paw. He craned his neck to see Tick, who swiftly placed the orc on her shoulder.

Sure enough, the rotting chromatic dragon was flying full-tilt toward his adversaries. "Did you really think we would not come for you?" called a voice that did not belong to Chromatus. Thrall peered, straining to see in the moonlight, and realized there was a small figure perched on Chromatus's gigantic back.

It had to be the Twilight Father.

What cultists were left after Torastrasza's razing of their ranks had also climbed on dragonback. They wielded weapons Thrall could see glinting in the dim light, and doubtless others knew spells and would be even more dangerous foes at a distance. He realized that they intended this to be the final confrontation, and the Twilight Father was clearly prepared to lose what he must in order to ensure victory.

Thrall took precious minutes attempting to firmly ground himself in the present moment. He had no way of knowing if the ceremony he had just led had done what it was supposed to have done. He had wanted more time—time for the Aspects to fully integrate, to blend, and to settle into this new way of being, before turning their full attention toward Chromatus and the cult. But such thought was not being truly in the moment, as he had learned. He had done what he could in the time he had, and there was a curious peace in his soul at the thought.

From what he could see, the Aspects had recovered faster than he had, even though they had been unfamiliar with the sort of ritual he had taken them through. Thrall dared hope it was because they were doing what was right, what was needed—what they were supposed to have been doing all along. They moved swiftly and with grim purpose toward Chromatus, who paused and hovered in the air, flapping his strangely jointed wings before opening the mouths of all five heads. Flame, ice, sickly green energy, sand, and a terrible black cloud buffeted the Aspects simultaneously. All four were knocked backward, pummeled by the force of five striking spells.

"No!" Thrall shouted, but no sooner had the cry left his lips than the Aspects had recovered. They halted their tumble and, graceful and unified as they had been before, renewed the attack.

It took Thrall a moment to realize that he could see them more clearly than he ought to be able to. And he suddenly realized that each form, while its color remained unchanged, was limned with golden-white light. Even as he watched, the illumination seemed to crackle and pulse. Their poses seemed . . . calm, somehow. Focused, yes, but not urgent. They had a purpose, a goal, and were approaching it as a single unit, not four individuals.

Chromatus, too, seemed to notice. He suddenly rose straight in the air and wheeled about, his body tense and alert. "So," the black head bellowed, "you think to defeat me by joining against me. I can sense the new unity among you. Know that it will ultimately fail. How precious. But you will never be complete! You are missing someone, or have you forgotten? Deathwing is my patron, and he will see all of you destroyed!"

The voice was louder than it had been, booming and terrifying. Thrall found that, while he wanted desperately to aid his friends in this perhaps final battle, he could not tear his eyes away from the spectacle. He suddenly realized that it was because he, too, was an integral part of it. That was why he was having such trouble becoming just himself again: because part of him was still connected to the Dragon Aspects.

They did not need Deathwing for the ritual. And despite Chromatus's challenging words, Thrall realized they did not need Deathwing now. They had Earth. They had *Thrall,* and for this little while, the Spirit of Life had granted him the strength to hold something so strong, so profound, that it had once been granted by the titans themselves.

Just as he had exchanged his armor for robes in order to fight another sort of battle—one to calm and heal the earth—Thrall realized he had exchanged his ability to help as an individual for something far greater. He was not, could never be, an Aspect.

But he was what helped bind them together, to do what they needed to.

Tick did not question Thrall's sudden inaction, but neither did she cease her own fighting. She cast a spell that seemed to freeze several twilight dragons in place, and Thrall realized that for those unfortunate ones, time itself had stopped. Tick now dipped and dove and attacked, raked with her powerful claws and lashed hard with her massive tail. Thrall observed, but his true attention was deeply focused on helping the Aspects maintain this newly discovered unity.

He shook his head, suddenly finding it difficult to concentrate. Why? He had been focusing so clearly a moment ago. His thoughts were jumbled, slipping from his grasp. Sudden fear gripped him. He was the anchor, what helped the . . . what?

Angrily Thrall clawed at his right arm with his left hand, the pain helping him focus. His thoughts were being twisted, crippled. He looked up and saw the figure astride Chromatus extending his hands toward the orc—and that figure was now shades of purple-blue, an undulating shadow about him. Thrall growled, digging his nails deeper in his arm, and wrenched back his mind.

Chromatus shook his ugly heads. The sickly purple glow that radiated from all ten eyes was a dark imitation of the radiance that enveloped the Aspects as they flew acrobatically around his larger, comparatively squat form. The purple illumination highlighted his misshapen features ghoulishly, and when he drew back and opened his mouths, Thrall felt as though he were again fighting something as dark and evil and unnatural as the Burning Legion itself.

Whereas before, the five heads of the monstrosity attacked as separate entities, now they acted in eerie unison. Each head drew back, inhaling deeply, and then five sets of jaws opened to attack. This time, instead of five separate hues from five separate heads, the flames the creature spewed were dark violet and attacked the shimmering gold-white illumination. More than one of the Aspects bellowed in pain, and Thrall watched as Kalecgos and Ysera faltered for a moment. Their colors darkened as the radiance subsided but then flared to renewed brilliance.

They dove as before, coordinated and elegant, and when they opened their mammoth jaws, white fire exploded forth. It was not the slightly lavender tint of arcane magic, nor did it look like any spell Thrall had ever seen. It was breath in the shape of a flame, the purest white hue Thrall had ever seen. They all aimed for the same place: Chromatus's chest, exposed as all five necks reared back up to draw a second breath to attack.

Thrall had to shield his eyes, so blinding was the light as it struck. Four streams of brilliant white from each Aspect slammed into the great dragon, sending him tumbling wildly. Chromatus screamed in agony. He fell out of control for a long moment before awkwardly flapping his wings to bring himself back up. His heads, no longer acting in beautiful unison, but jerkily and wildly, again breathed dark flame, but missed their targets widely. In his struggle to bring himself back into the battle, he did nothing but expose his already-blackened chest. Again the Aspects, drawing in breath as one, breathed this strange flame that was not flame upon the chromatic dragon's heart.

He bucked and spasmed, his heads contorting and screaming curses even as his body convulsed.

"You cannot stop me!" the blue head cried, and then it fell back, eyes closed.

"I know all your secrets," warned the red before its eyes, too, ceased to glow with life.

And, most chillingly of all, the black head cried, "It took all of you to even attempt to destroy me! Think you Deathwing will be easier? He will rip this world apart to crush you for what you do! And I will be there with—"

There was one final spasm, a hoarse croak from the black head, and then Chromatus fell.

The Twilight Father clung desperately to Chromatus as the two of them hurtled earthward. His mind was numb with horror. He barely had enough wits about him to cast a protective shield about himself. Moments ago, after the first strange breath that had so harmed the dragon, the Twilight Father's mind had reeled with questions. What had happened to the Aspects? Where had they gotten this newfound ability? What was it? How could this possibly be happening? Chromatus was invincible!

And then all those questions vanished before the frantic terror of clinging to a dead dragon as he fell toward jagged rocks and snow.

He closed his eyes. The great body landed with a huge thump, and the Twilight Father cried out as he slid into a pile of snow. Shivering, frantic, he clawed his way out of the powder, grateful to have somehow survived, terrified of the repercussions of failure. He reached out to Chromatus, trying to sense any signs of life.

There were none. And yet . . . the dragon was not dead, or undead. No breath, no movement, no heartbeat, but neither was there the emptiness of a shell of a body. He was in some sort of in-between state. He lacked the spark of life, but the Twilight Father knew that if there was another way, the body could be reanimated. It was something. If Chromatus had been completely destroyed, the Twilight Father knew he would rather have died in battle. It would have been sweet and painless compared to what Deathwing would have done to him. Might still do to him.

His robes were soaked and clung to him, threatening an ignoble death from freezing as he picked his way through snow and over rocks, past the fallen body, to a small overhang. The small orb he used to speak with Deathwing was still intact; it would take more even than so great a fall to damage this artifact. With numb fingers he removed it from a pouch at his waist and regarded it for a moment. He debated simply trying to vanish—but how? He was alone, in the middle of nowhere, with red, green, bronze, and blue dragons everywhere the eye could see—not to mention four Aspects who had somehow managed to tap into more power than he could ever have believed.

No. Deathwing had invested much time and effort in the making of the Twilight Father. He would not destroy such effort on a whim. Chromatus was not alive—but he was not dead, either. That might be enough.

Huddled beneath the pathetic shelter, the Twilight Father placed the orb in the snow and knelt before it, shivering violently. The clear globe filled with an inky blackness, relieved only by the orange-yellow gleam of an eye. An instant later the orb cracked open. Thick black smoke wafted up, filling the limited space. The image of the monstrous black dragon was contained, but the terror he inspired was in no manner lessened.

"They are not destroyed," Deathwing said without preamble. "I would have felt it."

"I know, my m-master," stuttered the Twilight Father. "They did . . . something, and they d-d-defeated your champion. He lies without life, but not in death."

There was a long, terrible moment. "Abysmal failure, then."

The cold words were worse than a bellow of anger. The Twilight Father cringed. "Nay, Chromatus cannot be slain! He is defeated, but only for the moment."

He heard the sound of wings above him and peered upward. His eyes widened and he crouched back in his poor shelter. "My lord, I would continue doing your work in this world. But I will not be able to do so for much longer. They are searching for me, and—and it seems as though the twilight d-dragonflight is fleeing. . . ." He tried and failed to keep the panic out of his voice.

"You are a serious disappointment," rumbled Deathwing. "We had certain victory within our grasp. Yet the Aspects live; Chromatus is . . . damaged; and the cult has been dealt a severe blow. Why should I not throw you to my enemies?"

"I—I know much that is still of use!" the Twilight Father cried, clutching the orb as if he were clutching a master's hand. "I have those who trust me—you know I do. Let me return to them. Let me lead them eventually to you. The cult is all over this world; even if the dragonflights destroy it here, they will not destroy it entirely! Think how much time you would waste putting someone else in my position!"

"Humans are pathetically greedy and easy to manipulate," growled Deathwing. "And yet you speak sense. We have already lost enough time. I do not need another setback. Come, then. Surrender to the smoke," he said, letting his image, formed of the dark, silky smoke the orb had emitted, dissolve. Shadow tendrils reached out and caressed the Twilight Father, and even he shivered. "The portal will take you home. There, you may continue betraying the trust of those who honor you, and work my will again when next I ask it of you."

The Twilight Father cast off his cowl and embraced the transporting shadow-smoke, clad in his more familiar, traditional clerical robes.

"Thank you, my lord," whispered Archbishop Benedictus. "Thank you!"

TWENTY-TWO

They stood on the topmost level of Wyrmrest Temple as
dawn approached: four Aspects and an orc. All were weary
yet triumphant. The intervening hours between the fall of
Chromatus and this moment had been filled with the grim necessi-
ties that accompany the aftermath of battle: counting and naming
the dead, healing the wounded, and searching out any stragglers.

Many—too many—had fallen with each attack, and the solemn
task of gathering and disposing of the bodies would commence
once the sun raised its head over the horizon. For now, though, all
that could be done had been.

They had not found the Twilight Father among the slain
cultists—although Thrall had pointed out that there were quite
a lot of charred bodies, some of them clearly human and male.
Kirygosa had shaken her blue-black head. "No," she said. "I would
know him. I would know him anywhere."

Kalecgos had regarded her with a worried expression. Only time
would tell if Kirygosa would heal from her months of torment.
But she had returned to her flight, and was held dear in the heart
of the Life-Binder. Thrall suspected she would be all right.

The only twilight dragons they had found were corpses. The rest had fled, leaderless and afraid. And Chromatus—

Concerned that some other dark power might try to revive Chromatus, the dragons had attempted to destroy the corpse.

They had failed. Some powerful spell, probably woven into the dark marriage of magic and technology that had animated him in the first place, protected the body from all their efforts to obliterate it.

"Then he must be guarded until such time as we can find a way to completely destroy him," Alexstrasza had decided. "Representatives from our flights will stand watch over him. He is not dead . . . but if he lies without the spark of animation, he will harm no one again."

"During the Nexus War, Malygos created arcane prisons," Kalecgos had said. "We know how well they worked. We can construct one large enough—and strong enough—to hold him."

Now five figures stood, four dragons and one orc, gazing to the east. "We will go our separate ways shortly," Nozdormu said quietly. "But we will never be truly apart. Never again." He lifted his head to regard them. "Thrall . . . I told you something of what I had learned." Thrall nodded, and listened as Nozdormu shared with the other Aspects the dire news he had imparted to Thrall earlier.

"Thrall found me becaussse I was attempting to find the answer to sssomething. You all know that I was given the knowledge of the hour and manner of my own death. While I would never sssubvert what I know to be true and right—in my travels, in one timeway—I became leader of the infinite dragonflight."

They stared at him, horrified. For a long moment no one could even summon the ability to speak. Then Alexstrasza said very gently, "You said one timeway. Is it the true one, my old friend?"

"I do not know," he said. "I was searching to discover that very thing. To—to find some way to avoid becoming something so antithetical to all that I stand for. And it was while on that quest that I learned what I asked Thrall to share with you: that all of the suffering we have had to deal with—the madness of Malygos and Deathwing, the Emerald Dream turned to a nightmare, the Twilight Cult . . . everything—it is all intertwined. This much I shared with Thrall. And the reason I was late in coming to your aid was that I was following another thread of information. I have discovered who is behind this vast and dreadful conspiracy."

His eyes gleamed, brilliant with righteous anger in the coming dawn. "It . . . I can barely ssspeak of it, even now. It is"—his mighty voice dropped to a low whisper—"the Old Gods!"

The three other mighty Dragon Aspects stared at him, their own eyes wide with shock and worry. At their expressions, Thrall's own heart sped up with dread. He knew something of these figures, ancient and evil; two of them lurked in Ulduar and Ahn'Qiraj. "I have heard of these beings," Thrall said, "but you clearly know more."

For a moment no one spoke, as if to speak of them might cause them to appear. Then: "You have heard old tales, Thrall," said Alexstrasza, her vibrancy subdued. "Tales of evil whisperings in one's mind, that urge one to do dark and terrible things. Subtle whispers that sound like one's own thoughts."

And Thrall realized he had. "The tauren say that the first time evil ever left its mark on them was when they heard and harkened to dark whispers."

Ysera nodded, looking miserable. "The whispers penetrated even into the Emerald Dream," she said.

"Even," Kalecgos said, "into Deathwing's mind, when he was still Neltharion the Earth-Warder. It is the Old Gods who drove him mad, Thrall. Drove *all* the black dragons mad."

"They are old, older even than we," said Nozdormu. "They

were here even before the titansss came, and would have ruined this world had not our creatorsss intervened. A battle sssuch as this world has never seen since raged. They were locked away—hidden in the dark placesss of the earth, drowsing in enchanted slumber."

"Only with their whispers could they reach us," said Alexstrasza. "At least . . . until very recently." She lifted stricken eyes to Nozdormu. "And you say they are the ones behind everything? Neltharion's corruption, we know of, and at least one rift in the timeways—but everything? For so many millennia?"

"To what end?" asked Kalecgos.

"Do they need one?" asked Ysera. "Who knows how the Old Gods think, or dream? They are evil, and even in this slumber, that evil seeps out."

"What is sure is that all those dark events—they caused. Did they do it sssimply because they hate, or because they plot? We may never know. All we need to know is that they happened, and they had terrible consequencesss."

He looked at them intently. "Think of how each of these things wounded us ssso. They tore us apart. They made us mistrust one another. Recall how quickly we turned on Korialstrasz, when in reality his deed was ssself-sacrificing and heroic. Even you doubted, my dear," he said gently to Alexstrasza, who lowered her crimson head.

"I think that even my becoming leader of the infinite dragonflight, if it mussst happen, is traceable to them. But today . . . we learned. We, so old, so ssseemingly wise." He chuckled slightly. "We discovered that we must work together as one if we are to ssstand firm against what is coming." He turned to Ysera. "Will we stand otherwise?" he asked very gently.

She shook her head. "No," she said. "Without the unity we have found—without the unity we must continue to find, again and

again and again—we will never be able to stand against the coming Hour of Twilight and—and the vision I saw."

"I thought this was the Hour," Thrall said, confused.

She shook her head again. "Of course it wasn't," she said tol-
erantly, as if he were simple. Thrall's only comfort was that the
other dragons assembled seemed to be as confused as he. Ysera
was powerful, and benevolent, but she *did* truly exist slightly apart
from other beings.

"You have helped us, as I saw that you would," the green Aspect
continued. "I wasn't sure how . . . but you have. The mosaic is no
longer simple chips of colored stone. It is taking shape and form
now. The visions and dreams I have had—they will manifest. It
has taken one who is not one of us to bring us together so. And
because we are together . . . when the true Hour comes . . . we
shall not fail."

"I came here with a hope for unity among the dragonflights in
my heart," said Alexstrasza. "And after so much pain and loss and
struggle . . . it has happened in a way that I could never have foreseen. My reds will always welcome you, Thrall, son of Durotan
and Draka. Take this, as a token of that pledge." Delicately, using
one massive foreclaw, she scratched at her heart. A single small
scale fell to the floor, glittering crimson. Thrall picked it up and respectfully put it in his pouch—the same pouch that had once held
the acorn of an ancient, and still held the necklace given to him by
a young human girl.

"As will my bronzes, friend to the timeways," said Nozdormu.
He, too, gifted Thrall with a precious, gleaming scale.

"The Emerald Dream is not your realm, shaman, but know that,
from time to time, I will send you dreams of healing. My scale,
too, you may have. With all my heart, I thank you for accepting my
request," said Ysera.

Kalec bent his great head down, and in the first hints of the warm rose light of dawn, Thrall was certain he saw a single tear shining in the bright eyes as the blue Aspect offered a scale from over his heart.

"You, without any doubt or exaggeration, have saved the blue dragonflight. Anything you ask of me, you will have."

Thrall was almost overcome. He took a moment, struggling for composure.

"While I am grateful for the gift of a scale from each of your flights, truly, I ask only your friendship," he said to them all. "And"—he smiled a little—"a way to return to my beloved."

Thrall mused wryly that he was becoming used to traveling on dragonback. Particularly the back of this dragon. He and Tick had grown to become friends over the last several weeks of traveling and fighting together, and Thrall knew he would miss her. Thrall had been curious when Tick had offered to return him, concerned that the flight from the continents to the Maelstrom would be too far for an ordinary dragon to travel. Tick had chuckled.

"We have the ability to slow or speed up time, remember?" she told Thrall. "I will speed it up for us . . . and will therefore fly much faster and farther." Thrall was, again, astonished and humbled by even the abilities of so-called ordinary dragons. And sure enough, after only what felt like a few moments, they were flying over the Maelstrom. Thrall felt the bronze inhale swiftly as she beheld the churning, angry whirlpool.

"So this is where Deathwing entered our world," Tick muttered. "It is no wonder the earth is still in so much torment."

"You sound like one of my tauren friends grieving for the Earth Mother."

The great creature craned her neck to regard Thrall closely. "Who is to say they are wrong?"

Thrall laughed. "Not I," he said. "Never I."

There was a stable-looking spot some distance away from the main settlement. Carefully, mindful that the earth was unhappy, Tick made a gentle landing. Thrall slipped off the bronze's back and regarded her for a long moment.

"You have earned the gratitude of our flights," Tick said soberly. "You have the scales. Use them if you are in need of our aid, and you shall have it. I can only hope that this wounded Azeroth can benefit as much from your care and focus as we have."

"You embarrass me, my friend. I only did what I could."

A wry, amused expression crossed the scaly face. "You would be surprised at how few even attempt to do that much. You are home now, Thrall. I must return. The Hour of Twilight is still to come one day, and I must be ready to stand with my lord, Nozdormu, when that time comes. Thank you again . . . for helping us find ourselves and one another."

She bent her head low, only a few short feet from the ground, in what Thrall knew to be a deep obeisance. He felt his cheeks grow hot and nodded, then watched as Tick gathered herself and leaped skyward. Squinting against the brightness of the sun, Thrall watched until the mighty dragon dwindled to the size of a bird, then an insect, and then vanished altogether.

Then, a solitary figure, he closed his eyes and, sending a whisper on the wind, called a wyvern to him. Patting the creature, Thrall climbed atop him and headed for the encampment.

Guards spotted him, and by the time Thrall reached the Earthen Ring encampment, many shaman were already gathered there.

"Welcome home," rumbled Muln Earthfury, striding forward to grasp the orc's shoulders. "Long have you been gone, but at last you are returned to us."

Thrall smiled up at the tauren. "Sometimes lessons take time to learn," he said quietly. "I think you will find that I have settled my own . . . demons, and return to you with knowledge and information that will benefit our workings—and our world."

"I am even better pleased to hear that," Muln replied. "Not just for the benefit it will bring to us, but from what I can sense from you, my friend. You are"—he cocked his horned head, searching for the right words—"settled. Calmer."

Thrall nodded. "Indeed I am."

"You have returned!" It was Nobundo, who approached and squeezed Thrall's shoulder affectionately. The Broken smiled warmly, his homely face alight with pleasure.

"Welcome back," Nobundo said. "I overheard some of what you told Muln. And I am so pleased to hear of this. Are you hungry? Your journey must have been arduous, and there is meat roasting on the fire even as we speak."

"Thank you all," Thrall said. "And while it is good to see you, there is one here I do not see. Excuse me, I must find her."

He bowed to his colleagues.

Aggra was not here; she would have come out if she had been. He suspected he knew where she was.

There was a small rise that seemed less harmed than most places in this area. Certain herbs grew here, struggling but surviving, and Aggra often came here to harvest carefully and, Thrall knew, simply sit and meditate.

She was there now, sitting calmly on the rise, legs crossed, eyes closed.

For a moment Thrall permitted himself to watch her while he remained unseen. For so long he had dreamed of this moment: returning to this amazing, inspiring female, who filled his heart and soul with a love so bright and strong he could barely contain it. This was the face—brown, strong-boned, tusked—that had kept him from surrendering to the cold. This was the body, muscular and curvaceous and powerful, he wanted to hold in his arms for the rest of his life. Her laughter was the music of the universe to him; her smile his sun, moons, and stars.

"Aggra," he said, and his voice broke on the word. He was not ashamed.

She opened her eyes, and they crinkled around the edges in a smile. "You have returned," she said quietly, though joy hummed in the words. "Welcome home."

Thrall crossed the space between them in two huge steps and before she could say a word, he had swept her up into his arms and held her tightly to his chest.

She laughed in pleased surprise, and her arms encircled him. Her head was nestled on his shoulder, where it fit perfectly. He could feel her heart beating against his chest, rapid with excitement and delight.

For a long, long time he held her thus. He didn't ever want to release her. She, too, clung to him and didn't protest as the moment lasted.

Finally, though, he moved away slightly and cupped her face in his large green hands.

"You were right," he said without preamble.

She raised an eyebrow, indicating he should continue.

"I was hiding behind the mantle of warchief. A thrall to the Horde, to what I thought was my duty. And that kept me from having to look deeply at myself, and seeing things I did not like. And if I didn't do that, I couldn't change them. I couldn't become better."

He stepped back, reaching for her brown hand. He entwined his fingers with hers, fully present, seeing as if for the first time the nicks and scars on both their skins, green and brown, feeling the rough textures rub against one another. He then lifted her hand and touched it to his forehead before lowering it and looking deep into her eyes.

"I couldn't truly appreciate either the great things or the little things. Like this strong hand in mine."

Her eyes were bright; were they glittering with tears? But she was smiling broadly, remembering the moment as he was.

"I do appreciate these things now, Aggra. Every raindrop, every shaft of sunlight, every breath that fills my lungs, every beat of my heart. There is peril and there is pain, but here is also quiet, constant joy, if we just remember and know it is there.

"I did not know who I was, or who Thrall would become, after leaving all I had built. But I do now. I know who I am. I know what I must do. I know . . . who I want."

Her smile grew, but she stayed silent, listening.

"And I know in my heart that when the time is right, I will be able to do what is necessary."

"Tell me," she said quietly.

And standing there, their arms wrapped around each other, he did. He told her of the ancients, and of Desharin. Of the killer who turned out to be an old, old enemy made new and thrust into the rightful timeway. Of the pain of choosing not to interfere with his parents' murder, mixed with the joy of reassuring Durotan that his child would live.

He wept as he spoke of this, recalling all he had seen, and felt, and done, all the horrors and kindnesses that had come his way, and a strong brown hand smoothed away the salty tears from his green face.

He spoke of Taretha and Krasus, of Nozdormu, of Alexstrasza and Kalecgos and Ysera and Kirygosa. Of his own experiences in understanding, and appreciating, and being truly present. Of the experiences he, a simple mortal orc, had endured, and the lessons he had been able to bring to beings as powerful as Dragon Aspects.

"You were given a gift," Aggra said when he fell silent. "You were given the chance to see who you were, to learn from mistakes, and to change and grow. Few are granted such insight, my heart."

He was still holding her hand, and he squeezed it tightly. "It was you who got me through the worst moment," he said. "And enabled me to recall the broken Life-Binder to herself."

Softly, whispering the words, he told Aggra of his need to be with her, to gaze upon her face. Her eyes did fill with tears as she listened, and Thrall realized that it was indeed possible to see a loving heart reflected on a beloved face.

"So I have come home," he said at last. "Humbler, but proud of what I have been able to participate in. Ready to do more. To be my best, my highest self, at all times, to honor you, and my friends, and my world. I stand ready."

For a long moment Aggra didn't speak. Then finally, in a voice that was thick with emotion but bursting with pride and delight, she said, "There. *That* is my Go'el."

Thrall's lips curved around his tusks in a grin. "Go'el," he said, the word feeling oddly comfortable in his mouth. "The name of my birth." He regarded her for a moment and again started to speak. But before he could do so, he heard a cheerful voice behind him.

"Thrall! I only just heard. Made it back alive, I see!"

It was Rehgar, either oblivious to the intimate moment he was interrupting or, more likely, simply not caring. He hurried up to

Thrall, beaming, and clapped the other orc on the shoulder. "I will wager you have many a tale for us!"

Thrall stepped back from Aggra slightly, turning to face his friend. He reached and clapped Rehgar on the shoulder.

"Rehgar, my old friend . . . the Thrall you knew is no more. I am Go'el, son of Durotan and Draka. Thrall only to myself"—he turned back to Aggra, squeezing her waist and smiling—"and to my love."

Rehgar threw back his head and laughed. "Well said, my friend. Well said. I will let you tell the others, but be quick. The roasting meat is almost done, and we are ravenous. We wait upon you, but we will not wait forever!"

With a final wink, Rehgar turned and headed back to the encampment. Go'el watched him, smiling, then turned back to Aggra. He grew serious and, taking both her hands in his, said more quietly, "I meant it. I will be a thrall only to myself, and to my love . . . if she will have me. For the rest of our lives."

A joyful grin spread across Aggra's face. She squeezed his hands so tightly that he almost winced.

"I was willing to follow Thrall to the end of this world or any other," Aggra said. "How much more would I be willing to bind my life to Go'el's?"

He couldn't stop smiling. He did not think he had ever been happier. He leaned his forehead on hers, grateful beyond measure that he had learned how to savor a moment, for this one was assuredly sweet. At last he pulled back, letting the moment pass into the past, and welcoming the present. For it, too, was joyful.

"Let us go back to the camp and tell the others. We have challenges and grim duties ahead. We will triumph over some, and struggle with others. But we will always do so . . . together."

Hand in hand with his future lifemate, Go'el turned back to

where the other members of the Earthen Ring awaited. There would be laughing and feasting tonight, celebrating his return and his future plans. On the morrow, the solemn duty of working to heal a wounded world would resume.

And Go'el would be ready.

NOTES

The story you've just read is based in part on characters, situations, and settings from Blizzard Entertainment's computer game *World of Warcraft,* an online role-playing experience set in the award-winning Warcraft universe. In *World of Warcraft,* players create their own heroes and explore, adventure in, and quest across a vast world shared with thousands of other players. This rich and expansive game also allows players to interact with and fight against or alongside many of the powerful and intriguing characters featured in this novel.

Since launching in November 2004, *World of Warcraft* has become the world's most popular subscription-based massively multiplayer online role-playing game. The latest expansion, *Cataclysm,* sold more than 3.3 million copies within its first 24 hours of release, making it the fastest-selling PC game of all time and surpassing the previous record held by *World of Warcraft*'s second expansion, *Wrath of the Lich King.* More information about the *Cataclysm* expansion and upcoming content, which continues the story of Azeroth where this novel ends, can be found on WorldofWarcraft .com.

Further Reading

I f you'd like to read more about the characters, situations, and settings featured in this novel, the sources listed below offer additional pieces of the story of Azeroth.

- The Cataclysm recently altered the physical and political landscape of Azeroth forever. The events preceding this catastrophe, including the death of Thrall's close friend Cairne Bloodhoof, are depicted in *World of Warcraft: The Shattering: Prelude to Cataclysm* by Christie Golden.

- Thrall makes the difficult decision to step down as Horde warchief and focus on the elemental instability affecting Azeroth in *World of Warcraft: The Shattering* by Christie Golden. Other details concerning Thrall's past, such as his time as warchief, his slavery under Aedelas Blackmoore, and his friendship with Taretha Foxton, are portrayed in *Warcraft: Lord of the Clans* and *World of Warcraft: Rise of the Horde* by Christie Golden, *World of Warcraft: Cycle of Hatred* by Keith R. A. DeCandido, Sarah Pine's short story, "Garrosh Hellscream: Heart of War" (on www.WorldofWarcraft.com), *Warcraft: Legends*, volume 2, "Fear" by Richard A. Knaak and Kim Jae-Hwan, and issues #15–20 of the monthly *World of Warcraft* comic book by Walter and Louise Simonson, Jon Buran, Mike Bowden, Phil Moy, Walden Wong, and Pop Mhan.

- Before succumbing to the corrupting influence of the Old Gods, Deathwing was known as Neltharion the Earth-Warder, the respected Aspect of the black dragonflight. His sudden chilling betrayal of the other dragonflights is revealed in the War of the Ancients trilogy (*Warcraft: The Well of Eternity, Warcraft: The Demon Soul,* and *Warcraft: The Sundering*) by Richard A. Knaak. A number of his other schemes can be seen in *Warcraft: Day of the Dragon* and *World of Warcraft: Night of the Dragon,* also by Richard A. Knaak, *World of Warcraft: Beyond the Dark Portal* by Aaron Rosenberg and Christie Golden, and the *Shadow Wing* series by Richard A. Knaak and Kim Jae-Hwan.

- You can find more information about Alexstrasza, Ysera, Nozdormu, Malygos, and their respective dragonflights in the War of the Ancients trilogy, *Warcraft: Day of the Dragon, World of Warcraft: Night of the Dragon,* and *World of Warcraft: Stormrage* by Richard A. Knaak.

- The creation of a clutch of malefic twilight dragons by Deathwing's former consort, Sinestra, is shown in *World of Warcraft: Night of the Dragon* by Richard A. Knaak.

- The strong-willed orc Aggra first encountered Thrall during his stay in Nagrand while searching for answers to Azeroth's elemental instability. This meeting, as well as further development of their relationship and Aggra's decision to accompany Thrall back to Azeroth, is explored in *World of Warcraft: The Shattering* by Christie Golden.

- You can read about the wise tauren Muln Earthfury and the beliefs that guide him and his fellow Earthen Ring shaman in *World of Warcraft: Shaman* by Paul Benjamin and Rocio Zucchi.

- Although Nobundo is now a respected shaman of the Earthen Ring, he was once an outcast on the shattered realm of Outland. His path to becoming a shaman is featured in Micky Neilson's short story "Unbroken" (on www.WorldofWarcraft .com).

- Before aiding the Earthen Ring at the Maelstrom, Rehgar Earthfury was a trusted advisor to Thrall, a member of the new Council of Tirisfal, and the owner of Varian Wrynn during the human's time as a gladiator-slave. These exciting events in Rehgar's life are documented in the prologue and issues #1–3, #15–20, and #22–25 of the *World of Warcraft* comic book by Walter and Louise Simonson, Ludo Lullabi, Sandra Hope, Richard Friend, Jon Buran, Mike Bowden, Tony Washington, Phil Moy, Walden Wong, and Pop Mhan.

- Korialstrasz—also known as Krasus—has been involved in many influential events throughout Azeroth's history. His role in the War of the Ancients is disclosed in the War of the Ancients trilogy by Richard A. Knaak. More on Korialstrasz, including his relationships with Alexstrasza and Kalecgos, is offered in the *Sunwell Trilogy* by Richard A. Knaak and Kim Jae-Hwan; *World of Warcraft: Stormrage, World of Warcraft: Night of the Dragon*, and *Warcraft: Day of the Dragon* by Richard A. Knaak; *World of Warcraft: Tides of Darkness* by Aaron Rosenberg; and *World of Warcraft: Beyond the Dark Portal* by Aaron Rosenberg and Christie Golden.

- Insight into Kalecgos, such as his mission to investigate magical disturbances related to the Sunwell and his interactions with Korialstrasz, can be found in the *Sunwell Trilogy* by Richard A. Knaak and Kim Jae-Hwan and *World of Warcraft: Night of the Dragon* by Richard A. Knaak. Kalecgos also makes a brief appearance in volume 2 of the *Shadow Wing* series by Richard A. Knaak and Kim Jae-Hwan, a story that recounts the discovery of the mysterious and powerful nether dragons.

- Many centuries ago, Arygos took part in the War of the Shifting Sands between the malevolent qiraji empire and a combined force of night elves and dragons. Arygos's involvement in this conflict is briefly depicted in the short story "The War of the Shifting Sands" by Micky Neilson (on www.WorldofWarcraft .com).

- The true fates of Aedelas Blackmoore and Thrall's friend Taretha Foxton are revealed in *Warcraft: Lord of the Clans* by Christie Golden. Additionally, further details about Blackmoore can be found in *Warcraft: Legends,* volume 5, "Nightmares" by Richard A. Knaak and Rob Ten Pas and *World of Warcraft: Arthas: Rise of the Lich King* by Christie Golden.

THE BATTLE RAGES ON

The major seismic upheavals caused by the Cataclysm have subsided, but the effects of this disaster linger. As sporadic fighting between the Horde and the Alliance consumes the attention of both factions, the corrupted black Dragon Aspect, Deathwing, and his servants in the Twilight's Hammer cult work feverishly to ensure that the world will never recover from its dire state. . . .

In *World of Warcraft*'s third expansion, *Cataclysm,* you can battle Deathwing's fanatic minions and assist factions such as the shamanic Earthen Ring as they struggle to defend a world under siege. The previous two *World of Warcraft* expansions, *The Burning Crusade* and *Wrath of the Lich King,* take players to the ruined world of Outland and the icy wastes of Northrend. *Cataclysm* allows players to explore once-familiar regions in Kalimdor and the Eastern Kingdoms forever transformed by Deathwing's assault on Azeroth. The battle lines between Azeroth's defenders and their adversaries have been drawn. All that remains is to decide whether *you* will join in the fight to save the world from annihilation.

To discover the ever-expanding world that has entertained millions around the globe, go to WorldofWarcraft.com and download the free trial version. Live the story.

CLASS STARTER DECKS

BRING YOUR WORLD OF WARCRAFT® CHARACTER TO THE GAMING TABLE!

For more information,
visit:
www.wowtcg.com/products